Praise for the Books of Brianne Sommerville

What She Left Behind

"Brianne Sommerville has done it again! WHAT SHE LEFT BEHIND is a gripping thriller with characters to care about and a story that pulls you in and won't let go until the very end. Sommerville has created a setting that transports you with its quaintness while at the same time has you questioning everyone in it—who can be trusted, who has done the unthinkable and who will stop at nothing to keep their secrets." —Jessica Hamilton, author of *What You Never Know* and *Don't You Dare*

"Taut like a tightrope, WHAT SHE LEFT BEHIND is a profoundly impactful suspense about a woman who becomes entwined in the decades-old death of a teenager. With an ominous small town setting where secrets are well-hidden, this beautifully written and exquisitely tense sophomore novel kept me pinned to the pages, jaw dropped. The spine-tingling twists are staggering, and the perfectly timed reveals chilled me to the core. It's an exceptional read." —Samantha M. Bailey, USA TODAY and #1 international bestselling author of *HELLO, JULIET*

"Set in a small town where everyone knows everyone else (or do they), WHAT SHE LEFT BEHIND, weaves plot twists, dual timelines, family dysfunction, and reckoning with the secrets of a very dark past, all at an absolute breakneck pace." —Ashley Tate, #1 national bestselling author of *Twenty-Seven Minutes*

"What She Left Behind satisfies that itch for a classic mystery while also delivering complex characters and a page-turning, dual timeline narrative. Throw in an old, creepy house and a dead girl's diary, and you've got a gothic-esque thrill ride." - Jacquie Walters, author of *Dearest*

"Directionless and jobless, Charlotte finds herself tangled in a small town's big secrets. A page-turning, twisty mystery where the past and present collide." —*Marie Still, Author of MyDarlings*

"In her signature enticing voice, Sommerville weaves a haunting, heart-pounding mystery where past and present blur, and nothing is as it seems. In an eerie, secret-filled small town, a murderer lurks in plain sight. Spooky, gripping, and unpredictable, this story will keep you questioning the past as the present sneaks up on you." —Maggie Giles, author of *The Art of Murder*

If I Lose Her

"Sommerville captures the bone-deep fears of new motherhood with raw and poignant accuracy. Using the landscape of a mother's sleepless nights and pressure for perfection coupled with a strained marriage and her own dysfunctional family past to create an edge of your seat thriller in which everyone is a threat to her child, possibly even, herself." —Best selling author of *What You Never Knew*, Jessica Hamilton

"Debut author Brianne Sommerville makes a splash in the thriller genre with her captivating, compelling IF I LOSE HER. I flew through this riveting, suspenseful story of a new mother whose past traumas might be unraveling her current reality, or someone else could be pulling the strings. As the list of suspects grows, Sommerville beautifully balances a woman trying to figure out who's putting her child in danger with a deep, raw look at motherhood, marriage, and family that skyrockets in intensity on every new page. A fantastic read!" —Samantha M. Bailey, USA TODAY and #1 national bestselling author of *A Friend in the Dark*

What She Left Behind

Brianne Sommerville

Text copyright © 2025 by Brianne Sommerville

Cover Illustration © Nat Mack
Distributed by Simon & Schuster

ISBN: 978-1-990253-93-5
Ebook: 978-1-990253-68-3

FIC031080   FICTION / Thrillers / Psychological
FIC031100   FICTION / Thrillers / Domestic

#WhatSheLeftBehind

Follow Rising Action on our socials!

Instagram: @risingactionpublishingco
Tiktok: @risingactionpublishingco

To Sean – spelled the right way – my first and final love

What She Left Behind

Chapter One

LARK

He's been watching me. Searching for signs that my belly is swelling. Waiting for my lips to part—the truth to seep out between sobs.

I'm nearly two months along, and soon my dancer's frame will betray me.

Miss Lindsay will discover the truth first. She's paid to study her dancers' bodies. Study our pliés, our pirouettes. Our inconsistencies. My mulberry leotard will pull at the front by the time of the showcase, and she'll have no other choice. *Skip this year's performance.* She'll have the talk with me in the dressing room after the others leave. *You have options, Lark. You have a future, and you are in control of it.*

I don't have a future, and I've lost control.

He knows that.

I know that.

Chapter Two

CHARLOTTE

Sixteen years later

The subway grinds to a stop with a high-pitched screech, forcing the standing passengers to grab hold of a nearby pole. Charlotte stands, wedged tightly between an older woman with a pull cart overflowing with meats and cheeses and a man in an Italian-cut suit, likely headed to the financial district. In a wide stance, Charlotte transfers weight from side to side, steadying herself against every jerk of the train. Occasionally, she rises on her tiptoes to reach the handle above her but then her arm grows tired, her fingers numb.

She loosens her wool scarf and slides two fingers along her throat, feeling the *thump, thump* of her rising pulse.

She unzips her parka, but it's too late; she's overheating and her head throbs.

The smell of cheese doesn't help.

The bass from a nearby teenager's headphones distracts her. What song is that? Nineties hip hop.

Perhaps she can change her boss's mind. She can head back to the office before most of her colleagues arrive for the day and discover the news. She had been caught off guard this morning, stuttering, "Thank you for the opportunity," after handing over the takeout trays of her colleague's coffees.

"It's just not a great fit," Toni had said with a shrug, as if the decision of Charlotte's termination was made on a whim.

But now, as Charlotte fans herself with a glove, she mulls over her recent behaviour—calling in sick every other day, the hard days making it next to impossible to get out of bed, the aches restricting her breath.

"Stand clear of the doors. Doors are closing," the conductor mumbles over the speaker.

Charlotte must find a seat. She must hang tight for one more stop, and then most of the finance workers will exit and give up their coveted spots. A young man seated a few feet away avoids eye contact. *Okay, fine, don't offer your seat to a woman in her early thirties.* But hasn't he noticed the older woman hunched over with the cheese?

Charlotte rummages in her purse in search of a mint or granola bar. "Your blood sugar is low," her mom always says in these situations. It's nothing more than that. Charlotte just needs to eat something. She checks her pulse again. *Thump, thump, thump.*

She opens her purse wide and retrieves her spiral-bound notebook with this morning's to-do list written in flawless penmanship:

  `-Take the subway`
  `-Get coffee for the team`

—Tell Toni about your mentorship idea. It will land!

The conductor's voice echoes through the speaker again, but this time Charlotte can barely make out his words. The noises of the busy subway fade away—her pounding heart taking center stage—and her grasp on the journal wavers. The book falls to the floor seconds before her bag, followed by Charlotte herself.

When she comes to, she is slumped on the ground with her head between her knees, keenly aware that she is wearing a skirt. Cool sweat covers her back and neck, and she paws at her strawberry blonde bangs that have plastered to her forehead. Sound finally resurfaces, the rhythm of the hip hop reverberating through the train.

"Doo-Wop" by Lauryn Hill.

The older woman with the cart fans Charlotte with her newspaper. "Do you want a nibble of cheese, dear? You took a spill."

Charlotte shakes her head but can't find the words to pass or explain that the smell of Gruyère is making her feel worse.

The woman continues to flap the folded paper like a wounded butterfly with one working wing. "My grandson has the same thing. He gets overwhelmed. Stressed. Takes a pill now and sees Dr. Avery at the medical center near St. Clair station." She squints at the fluorescent light above them. "Or is it Dr. Avon?"

This isn't stress, Charlotte thinks. *There's something bigger going on here.*

The doors open with the bell's descending chimes, and most of the commuters clear out.

"Get some help, dear. The Devil comes for the weak ones." The woman shoves a brick of cheese toward Charlotte, who politely declines and crawls to the closest seat.

Charlotte opens her call history, and the word *Mom* repeats itself in an infinite log. Her parents will put her up in the guest bedroom like last time.

Her parents will make everything better.

At least, until they abandon her.

Chapter Three

CHARLOTTE

The familiarity of the Boyds' kitchen wraps Charlotte up in a hug as she sits at the table, her legs crossed in front of her, a thermometer dangling from her mouth. She has swapped the restrictive pencil skirt for a pair of her mom's flannel pyjamas, which are pilling from too many washes. Avoiding eye contact with her parents, she traces the flowers on the plastic placemat with her index finger.

The thermometer beeps, and Charlotte's mother, Sheryl, runs over to consult it. "Nope, completely normal range. You're not sick. Just need to eat something." Sheryl replaces the thermometer with a banana, bringing it to Charlotte's mouth. "Eat the banana, Char. You need to raise your blood sugar."

Charlotte grabs the snack. "Got it." The fruit rolls around in her mouth, its flesh pasty, its flavour potent. "It was so embarrassing. Everyone was staring."

Sheryl tousles her fresh bob, drawing Charlotte's attention to the caramel blonde highlights masking the usual grey. "Oh, don't worry about it. We've all been there." Her mother's voice is steeped in forced optimism.

"You've fainted on a subway?"

This is how Sheryl always reacts to Charlotte's spells. *We've all been there. It's not a big deal. You just need to eat a snack.*

"It was the third time this week, Mom. There's something seriously wrong with me."

Sheryl slides her glasses down the bridge of her nose, peering over them suspiciously. "Are you eating breakfast before you go to work? Don't wait to eat at the office."

"I was fired this morning." Charlotte averts her eyes. Surely, it's better to rip off the bandage.

"Oh, Charlotte." Sheryl says, dipping her head.

Her father, Jared, looks up from his 5000-piece puzzle that covers the entire table. "Oh? At the architecture firm? That one sounded promising." He places the eye of a sea turtle he has been holding into its rightful spot. "Gotcha." He chortles.

Lately, everything is about sea turtles as her parents count down the days until they can escape Toronto's frigid winter for the Florida Keys. Charlotte still can't believe they are acting upon their retirement dream. And without her.

Sheryl places a hand on Charlotte's. "That's okay. We'll find you something better." She rises from the table with purpose and retrieves the address and telephone notebook she keeps on a desk by the landline. "They weren't very nice there, anyway. Made you do the coffee runs. You have too much experience for that. You're not some fresh-out-of-school twenty-year-old." She jabs her finger at a name in the book. "Jared, what about calling Olivia? Charlotte could shadow her at the event planning company. At least until she finds her passion."

Passion—a lie the nineties generation was sold by their parents who were tired of working nine-to-five office jobs. *Find a job you love, and you'll never work a day in your life.* They clearly had no foresight into Toronto's housing crisis. Passion doesn't pay the mortgage.

"Event planning could be fun. It's very glamorous, I bet. Maybe you'll even meet someone." Sheryl nudges her daughter, but Charlotte only rolls her eyes. "You're young. You're beautiful. You should be taking full advantage of the city."

Charlotte chews on her lip. The only child gets it the worst, with all the opportunity and responsibility landing on one pair of shoulders. And Charlotte's parents have placed her on a particularly high pedestal.

She is the one who survived, after all.

Charlotte tilts her head, imagining the logistics of coordinating caterers, managing guest lists, and ultimately, the humiliation of sucking up to entitled hosts. "I don't want to start over again. It's too much right now."

Sheryl nods. "I understand. It's been tough for you. But honey, the accident was fifteen years ago." She brings her hand to her mouth. Then she fills her lungs with practically all the air in the room, the silence suffocating. "We just want you to find your way back."

Charlotte rubs her face in her palms. "Can I stay here for a while? We can sublet the apartment."

Jared and Sheryl shoot each other glances. Only then does Charlotte realize they are wearing matching apricot shirts.

In front of Jared sits a collection of seafoam green puzzle pieces that will make up one of the turtle's underbellies. "That's actually not going to work this time, Char. We've moved up our trip."

Sheryl clears her throat. "We leave in two days."

The room begins to spin, and the teacups on the kitchen wallpaper twirl. "I thought you were staying until January." Charlotte feels for her pulse.

Jared shrugs. "Someone's gotta save the turtles."

"A spot opened earlier," Sheryl explains, her eyes flitting from Jared to Charlotte. "The renters before us need to get back for a wedding. On New Year's Eve, actually. What fun?" she adds, her voice travelling several octaves higher.

The reality that she'll be spending Christmas alone hits Charlotte like a punch to the gut. She shakes her head in bewilderment. "Why can't I stay here while you're gone?"

Sheryl's voice returns to its rightful pitch. "The realtor is showing the house next week."

Jared raises his head from the puzzle, a goofy grin smeared on his face. "There are already three viewings booked." He rubs his hands together excitedly. "I smell a bidding war."

Banana and stomach acid churn behind Charlotte's breastbone, threatening to claw their way back up her throat. "I might throw up."

Charlotte's nausea grows as she watches her mother rush to the cupboard to retrieve a bowl. Sheryl shoves it in front of Charlotte and takes position behind her, grasping her hair out of the way.

Jared, who appears to be unfazed by the event, says, "I've got it! Charlotte will be our project manager on the Anville renovations. She needs a job. She needs a place to stay. Two birds with one stone." He nods to himself, appearing satisfied to have solved at least one puzzle in the room.

Outside, a cloud drifts in front of the sun, darkening the kitchen, and a chill travels up the nape of Charlotte's neck.

Part of her parents' retirement plan included purchasing a late-nineteenth-century home in Anville's wine country, two hours west of the city.

"We'll spend the winter months on the beach and summer months sipping on Riesling and maple ice wine," Sheryl had said months earlier when she showed Charlotte high-contrast photos of the derelict four-square with a tragic past.

Charlotte shakes her head frantically. There is no way she will move to that house. Especially not alone.

Sheryl releases Charlotte's hair and claps her hands together. "A great idea! Put her architecture experience to good use."

"Architecture experience?" Charlotte scoffs. "I was barely an office manager." At the firm, Charlotte's main responsibilities involved fulfilling the coffee and lunch orders and changing the printer cartridge when the ink ran dry, yet to her parents, she was the next Antoni Gaudí.

Sheryl waves Charlotte's comment off and begins rummaging in the desk drawer, completely oblivious to the grimace Charlotte wears. "We've already put together a guide for the contractors. You'll just need to make sure they follow it. Ensure they don't take any shortcuts."

Charlotte jerks her head toward her mother. "I'm not going to the middle of nowhere to stay in that creepy house."

"It's not creepy. It just needs a little freshening up," Jared says.

"Dad, a girl killed herself there. Right in the house. That's the only reason it was cheap."

Sheryl loses her cheery disposition, her voice firm and her lips pursed. "Don't talk like that!"

Charlotte's mouth falls open, her mother's words hitting like a slap. How can she be expected to stay there without them?

Sheryl softens her tone. "Char, babe, we can't help you if you don't want us to."

Charlotte lurches forward and lets the half-digested banana fill the bowl. Without her mother holding her hair, strands sneak in and mingle with the vomit. She wipes her mouth on her purple and green flannel sleeve.

With opportune timing, Sheryl rushes to her daughter's, washcloth in hand.

"It's not that I don't want to help." Charlotte dabs her mouth with the warm cloth. "It's just—this is my home. Everything I need is here."

"I thought it would be a fun project you could see through from start to finish for once," Sheryl says.

Charlotte's throat burns from her stomach acid, but her heart aches far more.

Sheryl finds her seat. "We can float next month's rent, but you'll be responsible for February."

Charlotte's shoulders sag as she considers her future. She'll need to contact the temp agency when she gets home, but finding a new position could take weeks.

"It would be a paid position," Jared says, raising his eyebrows.

Sheryl nods in agreement. "Absolutely, we'd pay you. We'd have to hire a project manager anyway."

"You'd be doing us a solid," Jared says with a wink.

"At least think about it," Sheryl says, patting Charlotte's knee. "But we'll need to know soon so we can sort out your apartment."

At least being a project manager would mean managing her hours and working from "home"—if she could call it home. She breathes deeply, assessing the tightness in her chest. A niggling feeling remains that goes beyond annoyance at leaving the comforts and conveniences of the city behind. When she thinks about her parents' impulse purchase and the sinister events it housed, her abdomen grows more unsettled.

"What do you say, sweet pea?" Jared's grin has shrunk, his smile more tender.

She considers agreeing, knowing how it will ease their consciences to believe she is taken care of while they are basking in the Florida rays. If she rejects the offer, they might postpone the trip. They'll put her first like they always do. She tilts her head to the side, inspecting her mom's uncharacteristic new hairdo. It suits her.

"Will you at least pay me like a real project manager?"

Sheryl lets out a squeal and squeezes her daughter's shoulders before Charlotte can change her mind. "Oh, this will be great for you!"

Charlotte sinks into her seat, the heaviness in her chest swelling.

`Tonight's to-do list:`

`-Wash hair`

`-Order Mom and Dad a going-away present (something with sea turtles)`

`-Find out more about Anville and the house on Elizabeth Drive`

Chapter Four

CHARLOTTE

C harlotte lies stretched across her bed, not wanting to leave the freshly washed linens. It's a scent she is embarrassed to admit she hasn't smelled in a while, but struggling with fitted sheets and duvet covers without help from a partner isn't something she wants to tackle weekly.

In a few days, someone else will be lying in her bed—a twenty-some-thing-year-old business student taking advantage of the four-month, fully-furnished sublet while they finish their degree. The student wanted the place right away and offered slightly over asking, which Charlotte's parents accepted without missing a beat. The convenience of it all makes Charlotte wonder if her parents had a tenant waitlist ready, knowing she would fuck up again.

Charlotte squeezed what she could of her life into the two eigh-teen-inch suitcases that sit at the foot of her bed, reminding her she will be far from the city and its buzz by tomorrow evening.

She is still in shock that she agreed to her parents' plan to pack up and leave what Toronto offers—everything walkable from Pad Thai to tampons and batteries. Even if she isn't taking full advantage of its opportunities yet, she's at least near the action; she is among other thirty-year-olds, some of whom, like her, are still trying to figure their lives out.

The average age of Anville is sixty-five, so her parents will fit right in when they return in the spring. Perhaps Charlotte can pick up the game of bridge while she's there or learn to knit a pearl stitch.

She rolls onto her side, reaching for her vibrating phone.

A message from her mother appears on the screen.

Are you coming by to get the car today?

Charlotte trudges to the window, phone gripped tightly in her hand. Outside, the snow falls lightly, collecting in small clumps on the street below.

Weather isn't great over the next few days. Maybe I'll just take a cab there.

She doesn't have to wait long for the response.

Really? You don't want access to a car for four months? I have no idea what Anville transit is like.

A pulse throbs in Charlotte's tense neck. It's as if her mother has forgotten everything Charlotte's been through with Sheryl's focus on Florida and their retirement dream. While Charlotte considers a response, an ellipsis reveals her mother isn't finished with her thought.

If someone offers on the house, you might have to come back and get the car anyway. Let us know either way. We were hoping you'd drop us off at the airport ...

Charlotte never agreed to an airport drop-off. Airports can be confusing for a confident driver, not to mention someone who took four attempts to pass their full license and has avoided driving for years.

Sorry to disappoint. If you can make other arrangements to get to the airport, that would be best. Safe trip. Love you.

Charlotte tosses her phone on the bed and doesn't bother to retrieve it when she hears another buzz.

The photo in the corner of her full-length mirror catches her eye. It has followed her to every apartment like a trailing shadow. Charlotte sits on a balance beam in the middle of four girlfriends. They wear competition make-up—winged eyeliner and lipstick the colour of blood. Their eyelashes are fringed curtains, making them appear doll-like at sixteen. There is a reason this is the photo she chooses to display rather than something casual and barefaced. It keeps them at just enough of a distance—suspended in time like the beam they sit on. She takes the photo in her hands, flipping it over to read the ink that has bled from water damage. The names of her friends, once written in cursive, now blur together, nearly wiped away. She tucks it into the front pocket of one suitcase.

Walking aimlessly around her apartment, Charlotte considers how she'd like to spend her final night in the city. She settles on ordering takeout from her favourite Thai restaurant and sets herself up with her laptop in front of the TV to continue binge-watching *Black Mirror*. Her internet is good until the end of the month, so she might as well take advantage before she's out in the boonies with weak cell service. She gulps at the thought of being stranded without data.

Charlotte has avoided researching Anville, fearing she'll discover more unnerving details about the family who lived in the house she will call home for the next few months, but something in the pit of her stomach urges her to type two words into the search engine: *Anville suicide*. She quickly selects the "news" filter, not wanting to see the images conjured by the second word. A few stories down, she encounters a headline in the local Anville paper.

Family is shocked by local teen's tragic death.

While there is no direct mention of Lark Peters' suicide in the news report, likely out of respect for the family, clues sprinkled throughout the story point the death in that direction. Charlotte finds herself particularly drawn to a quote from the brother, nineteen years old at the time of Lark's death, and rereads it a few times.

Lark was a passionate, creative, thoughtful young woman. She was deeply inquisitive and self-reflective, which often meant she would look at herself with a critical eye. While Lark kept most of these thoughts to herself, she would confide in me with the big stuff. Lark knew she could come to me with anything, so this still doesn't make sense to me—probably never will.

Charlotte closes the laptop without exiting the story. She wonders if the brother still lives in town—if he's finally come to terms with his sister's death or if he still asks the higher powers that be, *why her?* A feeling Charlotte knows all too well, though in her case, the question is, *why not me?*

She continues to ponder this while she shovels green curry and rice into her mouth, and she has trouble thinking about much else as she lies in her bed for one last sleep in the apartment.

Chapter Five

CHARLOTTE

The next day, a ceaseless pulse hums through Charlotte's body as she swings the door shut on the bare apartment. There's no turning back now. Her parents are out of the country, the new tenant is set to arrive first thing in the morning, and an extensive to-do list awaits her in the renovation binder that is currently weighing down one of her suitcases.

Charlotte had wanted to hit the road before sundown, but last-minute errands stole the hours away, and now, as she enters the cab at midnight, she feels as though she is a runaway, escaping her past and skulking into a new life.

Charlotte clenches her eyes tight as her cabbie merges onto the highway, and she eases into her seat only slightly upon discovery that the roads have minimal traffic. An hour and a half into the trip and a third of the way through her playlist, her eyes grow heavy, the lids bobbing, but she dares not fall asleep. No, she must stay alert. Anville's exit won't be far now. When they pull off the highway, turning onto a rural road, the snow squalls drift across the asphalt, masking what lies ahead, and Charlotte inches forward in the back seat, prepared to warn the driver of impending brake lights.

Charlotte's whitened fingertips unravel their tight grip from the door handle as the cab scrapes a snowbank, slowing to a halt on the residential street in front of Charlotte's new home. She attempts to force open her door, but the snowbank prevents her from freeing it more than an inch. She concedes and climbs out the other side.

The driver unloads her two suitcases onto the street and then speeds away, leaving her to fend for herself up the icy steps.

With the December snow falling and in the quiet of the night, the four-square resembles a scene from a Hallmark holiday film. But as she gets closer, she realizes it's not movie-picture perfect.

Stacked bay windows grace the left side of the house. Their overhead gables match the green roof and front door. Charlotte's parents want the accents painted black. "The green is dated and the paint's chipped," Sheryl had told her before leaving for Florida.

Charlotte finds it hard to imagine her parents, who both grew up in the city, living in this sleepy town. Did their new dream include buying side-by-side rocking chairs and spending their days on the sagging grey porch drinking their morning coffees and nibbling peaches from a nearby fruit stand? Saving sea turtles in the winter? Where does she fit into this?

When Charlotte unlocks and opens the front door, an overwhelming, putrid smell greets her and adrenaline courses through her veins. She uses the blue glow of her phone to find a light switch. With a flick, the foyer comes into view, and Charlotte follows the dark wooden beams on the ceiling. She stands, dripping slush onto the floors, and hears her mother's voice in her head, "We'd like to keep the original hardwood." She quickly removes her boots and places them at the front door.

As she turns left to head into the living room, she nearly trips.

Oh, dear God.

Charlotte flicks on the living room light and considers fleeing. At her feet, red and black milk crates sit stacked high, full to the brim with worn board games and gimmicky kitchen appliances with food remnants caked on them. Junk that the previous owners couldn't be bothered to take with them. And amongst these piles of crates is a kitty litter box—which explains the smell.

Tomorrow's to-do list:
-Order a dumpster
-Shovel the steps
-Buy a shoe mat and air freshener spray

One task at a time. It's the only way Charlotte can get through the day.

She considers retiring upstairs, the long day catching up to her, but her eye catches a cardboard box labelled *Lark*, and Charlotte finds herself closing the gap. She traces the young girl's name with her finger, her stomach free-falling as she does so. How strange it feels to touch a dead person's things. But Charlotte is drawn to it, her morbid curiosity winning over respect, her fatigue disregarded like the belongings she eyes.

Charlotte unrolls a creased poster of the band Broken Social Scene and lays it on the hardwood, weighing down the edges with a porcelain piggy bank and a ballerina jewelry box that plays a tinny "Clair de Lune." She runs her fingers through a collection of CDs her father would call melancholy rock: The Shins, Brand New, Death Cab for Cutie—bands Charlotte enjoyed in her youth.

From the box, Charlotte lifts a framed dance examination certificate awarded to Lark

Peters. Charlotte practiced ballet when she was young but gave up her commitment when she peaked at five feet, two inches. She pivoted to gymnastics but quit that at seventeen for more dire reasons.

She is poking around a box of Disney VHS tapes when she spots *Alice in Wonderland*. It was once her favourite Disney movie until a Victorian Literature class exposed Lewis Carroll's inappropriate relationship with eleven-year-old Alice Liddell, leaving a bad taste in her mouth whenever she thought of the character whom Liddell inspired. Charlotte turns the case over to scan the back copy, but something shifts inside. She opens the case to reveal a moleskin notebook. She feels a surge of excitement as she runs her finger along the front of the journal, which is embossed with the word *Bird*. She should leave it alone, return it to the case. It doesn't belong to her. She bites her lip as she flips it open, settling on an entry dated sixteen years ago.

Then, she swats it closed and backs away as though someone will witness her transgression.

Charlotte catches a glance of a dark form out of the corner of her eye, and a loud bang echoes throughout the room.

"Jesus," she utters, turning around to find the stack of board games strewn across the floor, a spinning top twirling frantically around the hardwood.

A black and white cat stares up at her. The feline lets out a groan.

"Where did you come from?" Charlotte's voice warms. "Come here, baby."

The cat weaves through Charlotte's legs, scratching its back in the process. Before she can pet it, the cat trots up the stairs.

"Hello?" she calls towards the wooden staircase, her voice wavering. Maybe there was a misunderstanding. A miscommunication around the closing date. Charlotte can't fathom an owner leaving behind all their belongings, let alone their family member.

She tiptoes through the kitchen toward the back door. Once she confirms it's locked, she presses her forehead to the glass. In the wintery night, an oak tree towers, its naked branches reaching for Charlotte as if summoning her.

It is just her mind playing tricks on her.

She gathers her bags, pausing for a moment to eye the moleskin journal. She can almost hear it calling her name, tempting her conscience to give in. She tucks it under her arm and climbs the creaking stairs until she reaches the top, where she is met with a bathroom. The black and white checked floor reminds her of one of her dad's unfinished puzzles, the tiles chipped in various sections. The claw foot bathtub needs bleaching. Charlotte hopes the stains are from hard water, though she can't help but consider whether they are bloodstains, and this is where Lark took her own life.

Charlotte counts a total of three bedrooms, which are all empty, allowing her to breathe easily. She settles in a room at the front of the house with butter yellow walls—farthest away from the room painted purple, which she assumes belonged to Lark.

She unrolls her foam mattress and sleeping bag, positioning them against the wall. Then, she climbs into her bedding and turns onto her side so she has a view of the door. Pulling the fabric above her eyes, she allows her warm breath to fill the space. She can't shake the feeling that she isn't alone—that someone or something lives here, too. She uncovers

21

her eyes. She'd rather see it coming—whatever *it* is. Tonight, she'll sleep with the light on.

Her eyelids flutter as she finally succumbs to her sleepiness until a bang interrupts the stillness. Her feline friend must have knocked over something else. Charlotte holds her breath for a moment, clutching her sleeping bag to her chest. *Thump, thump, thump.* The sound of her heartbeat rises. But that is the only sound she hears.

It will take some time to become familiar with the nightly noises of this home, but she suspects she'll be gone before she's acclimatized.

She drags Lark's journal closer to her. Flipping through its pages, marked with blue, black, and red ink, she rebels against her moral compass. The entries of poetry, sketches, and confessions whisper her name, inviting Charlotte to devour them.

Chapter Six

LARK

January 1, 2006

Dear diary? Dear journal? I guess it's up to me to address my own notebook.

Dear Darryl,

Yes, that seems more fitting since this was your idea.

As I sit down to write my first journal entry, I feel like a walking cliché. Starting my new journal on January 1st—who am I, Bridget Jones? I don't have any resolutions—I'm not trying to get the attention of a guy, lose weight, or launch a career in journalism. But I am attempting to capture my feelings more productively, as you suggested, and it is fitting to do this in January when the world tells us it's okay to feel depressed. It's the post-holiday slump, not a chemical imbalance in my brain.

School is out for another week, and you are practically living in Xander's basement (anything to get away from Mom and "Please, call me

Jake," and their honeymoon period). Thanks, Bro, leave me to watch him caress her while she washes the dishes.

Mom found the mark on my arm on Christmas morning of all days. I wonder if she bought that hideous charm bracelet because she wanted a reason to see my wrist up close. "This was the one you wanted, right?" she asked. "We were at the mall, and you pointed to it at that kiosk with the butterfly broaches." I didn't have the heart to tell her I had no fucking clue what she was talking about. But who did she mix me up with? It's not like she has any other girls to buy gifts for. She offered to help me with the clasp and then her eyes zeroed in on the scratch, her thumb brushing over it to verify it was real. She looked concerned but mostly just sad. I told her it was a dance injury. Made a joke about the competitiveness now that I am in the Intermediate level. She didn't buy it, but she also didn't offer much help. She's distracted, I guess. New love will do that. Sigh. We'll see how long this one lasts.

You've known about the cut longer than Mom. What went through your mind when you first noticed it? I guess you believe this journal will help me hash everything out. Big brothers have to look out for their sisters that way, right? Teach the bully a lesson. Beat up the asshole who breaks her heart. The journal is your attempt to fight the enemies in my head, but I'm guessing we'll need more than a leather-bound book to do that.

So, Darryl, this is for you. My attempt to sort it all out because the truth is, you are the reason I didn't cut deeper that day.

———— ◆ ————

January 3, 2006

What's worse than hearing Mom having sex? And sorry if this brings up memories of "Frisky Fred" and his moans that sounded like our dial-up internet. What's worse, is stumbling upon Mom's porn. Yes, her porn. Excuse me while I throw up my fish sticks.

I went into her room last night to grab my *Garden State* DVD. You know nothing cheers me up like Natalie Portman's tap dancing. I pressed the eject button and a nondescript DVD spit itself out, with text in all caps that read *NAUGHTY SCHOOLGIRLS VOL 4*. I. Kid. You. Not. Either naughty schoolgirls turn Mom on, or she's been watching porn with Jake. And the fact that it was volume four worries me this isn't the first time they've had a movie night ...

Anyway, if you're looking for material, she doesn't owe it back at the adult video store until Tuesday. Barf.

———————— • ◆ • ————————

January 6, 2006

When people say *those are the best years of your life,* are they referring to high school or college? Please tell me college because if these are the best years, I might as well just end it now. Dani is being weird, distant, and honestly a bit cold ever since the last day of school before break. How can you go from hanging out with someone practically all hours of the day to bailing three times in a row? And her excuses are getting ridiculous. Like, she might as well have said she was washing her hair.

Did I think we'd be best friends forever? Call me naïve, but I did.

I've been thinking about earlier this year, the Sunday before grade ten. She invited me over to wax our legs—some sort of rite of passage to womanhood. We were no longer the lowest on the food chain now

25

that we were "sophomores." We bought those pre-waxed strips and took turns tearing off layers of each other's skin. My stubble wasn't long enough to grip, and she ended up breaking out in hives, but it will always be one of my favourite hangs with her.

She told me how she was insecure that she'd just gotten train tracks. How she was worried she would cut someone's lip the next time she kissed them. I opened up about how some days I feel like a sadder version of myself. It's like an illustrator who has lost all the warm colours in their palette and was forced to draw me in only purples, greys, and blues. Then Dani adopted this whimsical grin, and she looked like a little pixie with her cute turned-up nose and a stray curl at her temple. She ran from her room and returned with a notebook and markers. She made me close my eyes for ten minutes, and then she passed me the notebook.

Dani had full-on invented a comic and "Birdie" was the hero. Birdie, a stick figure with thick fringe bangs and a triangle dress, made up of yellows, reds and oranges. In each scene, Birdie was thrown into troubling scenarios but always came out triumphant. On the first page, Birdie stepped on a banana peel, slipping in front of the entire school, but ended up inventing skates, complete with banana peel treads that everyone vied for. The second story featured Birdie getting a piece of broccoli stuck in her teeth on picture day (okay, I didn't say they were entirely original) but because of Birdie's influence, she started a new trend—food in teeth, the latest accessory, plus a snack for when you get hungry.

And at the end of every scene Birdie stood beside Dani, their three-pronged hands touching.

I think I've been playing this hangout over and over in my head because it was the last time I really opened up about my depression to her.

And I guess I wish our latest hangout had gone more like that instead of horribly, horribly wrong.

Chapter Seven

CHARLOTTE

The morning sun pours into the room, forcing Charlotte to face the new day. She rolls onto her side away from the exposed window, her aching muscles reminding her she spent the night on two inches of foam.

Lark's diary lies upside down on the floor beside Charlotte, a reminder of her rebellion, its pages playing tug of war with its spine. *No more.* She closes the book with a sense of finality. Lark goes back in the crate today.

Charlotte reaches for her phone. It's nine in the morning, and she's already missed two phone calls from her parents—or rather, bosses. She props her pillow against the wall and leans back, readying herself to return their call. After four rings, Sheryl's cheery voice booms through the speaker with a voicemail greeting. Charlotte hangs up before the receiver has a chance to record her stomach growl. She grabs her own notebook and plots out her day, adding grocery shopping to last night's to-do list.

Before Charlotte can write another line, a light thump issues on the bedroom door. It's followed by a series of taps which are punctuated with a murmur from her feline friend. Charlotte creeps across the room with careful steps as if she truly is a visitor in this house and might wake up the host. She hesitates for a moment before slowly opening the door. The cat rushes in, immediately heading for Charlotte's bed. It lets out another cry.

-Grocery shop (human food + kitty food)

"What is your name, little one?" Charlotte asks, consulting its collar for a clue.

The cat nuzzles into Charlotte's hand and then scampers back down the stairs, coaxing Charlotte to follow.

The stillness of the house jars Charlotte as she counts each step she descends. In the city, she was conditioned to hear car alarms, sirens, and dogs barking on a typical Monday morning. But in Anville, everything moves at a slower pace, and she isn't sure how to match it.

The cat trots over to an empty margarine container near the fridge and paws at a drop of water, her eyes flitting to Charlotte, who obliges, filling the makeshift dish from the kitchen tap. Out of solidarity, she pours herself a glass, but the mineral taste of the well water causes her to gag.

She moves about the room. It's her space now, though she feels like a guest. The plaster feels rough and uneven against Charlotte's fingers as she runs her hand along the surface of the archway that connects the kitchen to the living room. Soon, the wall will be knocked down and replaced with a wooden support beam, offering an open-concept area perfect for the Boyds' trivia nights. Lark and Darryl's names and ages climb up the drywall in graphite scribbles, displaying their heights. The siblings were tall, both surpassing Charlotte's current height before they turned fourteen.

Charlotte approaches the living room like it is forbidden. She eyes the stacks of black and red boxes, counting them curiously. Weren't there more yesterday?

"I need to get out of this place," she says aloud and then, as if in response, the doorbell rings, giving her an out.

Charlotte notices the colour of the woman's highlights first, the periwinkle blue complementing her otherwise white hair. Then she spots the cane, with its silver garland winding from the handle to the rubber foot.

The woman thrusts her arm toward Charlotte and clears her throat. "I'm Leslie, your neighbour." She gestures across the street. "I'm at the white house. But I'm not the POTUS. I'm POA." She cups her hand at the side of her mouth. "President of Anville."

"Oh," Charlotte says, returning the shake, her hand matching Leslie's firm grip.

"Not actually. But I am one to know because I know everything that goes on in this town. Which is precisely how I knew you moved in last night."

Charlotte sways uncomfortably, a tight smile pulling at the edge of her mouth. She imagines the woman peering out her window, eyes pressed against binoculars, and then launching a phone tree to advise the town of the new resident.

"I just wanted to invite you over for tea. A welcome to Anville."

Charlotte glances down at her slippers. "I'm not sure today will work. I'm still getting everything set up."

"Tomorrow?" Leslie offers.

Charlotte bites her lip, scouring her brain for an excuse.

Leslie taps her cane on the porch. "Wednesday?" She purses her lips. "Thursday, then. And I'm not taking no for an answer. One cup of tea—it's the least you can do to be polite."

Charlotte nods stiffly.

"Great," Leslie says, rocking back on her heels. "And you might want to give these stairs a shovel. A big storm is coming this afternoon." She turns to leave.

"What time do you want me on Thursday?" Charlotte asks toward Leslie's back.

Leslie swivels around, spritely for a septuagenarian with a cane. "Tea is always served at three, my dear. And if you bring a batch of baked goods, you can get in on my annual bake swap." Leslie taps the side of her nose twice. "Nanaimo bars would be suitable."

Charlotte stands stunned in the doorway, watching Leslie march across the road back to her four-square until the vibration from Charlotte's phone pulls her attention away.

"Mo-om," she says, the word getting caught in her throat.

"Char, baby! Sorry we missed you. You'll never guess what I'm doing right now."

Charlotte closes the door, securing the lock. "Saving sea turtles?" She leans against the door, the social encounter with Leslie having nearly winded her.

"That's planned for Wednesday, actually. No, I'm on a golf course, and I just shot—what was it, Jared? I just shot 200 yards. My first time golfing! Can you believe it? Dad says I'm a natural. Anyway, how are you settling in?"

Charlotte moves to the living room. "Not great." She overturns a crate of blankets, constructing a seat for herself. "There's a bunch of junk in the living room."

"Junk? What do you mean? Whose?"

"The previous owners left half their stuff here. I don't think they've fully moved out."

Charlotte feels gutted by the muffled chatter in the background competing for her mother's attention. "Mom? Did you hear me?"

"Sorry, say that again," Sheryl says.

"The owners left everything here. Even their cat. Are you sure they're gone?"

"Yes, of course, the closing date was two weeks ago. And, as far as I know, the woman moved into a facility in September, so I'm not sure whose cat that is. Maybe a stray got in somehow?"

"That's comforting."

"Oh, Char, everything is going to be okay, babe. You're just overwhelmed right now. Why don't you run yourself a hot bath?"

The thought of bathing in the stained tub upstairs causes Charlotte to shudder.

"Oh, it's the next hole, and I'm up. We'll call you later tonight and see how your day went."

"Love you," Charlotte manages, resisting the urge to beg them to come home.

"We love you, too."

Feeling restless, she moves to the mess in the middle of the room. She is circling the boxes, a bird homing in on its prey, when she freezes, sucking in a sharp breath. The box with Lark's name has disappeared. Gone without a trace. Charlotte hasn't left the house. The doors are locked and secured, yet the box no longer sits where she left it in the pile. Her throat tightens when she thinks of the diary upstairs.

Perhaps opening its pages was a bad idea—like unlocking Pandora's box.

Chapter Eight

CHARLOTTE

The snow has been falling since Leslie warned Charlotte of the impending storm. With nearly seven hours of wet, slushy flurries and more in the forecast, Charlotte decides the shovelling can't wait until morning.

She is on her way out the front door when a scraping sound gives her pause. Metal against asphalt, echoing throughout the silent winter's night. She's surprised someone else has the same idea at ten at night. Standing on the porch, she eyes the driveways across the street; all, including Leslie's, remain untouched. She grabs her shovel, which leans against the window ledge, and quietly clears a pathway to the other side of the porch. She stops for a moment when the wood gives away her position with a loud creak. Once she reaches the side railing, she leans on her forearms and cranes her neck to see who, like her, is out tonight.

Charlotte's eyes widen as she grips the railing. The scraping is coming from her laneway.

A man stands in front of her detached garage near the back of the house, zig-zagging a pattern into the driveway with a shovel of his own. He stops suddenly, forcing Charlotte to retreat and seek cover from behind the brick wall. Her heart beats fast, and she realizes she has been holding her breath, afraid to make any noise. She allows her breath to escape her mouth, and the white fog floats through the air, waltzing with the crystals of falling snow. The scraping resumes, and Charlotte reclaims her position, hugging the rough brick.

Who is this man?

Warm light seeps through the small semi-circle windows above the garage door, which appear to be frowning at her. Charlotte wonders if the light has been on this whole time, and she missed it in the daylight. No, it wasn't on last night when she arrived, she is almost certain.

The man wears a blue flannel jacket and heavy-duty snow boots. A toque covers his long, dark hair. It is hard to see his face in the dull glow of the garage light, so she can't determine his age, but she guesses he is under fifty by the way he effortlessly hurls heaping piles of snow. Charlotte grabs her phone from her pocket. She should call the police. This man is trespassing. It's late in the night. But she stops dialling after the number nine. How will she answer the question, "What's your emergency?" *A neighbour is shovelling my driveway.* She shoves the phone back into her pocket. Maybe he doesn't realize she's moved in. Maybe he lives close by and is trying to maintain the property while the house is unoccupied. Perhaps Leslie hasn't given him the memo yet.

Then, the loud creaking of rusted metal breaks the silence. She leans over the railing once again. The door to the garage has been pried open. And the scene inside wrenches Charlotte's stomach.

The garage has been transformed into a tiny home from a HGTV show. She gapes as she focuses on the furniture: a small kitchen table with a lawn chair tucked underneath, a floor lamp illuminating a floral recliner, a burnt orange carpet stretching from wall to wall, and a cot nestled against the back wall, complete with a knitted quilt.

Charlotte clasps her hand to her mouth.

The intruder removes his boots and then swiftly walks the length of the space, pausing to warm his hands in front of a space heater. He makes his way to a stack of milk crates—no different from the ones still stacked in Charlotte's living room. He rummages through a crate until he finds what he is looking for. Then, Charlotte watches as a puff of smoke escapes his mouth, and she smells his pastime, the earthy cannabis wafting over.

Charlotte ditches the shovel and rushes into the house, locking the door behind her. This man could be dangerous, and if he has access to the garage, he might have access to the house. She scampers to the kitchen, scaring the cat in the process, who clambers up the stairs. Charlotte flings open a drawer in search of a knife, scissors, or anything sharp that the owners might have left behind. She sinks to the floor, clutching a wine bottle opener, its spiralized metal protruding from her clenched fist. Then, she dials the police, stuttering that there's been a break-in at her house, and prays they arrive before the man makes his next move.

Chapter Nine

CHARLOTTE

C harlotte remains huddled in the corner of the kitchen, where she has a clear view of both entrances to the home. She holds her breath, trying to decipher whether the odd creak is from a floorboard or a gust of wind outdoors.

Who is he? Could it be Darryl, Lark's brother? The milk crates in the garage resemble the ones in the next room that hold his and Lark's memories. Charlotte crawls across the hardwood floor to the living room. That would explain the missing crates.

A pounding on the door jerks Charlotte from her trance and urges her to scramble to her feet. The knock is followed by a booming voice, "Anville Police."

Charlotte bolts to the foyer, pulling the door open slightly to reveal a uniformed officer who doesn't look much older than herself.

"Officer Armstrong. We received a call about a break and entry." His deep-blue eyes dart left towards the stacks of crates.

"Yes, I called it in. I only moved in a few days ago. It's my garage. A man is living there." Charlotte is still clutching the bottle opener close to her chest. "It's just out back."

Armstrong scratches his head, giving Charlotte the impression that he hasn't encountered a break-in before and isn't sure of the next step. She notes the state of his perfect, golden blonde hair and concludes a typical Anville police shift must be uneventful.

Then, as if he's given himself an internal pep talk, he exhales a breath. "I'll go take a look."

He turns to exit the house, and Charlotte adds, "He was doing drugs, too." She sinks into her stance, the guilt, a stone plummeting in her stomach. It was only weed, which is legal in Canada, but this intruder needs to leave, and the mention of drugs makes Armstrong quicken his pace.

Charlotte locks the door as soon as Officer Armstrong retreats, then consults the laundry room window, catching a glimpse of the officer approaching the garage. He pounds on the metal door a few times.

Charlotte snatches her coat and heads to the porch to spy from the spot where she first saw the man, but the garage now sits in darkness. The door is closed, and the lights are off as if nobody is home. Armstrong bangs on the garage door again and calls out, "If someone's in there, you better come out. This is private property."

Charlotte loses sight of the officer when he circles the garage, but he returns to the driveway a moment later with a shrug, as though he is satisfied with his inspection. Charlotte greets him at the top of the stairs, her eyebrows raised in anticipation.

Armstrong rocks on his heels, his hands shoved deep in his pockets. "I did a thorough search of the premises, and the garage is secure. Door is locked, lights are off. No one appears to be inside."

"That's impossible."

"Do you have the key to the garage? I could take a look inside for you."

"I don't know. I was only given a key to the front door. I haven't had a chance to change the locks yet."

"I did find a joint around the back of the garage. I bet some kids have been hanging out since the previous owners moved."

Charlotte zips up her coat to ward off the frigid air. "What about the son?" Charlotte pauses. It would be inappropriate to admit she knows about this family and their history. "My parents mentioned the woman living here had a son. Could it be him?"

"Darryl? Unlikely. We haven't seen him or his truck in weeks. We think he left town."

Charlotte nods, but it doesn't reassure her in the slightest. She holds out the key to the front door. "Any chance this key might work for the garage too? It's all I was given."

"Let's try it out." Armstrong's voice is filled with excitement.

Charlotte follows him down the steps and the back half of the driveway that was recently cleared of snow.

"There was definitely someone here. I didn't shovel the driveway."

"Helpful neighbour?" he suggests and then forces the key into the small opening beneath the handle. "In Anville, we look after each other." He tugs on the handle with a jerk, but the door doesn't budge.

Charlotte leans into the door, pressing her ear to its cold metal. The man must know they are out here. He's purposely being quiet.

"No dice," Armstrong says. "Must not be a universal lock. A good thing." He smiles, exposing a gap between his front teeth.

"Can you drive me to a hotel? I don't want to sleep here again until I can get the locks changed."

Armstrong consults his watch. "It's almost eleven. There's a B&B a couple of blocks over, but the owners won't be up. I'm sure they could get you a room in the morning."

Charlotte rubs her breastbone, trying to ease the tightness that grows. "No, no. That's not going to work," she says, her swirling thoughts escaping her mouth before she can suppress them. How can she be expected to stay here alone? "Is there another hotel? Motel?" She's certain her parents will cover whatever expenses she incurs. They'd want her to be smart in this situation. Safe.

Armstrong retreats to the house in a brisk walk, forcing Charlotte to trot after him.

"Or maybe you can stay to guard the garage? Or patrol the area for the night?" she pleads.

Armstrong rubs his hands together for warmth, and his eyes don't meet hers. The novelty of this exciting shift may be wearing off.

"I know what I saw," she continues.

When they arrive at the porch, he passes Charlotte the key, but he lingers.

She stares at the key in her palm, a false promise of security. "There's no way I'm going

to sleep here tonight."

"How about I take you to the Angel Pub in town?" he says, and Charlotte takes a step backward, unsure of the offer.

"They have a couple of rooms above the pub. It's nothing fancy, but I'm sure it'll be fine for the night."

The cat stretches in the open doorway on the other side of the screen door and lets out a cry.

"Do they allow pets?" Charlotte asks.

Chapter Ten

CHARLOTTE

-Spend the night at the dumpy Angel Pub
-Call to have the locks changed
-Did I mention get the fucking locks changed?

Officer Armstrong leans against the bar at the pub, engaged in deep conversation with an older man, also in uniform, who is settling his bill. The seasoned officer has deep-set eyes and a worry line between his brows that he wears like a badge of honour.

"I think he's back," Armstrong mumbles, and Charlotte catches herself staring at the men. She switches her gaze to her notebook, pretending not to eavesdrop.

The older cop wipes his mouth with the back of his hand. "Let's go to the house and do another patrol."

Charlotte shoves her notebook deep into the bag she packed within five minutes. The cat moans beside her and pokes a paw through a gap in the purple kitty crate, which Charlotte had managed to find amongst the junk in the living room.

The two policemen saunter towards the door and then the officer Charlotte has not yet met turns back to face her, his worry line still very much present. "Listen, sorry about your trouble tonight." He fishes in his wallet and presents a business card. "I heard they left you with quite the mess, too. Call this number, and they'll have that stuff taken to the dump for you. Tell them Officer Landry referred you."

Charlotte glances at the card, its sharp points digging into the pads of her thumb and forefinger. *Landry's Junk Removal.*

"My cousin owns it. He'll take care of it, no charge."

A smile pulls at the corners of her mouth. "Thank you." She can't help feeling bad about throwing out Lark's memories, as though keeping them there allows a piece of her to live on.

Charlotte watches the men exit through the door and disappear into the night with their matching midnight blue jackets.

"My wife's just making up your room. Can I get you a pint while you wait?"

Charlotte spins around on the stool to face the bar again. The owner of the inn is a middle-aged, bald man with a round, friendly face that has a purplish hue.

"I'm alright." Charlotte sinks into her seat, allowing her shoulders to slouch forward.

"Rough night? How about a drink?"

Once in her room, she'll be alone—truly alone—and the thought unnerves her. She glances up at the stairwell that leads to the inn's rooms.

The bartender sneaks a glance, too. "Cindy won't take long but let me at least get you a cider on the house."

Charlotte shrugs. She could use something to relax her, to ease the pressure beneath her ribcage. "Okay, sure. Whatever you have on tap."

Charlotte nudges an empty beer bottle out of her path, allowing her elbows to rest on the bar. She eyes a pile of peeled labels at the spot next to her where the officer sat. Christmas lights of red, green, and blue hang limply from the mirror behind the bar. Every few bulbs are burnt out and offer little festive cheer.

"You look like you saw a ghost," the bartender says.

"Something like that."

He tosses a pint glass and catches it behind his back with the opposite hand. Then, he consults Charlotte to see if she witnessed this display.

She smirks. "Fancy."

"I've been doing this a long time. You pick up tricks here and there. Anyway, it got somewhat of a laugh out of you, which was the point."

He fills the glass with a cloudy amber liquid and slides it across the bar. "It's a peach cider because, well, our town is swimming in peach orchards if you hadn't noticed."

Her parents had shown Charlotte a brochure on Anville from the town's culture and heritage department that had highlighted the many peach and wine orchards, the community theatre group that performs in the park during the warm season, and the award-winning botanical garden. This was right after they had mentioned the house's disturbing past, and Charlotte found it difficult to focus on anything but a lifeless teenager.

The cider is tart, and her cheeks ache in response. "How long have you owned this place?"

"Something like forty years? I'm Merle." He stretches out his hand, which is wet from the glass's condensation. "Cindy and I bought it in '82."

"Charlotte," she says and then discreetly wipes her palm on her leggings.

Merle sweeps the pile of labels into his hand and clears Landry's empty beer bottle. "I heard Landry and Armstrong talking. You've had some trouble with a break-in?"

Charlotte adjusts her position in her chair. In the city, bartenders don't have time for this kind of small talk. She wonders whether it stems from boredom, the residents seeking their daily gossip. But Merle's genuine look of concern, or perhaps the fact that he reminds her of her dad, is comforting. Especially since she hasn't been able to call her parents about the incident.

"Do you know the Peters? They used to live on Elizabeth Drive," she says.

Merle's mouth settles into a deep frown. He nods his head only slightly.

"Well, I've just moved into their house."

His eyes widen, revealing the whites. "You weren't kidding when you said you saw a ghost, then."

She scoffs. "I didn't see a ghost. But there's weird stuff going on over there."

"There's a lot of sad memories trapped in that house. You've heard what happened, I'm sure."

"It's terrible." Charlotte sips the drink. "But now someone's squatting in the garage."

"Huh. Living in the garage? You're sure? That would be frigid this time of year."

"Some guy has made himself at home. He has a bed and heaters and everything in there."

Merle twists his mouth to the side and narrows his gaze. "You have an odd sense of humour."

"I'm not joking. That's why I called the cops. Have any strange men been in here lately?"

Merle breaks into a hearty laugh. "That's *all* we get in here."

"Fair enough." She takes another swig, inviting the cider to numb her nerves.

Merle opens the dishwasher under the bar, and a rush of steam escapes. "That poor family. Sometimes tragedies hover around certain people."

"What were they like? The Peters."

He pours himself a pint of a darker, thicker liquid. "Lark was a sweet girl. Her death shocked everyone. It ruined the family."

Merle's eyes grow glassy, and Charlotte wonders whether he might cry. She shifts in her seat. "What happened to the brother?"

Merle takes a swig of his beer. "Darryl does odd-end jobs. Comes here some nights, always late and on weekdays when it's quiet. Keeps to himself, mostly."

A wave of dizziness washes over Charlotte, and she steadies herself, holding onto the bar counter. "So, he's still in town then? Officer Armstrong thought he'd moved."

"Nah, I don't think he'll ever leave this place. Although I'm sure it would do him good."

If Darryl Peters is frequenting local pubs, he must be living somewhere in town. And if his odd-end jobs can't cover rent, his family's garage seems like an appealing living arrangement.

Merle slings a towel over his shoulder and proceeds to unload glassware from the dishwasher. "I imagine living in this town would be haunting for someone like Darryl."

"Are you filling her head with ghost stories or gossip?" A woman appears through the doorway on the other side of the pub. "You'll have to excuse my husband. He's worse than the women at the hair salon." She laughs heartily as she makes her way to the bar, then playfully swats his arm. "I've got your room all made up. Sorry for the wait."

If Cindy hadn't introduced herself as Merle's wife, Charlotte would have guessed she was his sister with their similar stature and features. Cindy has the same round face as her husband and the warm smile that Merle was wearing before the talk turned to the Peters' family tragedy.

Charlotte hops off the bar stool. "Not at all." She takes a final gulp of the cider and slides the half-empty pint back to Merle. "Appreciate the drink. You'll just charge it to my room bill?"

"Oh honey, please, no charge," Cindy chimes in. "It's past two in the morning; we can't charge you a nightly fee for only a few hours."

The gesture makes Charlotte think of Officer Armstrong's comment earlier. *In Anville, we take care of each other.* Merle carries Charlotte's bag while she tends to the kitty crate, and they climb the narrow stairs to the second floor. Before Charlotte enters her assigned room, she turns back to Merle. "What does Darryl look like?"

"Why, you think it's him living in the garage? Probably didn't realize you were set to move in yet. I do think he's harmless."

Charlotte narrows her eyes. The way the officers were acting doesn't make her think Darryl Peters is harmless.

"He has dark hair. Wears it long now, usually with a hat," he says.

"Sounds like him."

"There's a picture of him hanging downstairs in the pub; I can show you tomorrow. An old baseball team photo. The 2004 championships, I think it was. We sponsor the under eighteens every year."

———— • ◆ • ————

Charlotte guides the flimsy hook through the one-way lock. It's at least better than sleeping in a home where she might not be the sole owner of a key.

She collapses on the double bed and melts into the mattress, which is a cloud compared to the floor she's been sleeping on. The room is cozy but dated, with burgundy, floral wallpaper and Royal Doulton figurines on the fireplace mantel that remind Charlotte of her mother's collection. The window provides a view of the street corner, and the snow, still falling, dances in the glow cast by the streetlights. In the five minutes since Charlotte entered the room, she feels more at home than in the house on Elizabeth Drive, which, at this point, she may never return to.

Charlotte didn't get a thorough look at the culprit's face, but even still, she is driven by the impulse to learn what Darryl looks like. Who is the guy that Lark poured her heart out to in those ivory pages?

Charlotte eyes her bag. Maybe another entry from Lark's journal would shed some light on Darryl. Is he harmless, as Merle suggests, or is he hiding something?

Chapter Eleven

LARK

January 10, 2006

The good news: Mom and Jake have started going to his apartment more. The bad news: when Mom is home, she's distracted and flaky. I want to ask if you've noticed the change in her, but I feel like you'd just brush it off as early menopause. It didn't happen overnight like that strange movie with Sissy Spacek where her kids trade her in for a new mom at the mommy market. This has been slow, like watching that playground on Park Ave get built—one pole at a time, literally years in the making.

Maybe it's in my head, but I find she'll get stuck in a memory—like so transfixed on something that happened a decade ago—and then she can't remember what she went upstairs to grab. On Tuesday night, she stopped home after her shift. She was surprised to find me in the kitchen, which was strange because it was half past four and where else would I be?

"Oh, my God," she said in this breathy voice. "You scared me."

Sorry? This is my house, too. I'm hunting for anything (literally anything) to snack on, but she's stopped grocery shopping, or at least she's stopped shopping for this household.

Then she sat down next to me at the kitchen table and practically begged me to stroll with her down memory lane.

"Do you remember the gravel pit Dad worked at?" she asked, nodding enthusiastically. "We used to go there and wade in the river valley. It was like our own private beach. One time we even brought our lawn chairs and a cooler of beers and jumbo freezies for you and ..." She paused then. Darryl, I think she forgot your name at that moment.

"Darryl," I finally offered.

And then she clammed up, rising from her seat. "Well, of course, Darryl. Who else would it be?"

I get it, we all lose words just like we misplace keys. I did search for menopause symptoms, and it can make you foggy. It's probably just that, right?

———— • ✦ • ————

January 14, 2006

Big brother to the rescue again. One of these days I'm gonna return the favour, by the way. How do you always know how to make things right? It's like you have a sixth sense with me. Let me ask you, last night, after we finished watching an episode of *Dateline* (Mom's pick, obviously), what was my tell that I needed a distraction? Now that I'm almost the age of some of these women who went missing, these shows hit harder. Of course, Mom went up to bed, completely oblivious that her choice in television has been giving me nightmares ever since I was twelve, and she first introduced me to *The Exorcist*.

But you shot me a look from the other side of the couch. It was after ten, and we probably both should have gone to bed, but you could tell I was off. How did you know?

"Alright, Bird, what's it going to be? Late-night infomercials or *Seinfeld* reruns?"

After we merged the two and ended up improvising our own ridiculous infomercials that could have been a stand-up routine, I barely remembered what was on my mind in the first place. I really want your Bat in the Cave nosepicker to be a thing. Maybe we should patent it?

———— ·◆· ————

January 18, 2006

I've gotten good at ignoring people's facial expressions. If you stare at a light—it has to be bright—for at least fifteen seconds, when you look away everything is blurry. Faces are distorted. Expressions muddled. You can no longer see the details, and it allows you to walk the school hallways looking above your shoes.

Yes, I am back at school after the holiday break. Joy to the world.

Blue Monday. I'm not talking about the New Order song, although I did play that as soon as I got home from school. How appropriate, right? No, today is Blue Monday.

Do you know what I thought when the news reminded me? That today is the saddest day

of the year? I was relieved.

I have another excuse to wallow, and others are joining in my misery.

But as soon as you heard New Order playing in my room, you were there, hovering at the door. Offering to bring me along to Xander's for band practice.

"You'd be doing us a favour, Bird. We need a girl's voice for the bridge of our new song. And I need someone else to tell Xander he keeps increasing the tempo when everyone knows it's the drummer's beat you follow."

Well, it worked. Thank you, Bro. You might just shake me from this trance after all.

Chapter Twelve

CHARLOTTE

Charlotte closes the diary and allows her face to fall into her palms. There is a heaviness in her chest after reading the sixteen-year-old's thoughts. A magnetic pull to continue to turn the pages but at the same time, a shadow, warning Charlotte of the risks—of what it might bring to the surface from her own past.

Lark's words provide a glimpse into Darryl and, so far, he appears to be a sitcom brother: caring, protective—perhaps a bit aloof. And as Merle suggested, likely harmless. So, is Darryl the man living in her garage? She'll sneak a quick peek at the photo of Darryl's baseball team. She won't be able to sleep until she does.

Charlotte flings the covers off and slides her feet into her boots. She escapes the comfort of the cozy room into the dark hallway. Using her phone's flashlight, she guides her way down the steep stairs of the inn. The phone has only three percent battery left, so she'll need to make this quick. She follows the dull hum of the mini fridge to the bar. The glow of the fridge combined with light pouring in from the front windows allows just enough illumination so that she can find her way to the wall near the front door where the frames of baseball photos hang in a haphazard pattern. The photos dating back to the eighties are faded, the years of sunlight having stripped away the vibrant reds and blues. But the championship photo from 2004 is still vivid.

Charlotte rises on her tiptoes to get a closer look. She is immediately drawn to the tallest boy in the back row. He stands in the middle, broad-shouldered and confident, wearing his fitted teal baseball tee, the Angel Pub logo centred on his chest. His dark hair creeps out the sides of his baseball cap, and his smile is warm and friendly. But it's his deep green eyes that are so familiar to Charlotte. She feels like she already knows him. It's Darryl. There's no doubt, and Charlotte is embarrassed to admit that he'd be exactly her type in high school. She does quick math in her head and estimates he is now around thirty-four, only a couple of years older than her.

Standing next to Darryl, and a few inches shorter, is another face she recognizes—Officer Armstrong. She recalls what he whispered to his partner just a couple of hours earlier—*he's back*—in a tone that leads her to believe Darryl's caused trouble before. This photo—the fact that they grew up together and even played on the same baseball team—proves Officer Armstrong knows what Darryl is capable of.

A pounding on the door sends off alarm bells through Charlotte's entire body. She spins around to locate the source.

"Merle, it's me. You gotta help me out."

Charlotte falls to her knees and scrambles under a four-top, willing herself to shrink into nothingness.

"Merle, come on. I need to crash here tonight." The voice is husky, with an air of desperation.

The pounding continues with urgency and then stops abruptly.

Charlotte eases her head out from the table. She keeps low as she crawls around the side of the four-top, attempting to improve her view of the glass door where the man was skulking just seconds ago.

As she inches closer to the doorway, he rushes to the window and peers in between his cupped hands. Charlotte falls to her stomach, flattening her position. Her breath is shallow as she attempts to keep still. She should never have left her room upstairs.

She counts backwards from ten, her thumb lightly tapping the filmy wood beneath her. She is biding time but also trying to calm her breath. When she arrives at number one, she accepts the risk and peers toward the window.

Her gaze meets the man who towers above her on the other side of the glass. Charlotte scrambles to her feet, but before she can turn away, she is held captive by his green eyes.

It's the same guy in the photo only he's eighteen years older and his hair is longer. He isn't the happy-go-lucky boy who just won his baseball championship. The man who stands before her is hardened.

Charlotte turns away from Darryl and rushes toward the back of the pub, eager to scurry up the steps. She fumbles in her pocket for her phone but smacks into something, which sends her and her phone tumbling to the ground.

"What in God's name?" The light at the staircase flicks on, and Merle hovers above her. "What on earth are you doing down here? I heard banging." He extends his arm to help Charlotte to her feet.

Charlotte rubs her shoulder, which throbs from their encounter. "There's someone at the door."

"What? At the front door?" Merle rubs his eyes.

By the time they make their way to the entrance, there is no one there. The only evidence of the visitor is fresh footprints in the snow.

Chapter Thirteen

CHARLOTTE

During the day, the pub bustles with regulars who are almost thrice Charlotte's age. They order tuna melts and bangers and mash and compete to be heard by their spouses wearing hearing aids. Walkers are parked in between tables, creating obstacles for the servers to dance around. Cindy places a club sandwich at Charlotte's table by the front window. The rye has the crusts cut off, as she requested through her server. She mouths "thank you" and then returns her ear to her phone.

Wayne Newton's cover of "Danke Schoen" is the hold music, tempting Charlotte to hang up and lose her spot in the queue. Before she can give it too much consideration, the music cuts out, and she readies herself for the voice on the other end of the line.

"Yes, hi. I'd like to make an appointment to get the locks rekeyed at my house."

The chipper voice spouts off a list of routine questions, barely leaving space for a response, and then confirms they can send a locksmith to the house in three days to do the job.

"That's the earliest you can get someone?"

Charlotte watches Cindy out of the corner of her eye. The woman hovers, fiddling with her apron. Charlotte hasn't spoken to the owners since last night's encounter, and she worries she might have overstayed her welcome. She's not even sure they believe Darryl was ever there, despite the footprints.

"Yes, okay, thank you." She places the phone down. "You probably think I'm weird for asking to have my crusts cut off."

Cindy smiles warmly. "Just like Mom's, right?"

Charlotte bites into the sandwich, the perfect ratio of mayonnaise to bread. "It's delicious,

thank you."

Cindy shifts her weight but doesn't attempt to leave. "Do you need to stay a bit longer? It's no trouble. We don't get bookings during the week."

"That depends. Is Merle expecting more late-night visitors?" Charlotte asks with a grimace.

Cindy shrugs. "I was so sorry to hear about that. It's so strange; Darryl's never asked to stay here before."

"That's because he's never been kicked out of his garage."

"A valid point ..."

"If it's not too much trouble, can I stay until Friday afternoon? That's when I'm getting the locks changed."

"The room is yours for as long as you need it."

Cindy leaves Charlotte to finish her club sandwich, though she might have welcomed the

company. After the accident, she swore off any new friendships or relationships, and now, without her parents around to confide in, she's realizing how lonely her life is.

She drags her pen in a line, crossing out today's first task.

-~~Book the locksmith~~

-Find a bakery that makes Nanaimo bars

-Call Landry's Junk Removal

She looks up from her notebook to confront the pub window, imagining Darryl staring back at her. She allows her mind to recount last night's scene. His deep green eyes. The intensity in his voice. She found she'd been both terrified and mesmerized. The easygoing brother described in the journal doesn't reflect the desperate man she encountered last night. But a lot can happen in a decade. People can become unrecognizable.

She glances around the pub, absorbing the energy of the conversations around her. She has no one to talk to. Her parents haven't returned her calls. It's Wednesday—their sea turtle excursion, so, likely, they don't have their phones on them. She rubs her breastbone with her fingertips. The tightness in her chest hasn't eased.

A woman rushes past the window with a collection of shopping bags dangling off her arms. With only a week until Christmas, the shops will be busy, but Charlotte can't avoid crowds forever. Besides, she could use the distraction.

After she settles her lunch bill, she strolls down Anville's main street, guided by Cindy's directions to the local bakery.

A chime announces Charlotte's presence as she steps into the quaint storefront. A wooden counter stretches the width of the store and is draped with a garland of greenery.

"Be right there," a voice calls out. Charlottes makes her way to the display of goodies that grace the countertop in search of the creamy, chocolatey delicacy she's come for.

A woman appears from behind the counter, the red hair piled on top of her head similar to the clump of dough in her hands. "Just took out a fresh batch of gingerbread if you're interested."

Charlotte considers buying the whole batch and binge-eating them in her bed at the inn based on the aroma alone, but another chime stops her before she can respond.

"Officer Armstrong, how are you?" the woman asks, and Charlotte turns on her heel towards the front door.

"Afternoon, Lou. It smells amazing in here."

"I've got your order ready; just give me five minutes to wrap it up." She turns to Charlotte. "I'll be with you in just a moment."

Charlotte nods and moves to the side to make room for Armstrong.

"It's you." He beams. "How was your stay at the inn? You've gotta try their potato skins if you haven't yet. They'll change your life."

"It was good—thanks for the recco."

He nods. "Hey, we did another patrol early this morning—no sign of anyone but we're on it. You've got nothing to worry about."

Charlotte chews on the inside of her lip. She wonders whether she should tell the officer about the run-in with Darryl. It seems he's already on Armstrong's radar, but after last night, she has proof that Darryl is in Anville and looking for a place to stay.

"Don't worry—I've got your back." He puffs out his chest, and Charlotte nearly rolls her eyes.

She glances at her boots and then at the shallow puddle of water she's tracked into the store.

"Everything okay?" Armstrong asks, inching closer.

"I don't want to get anyone in trouble, but I saw Darryl Peters this morning outside of the pub. He's definitely in town."

Armstrong's cheery disposition fades. "What time was this?"

"I guess it was around two-thirty in the morning. Sounded like he needed a place to crash."

"Damnit," he says and slams his hand on the counter.

Charlotte takes a step backward instinctively.

Armstrong quickly composes himself, the over-the-top grin returning. "Sorry about that—we just can't seem to get rid of this guy. Leave it with me. I'll handle it."

Charlotte turns to face the display of fruit cakes, their maraschino cherries sweating just like the nape of her neck.

Lou returns with a box wrapped with twine and what appears to be an authentic sprig of holly. "Your chocolate yule log. Hope the party is fun tonight!" She places the box on the counter and punches a few buttons on the cash register.

Armstrong counts out four five-dollar bills and slides them to Lou. "You've outdone yourself. You really don't need to waste your good boxes and ribbon on a bunch of tired cops. We don't care what it looks like, just how it tastes." He winks at Charlotte, and she averts her eyes, only looking up when the chime rings out.

Standing halfway through the doorway, Armstrong invites the piercing wind into the cozy store. He swivels to face Charlotte. "You did the right thing, telling me. We'll get him." He nods, his jaw protruding. "Maybe I'll see you tonight."

Charlotte scrunches up her face, not bothering to hide her confusion.

"At the pub—that's where the police department is having our holiday party. Stop by if you're around. I'll save you some yule log."

Charlotte smiles weakly as Armstrong lets the door swing shut.

Charlotte leaves the bakery with three things—gingerbread for Merle and Cindy, Nanaimo bars for her visit with Leslie, and a weary feeling in the pit of her stomach. She knows she should feel relieved about telling a cop that Darryl is back in town. She expected it would ease her mind to hear that an officer was taking care of it. But something about the way Officer Armstrong snapped makes her wonder if his problem with Darryl is personal.

By the time Charlotte makes it back to the inn after shopping and errands on Main Street, the sun has retired, and the quiet darkness covers the streets like a fresh blanket of snow. Charlotte wonders if Darryl will return to the pub tonight. She's unsure whether she's safer at the inn or in the house on Elizabeth, but at least here, Merle and Cindy can play witness.

Chapter Fourteen

CHARLOTTE

With her door opened a crack, Charlotte can finally decipher the song that had been blasting in the pub below her room and shaking the figurines on the mantel for the last ten minutes. A rowdy rendition of the Christmas tune "Fairy Tale of New York" by The Pogues plays for the third time in a row, the group of drunken cops shouting the lyrics louder each time.

Charlotte took cover in her room shortly after a quick dinner at the pub. She wanted to be out of sight once the Anville police department's holiday party began. Her mother would have offered the advice to rub elbows with the local officers, to lock in added security and patrol at the house. But cocooned in the quilt and nestled in her bed at the inn feels safer than schmoozing with Armstrong and his colleagues.

She jumps up and pulls the door shut when heavy footsteps trudge up the narrow stairs, sending a swirl of flurries through her core. She is a second too late turning out her light, given the light rap on the door.

"Charlotte, you in?"

It only takes her a moment to realize who is at the door, their bakery rendezvous still as fresh as the gingerbread she gifted to Merle and Cindy.

"I saved you some of my log." His voice erupts into laughter. "My yule log! There's a piece here with your name on it."

Charlotte doesn't need to see Armstrong to know he's had a few drinks. The slur in his voice confirms it. She remains frozen in place, not wanting to give the floorboards a reason to moan.

"I saw your light on. I know you're awake. Come on, it's me, Kyle. Don't you want to try the cake?"

Kyle. The name is unfamiliar, boyish, and Charlotte realizes this is the first she's heard his given name. With the most inconvenient timing, her feline friend hops off the bed and rushes to the door, patting it and letting out an elongated cry.

"It's the cat!" The shrill laughter returns, and it's unnerving. "I forgot you brought the cat. Come on, just let me give you the cake. I have an update on your case, too."

Charlotte concedes at the promise of an update and flicks on the light. "Give me a second; I was just going to bed." She consults the standing mirror on the back of the door. Crossing her arms, she attempts to cover her nipples that poke through the white T-shirt she wears without a bra. The rooms above the pub are heated by dated radiators that have a hard time hiding it's the dead of winter. She lets her hands fall to her side and then rushes back to the bed to retrieve her sweatshirt. She doesn't need another reason to feel uncomfortable in Armstrong's presence.

She pulls it over her head before opening the door a crack. "Hey, do you mind if we do this tomorrow? I can come down to the station." She uses her leg to block the cat from rushing into the hallway.

"But the log! You need to try this Yule log. Charlotte, it will change your life. And I really do have an update you should hear." He wears the pout of a three-year-old. What sort of tantrum will follow if she declines?

"Okay, just for a minute."

Armstrong saunters into the room, holding a plate with a slice of chocolate cake and a fork that teeters on the edge. "Did I wake you up?" he asks.

"No, but I was just about to go to bed." Charlotte leads him to the armchair beside the window and then drags over the wooden desk chair for herself. "So, you have an update on the case?"

"First, try some," he holds out the fork with a bite consisting mostly of icing.

Charlotte grimaces. "I'm actually allergic to chocolate." The lie comes naturally. She puts her hand to her mouth to stop the fork from entering against her will.

Armstrong's mouth falls open, and he drops the fork to the floor. "What a tragedy."

"It's fine. More for you. So, the case?" Her shoulders tense. She runs through the possible scenarios in her head. Darryl skipped town. The police have him in custody. His squatter's rights allow him to stay in her garage until he can find a new place.

Armstrong licks his lips, but chocolate icing remains in the corners of his mouth. If she had any attraction toward him, she might find this cute. "Officer Landry is on the case now, too. He's a pro, the best to have on your side."

Charlotte's shoulders fall, the anticipation deflating like a balloon. "Good to know," she says, her voice sinking as she realizes the case was only a ploy to get in. "Listen, I'm tired, and you're missing the party. I should let you get back to it." She rises and crosses the room to the door.

"I'm in no rush to get back to the boys. I see them every day. You are more interesting. With your cat and your chocolate allergy." His eyebrows dance, and his smile takes up most of his face.

Charlotte opens the door, again blocking the entry from her cat.

"Have you been to the Empire yet?" Armstrong picks up the fork from the ground and wipes it on his pant leg before taking another bite.

"What's the Empire?" she asks.

He sets the plate down on the coffee table with a clank. "The cinema! They get all the new releases. And they play classics too if that's what you're into." He looks her up and down. "You're one of those *Breakfast at Tiffany's* fans, aren't you?"

With the door ajar, Charlotte notices the music has faded; the party must be winding down. She consults her phone and realizes it is two in the morning, past the last call.

She exaggerates a yawn. "I need to get some rest. But thanks for the tip on the Empire."

The howls and laughter of men fill the night air as they spill onto the street from the pub. Charlotte rises on her toes to get a view of the street corner through the window by her bed. A few of them stumble onto the sidewalk, and she wonders what will happen when they are all gone except for the one cemented in her chair.

"Let me give you my digits—in case Darryl comes back tonight."

"Sure." Charlotte scoops the cat into her arms and opens the door wider.

"Unless you'd rather I stay? I don't mind. I can crash on this chair. It's actually pretty comfy."

"Not necessary. I'll take your number and call you if anything happens." Charlotte extends her arm, phone in hand.

Armstrong deserts the plate of half-eaten cake on the table and shuffles over to Charlotte. He grabs her phone and programs in his number.

Charlotte watches carefully as he makes his way down the stairs, his entire right side leaning against the wall for support. When he is out of view, she closes the door and places the flimsy lock into its rightful place.

The new contact mocks her on the phone screen:

Name: Kyle Armstrong

Notes: Empire tomorrow night. Pick you up at 7.

She lets out an audible sigh.

Tomorrow's problem now.

Chapter Fifteen

LARK

January 23, 2006

Tonight was fun! Actually fun. I didn't know what to expect from one of your shows, but the energy was like a music video. It was impossible not to let myself melt into the sweaty crowd. It helped that the dance girls came with me, seeing as Dani bailed again (seriously, what gives?) Whatever, I had fun without her. Invite four ballerinas to a concert and they'll dance circles around the punks.

I also enjoyed my moment of fame, so thank you very much for inviting me on stage for "Bleed My Heart Dry." I don't think my girls knew I had somewhat of a decent voice, so that was amusing to watch their jaws simultaneously drop. "Oh, you didn't know I could do a triple pirouette *and* hit a high C?"

Make way for Lark Peters!

And you! You were on fire! They have to move the drum set downstage, though. I could still see you, but I feel like you deserve to be front and centre with Xander. You write most of the lyrics he sings. It's criminal you're stuck in the back mouthing the words.

Hands down, my favourite part of tonight was at the end, hanging around while everyone else was being asked to leave. You have some serious fans. Maybe we should get buttons made or something. Sell them at your next show. They all just wanted a chance to say hi to the band, and I got to walk right past them backstage and sit captain on the way home in the band's van!

Do you ever feel like this when you come to my dance recitals? Probably not. It's not quite the same when there are hundreds of us dancers. Everyone getting a bouquet of red roses (which you know I find so cliché). It loses its specialness.

I wish I had something I cared about as much as you care about your music. Or as much as Mom with her fleeting passions—whatever the guy she's seeing is into. Can you tell I'm still bitter she splurged on that workout bike that has remained unused since she broke up with Carl?

I should really be telling this to your face instead of hiding it away in here. But it's not like you need a confidence boost. You don't need your lame sister idolizing you. Besides, you're barely around the house anymore, so when would I even have the chance to tell you all this?

So, I guess I'll settle for the next best thing—the diary you bought me—your way to fix me.

———— ◆ ————

January 25, 2006

You'll never guess who invited me over. Dani was standing by my locker after third period today, fiddling with her hoop earring, her curls wound tight in the white gold. She acted like her presence was normal, that she hasn't been ghosting me since Lex's New Year's Eve party.

"If you're not busy Friday night, my mom has been asking about you. She's making moussaka."

My face must have twisted into a frown because she followed it with a shrug and said she wanted to catch up too.

So, I guess I have Mrs. Poulios to thank for this sudden change of heart in her daughter. And I obviously said yes because she is the sweetest woman, and her moussaka tastes like home.

I wonder what Dani wants to catch up about—what it's like to hang out with the Tangerines? If Brittany visits the tanning bed one more time, her skin will be the shade of the fuzzy navel she was sipping on New Year's Eve before she decided to "accidentally" spill it all over my dress.

Can't Dani see they're just using her?

I want to talk to you about all this for real. I was so happy to see you were home after school and not at Xander's, but you were curled up with your copy of *The Perks of Being a Wallflower*, and I didn't want to interrupt you. I know how you love that book.

Chapter Sixteen

CHARLOTTE

C harlotte's grip strangles the bag of Nanaimo bars on the walk to
Leslie's from the Angel pub. She mutters to herself, asking why
she committed to the tea date. She would have rather stayed at the inn,
learning more about Darryl within the confines of Lark's diary. How
could the desperate man from two nights ago be the same guy Lark
idolized? The cute baseball player from the photo?

Leslie's home feels suffocatingly warm when Charlotte steps into the
cramped foyer. The woman resembles a doll, stiffly shuffling forward
into the kitchen with its delicate floral wallpaper. On the walls hang
mounted wooden crafts, cut in the shapes of bunnies and cats, Charlotte
suspects Leslie painted herself.

Charlotte cowers in Leslie's doorframe, mouth agape, realizing the
invite wasn't exclusive to her. Leslie, wearing a red and green sweater
that clashes with her grey-blue hair, guides Charlotte to a wicker seat at
a round table. Charlotte joins three other women who hold fanned-out

playing cards close to their chests. A wooden board with blue and red pegs is set up on one side of the table. There are cards laid out on display in a line in the centre where the tablecloth wears an intricate crochet design. Charlotte can't fathom what game they are playing, though she is fairly certain it is not *Go Fish*.

The oven stands open, allowing hot air to seep into the kitchen and emits smells of freshly baked sugar cookies. But instead of whetting her appetite, the scent is nauseating. Charlotte scans her surroundings for a bowl in case she needs to be sick.

"We're playing cribbage," Leslie says, removing the crumpled bag from Charlotte's grasp and setting it among the other baked goods that cover the cluttered counter.

"Hi." Charlotte offers a small wave. Then, she sinks into her seat, digging her fingernails into the flesh of her palms.

Leslie moves through the space with ease, her festive cane nowhere in sight. Perhaps it is more of an accessory, like a scarf or blue light glasses. She places a cup of tea in front of Charlotte and claims the seat beside her. "We're just in the middle of a round—playing in pairs. You can take Marie's spot when she leaves."

The woman on the other side of Charlotte, wearing a poinsettia sweater, leans in. "I'm getting my hair permed at four."

Charlotte nods politely, though she has no intention of joining this game or staying the afternoon.

"Ladies, this is Charlotte." Leslie lowers her voice in an almost whisper. "She's just moved into the Peters' house."

Marie raises her eyebrows. "Oh, dear. Didn't they tell you what happened before you moved in?"

Leslie shoots her friend a look. "Marie, it's your turn."

Marie scans her cards. "Go. I have nothing that works."

Leslie takes her turn and places a Two of Clubs in the centre of the table. "That makes thirty-one," she calls.

The women nod, taking note.

Marie switches her attention to Charlotte. "I hope they aren't charging you much rent."

"Charlotte's parents bought the house. She's helping them spruce it up," Leslie says.

Charlotte wonders if they'll continue to have a conversation about her as though she isn't sitting among them, and although it's off-putting, she'd rather not have to contribute.

A woman on the other side of Leslie, who appears to be younger than the rest, perks up. "Are you an interior decorator? My niece does that. She can make any room look like it's straight out of *House & Home*." She places a card in the centre of the table, presumably ending her turn.

"I'm not staying long," Charlotte says, finding her voice. "Just helping with the renovations, and then I'll move back to the city."

Marie tugs on the neck of her sweater, the poinsettia morphing into a new shape. "I don't blame you. I get the creeps coming to Leslie's. You can almost see the oak tree from here." She cranes her neck to look out the front window and then shudders, her upper body convulsing.

A sinking feeling emerges in the pit of Charlotte's stomach. "The tree?" She swallows hard and closes her eyes. The oak tree stares back at her, its shadow extending beyond the picture in her mind.

"Oh yes, the poor girl ended it all with the rope from her swing set," Marie says.

Charlotte's throat tightens, and suddenly Lark is hanging from a reachable branch, her lifeless body swaying, bloated and bruised. Charlotte opens her eyes before she can visualize the teenager's face.

The younger woman tosses her platinum hair. "She didn't have much of a role model. Their mother is a piece of work."

Leslie turns to Charlotte, offering clarification. "Their mother, Darlene, had her fair share of men over the years. She cut hair at the salon on Main Street until she lost her mind. Early-onset Dementia."

Charlotte flushes. Between the complicated card game unfolding in front of her and the vivid scene playing in her mind, the sinking turns into true nausea.

Leslie shakes her head. "It's just off-putting, what with that Darryl boy always lurking around."

"You've seen him?" Charlotte asks.

Marie pats Charlotte's hand. "We've all seen him, sweetie. He's like a ghost, haunting this town."

Blondie jumps in. "He's a strange one. My niece went to school with him."

"Well, the peach doesn't fall far from the tree," Marie says, sucking her cheeks in.

Charlotte releases the top button of her sweater. Is the oven still on? Why is it so hot in here?

The fourth woman of the group, a small, meek lady in a burgundy turtleneck and cat-framed glasses, takes her turn and places a card in the line-up. "I feel bad for the family. They've had a string of bad luck with Tom's death, too."

Charlotte leans closer in her chair. "Tom?"

The woman continues reluctantly. "The father. He died when they were young in a drunk driving accident. So tragic."

Marie tosses a card into the line, not bothering to straighten it. "Doris is putting it nicely. His head was taken clean off."

Charlotte stiffens in her seat, and her stomach lurches as she imagines the accident—the father's head being severed—and then she is back in her friend Chloe's sedan, a deafening ringing in her ear.

Leslie leans in. "I don't think either of the kids had many friends. Weirdos, both of them."

Charlotte feels the urge to come to Darryl's defence, but she can barely hold up her frame, her body weighed down—the same as it was when she woke after the accident. She wanted to move, to help her friends, but she was paralyzed with fear and rendered useless.

Charlotte shakes her head. This boy—man—has lost his whole family. No wonder he's tethered to this town. It's all he has left of them. She thinks of the memories trapped in milk crates, collecting dust in the living room. She sips her tea, leaving a trace of gloss on the yellow China. Her cup takes on weight, and she no longer has the energy to lift it. She leans forward and allows her elbows to rest on the table. *Don't faint. Not here. Not in front of the rumour mill.* She pushes her chair back with a screech and, using the table in front of her, pulls herself to a standing position. "Sorry, I don't feel well. I need air."

The women exchange glances.

Charlotte tugs her parka from the hook and escapes through the front door into the crisp winter day.

The cold wind is a welcome change from Leslie's claustrophobic kitchen. Charlotte stumbles down the sidewalk, clutching her parka in her arms. When she nears her parents' house, she finds herself automatically crossing the road, and before she realizes it, she's sitting on the porch trying to catch her breath.

Darryl's family—his father's horrific death, his sister's suicide, and his mother's dementia—all weigh heavy in Charlotte's heart. Who does he have left to turn to?

Charlotte pulls on her parka and reaches into her pocket, discovering the business card for Landry's Junk Removal. She thinks about the milk crates inside and imagines someone discarding her memories like they are trash. She thinks of her girls, the photo, and the trinkets she refuses to let go of. Chloe's half bottle of nail polish. A mixed CD from Madison. A ballpoint pen lid that Erica chewed on. She should give Darryl a chance to claim the boxes before they end up in a landfill.

Using the railing, she pulls herself to standing. She fumbles for her keys, approaching her front door. As she turns the key in the hole, she spots a yellow sticky note fluttering in the wind.

Sorry for the scare. I didn't expect anyone to move in for another month. I'll be out of the garage by the end of the week.

Charlotte's breath quickens, and her knees waver. She slides two fingers down her neck. Her pulse is rising quickly.

Charlotte spins around to find the railing and as her vision blurs, the form of a man emerges.

Chapter Seventeen

CHARLOTTE

C harlotte opens her eyes, and the white tiles materialize, a blank canvas ready to be marked. While attempting to roll onto her side, she discovers she is restrained, held in position by an unknown grasp. She struggles, kicking her legs and pushing until she releases herself from the taut sheets. Her hand grazes an object in her path, and she discovers she is caged in by a gray frame as if she were a baby in a crib. This isn't her room at the inn, but the sterile quality and sanitizer smell are familiar, and it causes heart palpitations. Before she can utter a scream, a voice from the other side of the room addresses her.

'You're awake. Good." A woman approaches the bed wearing dark blue scrubs, a clipboard dangling in her loose grip. "How are you feeling?"

"My friends. Chloe? Is she okay?"

The woman's brow furrows, and she consults the chart on her clipboard. Charlotte allows her body to sink into the hospital bed, realizing her mistake. She closes her eyes, thinking back to her last recollection, leaving Leslie's and walking to her porch. "I fainted. But ... how did I get here?"

"I'm Dr. Garrison. You're at Niagara Health Centre. You were brought here by ambulance earlier this afternoon after you lost consciousness. Let's check your vitals."

Charlotte tenses her muscles in response to the frigid stethoscope pressed firmly against her chest.

"Sorry, I should have warmed that up a bit," the young doctor says, tucking her hair behind her ear. "Okay, all good." She removes the ear tips and lets the stethoscope fall around her neck. She follows the standard routine of checking Charlotte's blood pressure.

Doctor Garrison looks like an attractive young resident in a medical drama, and Charlotte considers whether she is caught in a love triangle with other residents.

"You said you fainted. Do you remember what happened leading up to it?"

Charlotte recalls the fluttering note clinging to the screen door as she unlocked the door to the house. She remembers the man approaching, climbing slowly up the steps.

"I had left a tea party," Charlotte says, the words sounding surreal, immature. "It was at a neighbour's. I felt sick and needed air. I made it to my porch and then I don't remember much after that."

Doctor Garrison nods.

"Who called the ambulance?" Charlotte asks.

The doctor taps her pen on the clipboard. "It was your neighbour. He witnessed your fall. Or rather, he cushioned your fall, as he said you were close to hitting your head on the railing."

Charlotte instinctually feels for a bump on her head.

"We didn't find anything that leads us to believe you hit your head. Your neighbour was in the right place at the right time."

It's as if Charlotte has missed a step, her stomach free-falling. She thinks of a man cradling her fall, checking her pulse, and staying by her side while waiting for the ambulance to arrive. It is something Darryl from the diary might do—the kind optimist. But Darryl from the pub? She's not sure.

"Has this happened to you before?"

"Yes," Charlotte says with hesitation. "I've had fainting spells on and off since I was a teenager."

"Since you were a teenager?" Once again, Dr. Garrison consults her clipboard, and Charlotte wonders how much of her medical history Dr. Garrison is privy to.

"Since my ... accident." Charlotte twists her mouth and bites on the inside of her lip. She never meant to refer to it as *her* accident. As if she owns it. And then there is the matter of which accident. The two events will always be tethered in her mind as one: the second *accident*, the consequence of the first, wrapping up the worst year of her life.

"Accident?" Dr. Garrison asks.

Charlotte waves it off, realizing her medical history hasn't automatically followed her to this hospital. "It's probably unrelated. Can I leave soon? I have a cat to feed."

Doctor Garrison nods slowly, studying Charlotte like a specimen beneath a microscope. "Any other health concerns I should be aware of?"

"I think I just needed to eat something. Like I said, it was hot, and I needed air."

"Okay. Did you want to talk any more about the accident you referred to?

Charlotte shakes her head. "You never gave me the name."

"The name?"

"Of the neighbour. The one who called the ambulance."

"Oh, yes. I think we have it here." She flips over the page. "Darryl Peters."

Chapter Eighteen

CHARLOTTE

Charlotte expels a protracted breath when her fingers graze the house keys in her pocket. Her wallet, her phone. It's all there. But she can't shake the likelihood that she left the front door unlocked, maybe even wide open. She will need to return to the house on Elizabeth Drive. At least to lock up.

The ride from the hospital tests her resilience, even with the driver's leisurely speed. When they pass Leslie's house, and Charlotte spots a couple of women making their way down the driveway, she ducks out of view. Looks like the tea party is over. Did any of the women even bother to come by to check on her? She waits in the car, slowly gathering her items, until they pile into Blondie's SUV and disappear down the road.

The front door is locked when Charlotte tests it, and she imagines Darryl locking up for her, tucking the keys back in her pocket and zipping them up so they wouldn't fall out. She paces the length of the porch, then hovers in the spot where she first saw him. The garage looks secure, but what if he's just inside the door, sitting on his lounger with his copy *The Perks of Being a Wallflower*, the yellowed pages dog-eared? In just a couple of days and diary entries, Darryl has evolved from a creep hiding out in her garage to a thoughtful, enigmatic person who shares the same taste as her in music and literature and who practically saved her life.

Charlotte should leave, as the Uber driver is waiting to take her back to the inn, but instead, she waves him off. She slowly walks toward the garage, not knowing what her next move will be, as her lifeline reverses from the driveway.

The garage is silent when Charlotte presses her cheek to its cold metal, the peeling paint scratching her skin. She taps lightly on the metal, the knock barely audible. When there is no response, she sneaks around the perimeter, pausing at the back of the garage to inspect an entrance she had no previous knowledge of. Charlotte knocks on the wooden door, this time louder. She tries the door handle, and her stomach plummets when it swings wide open with help from the wind.

Charlotte steps into Darryl's home, which has lost some of its charm since she last peered inside. The carpet has been rolled into a lopsided cylinder, the crates stacked into two neat piles. It appears he's made efforts to pack up his things, causing Charlotte a strange sense of guilt, like she is the reason Lark's brother will be houseless.

She is eyeing a crate of books when a cough from the other side of the room makes her lose her footing. She stumbles forward, steadying herself on the armrest of the lounger.

She turns to see Darryl standing sheepishly in the doorway. He takes a cautious step toward her with his hands up as if to show her he's unarmed. "I—I'm almost done packing."

Charlotte's hand shoots up to her chest. "I was just—I came to—" Why did she come? She put herself in this situation without reason. She backs into the chair, slumping down onto its cushion. She hasn't eaten anything since before the hospital, and her energy has depleted.

Darryl steps forward and then pauses until she offers a nod of permission for him to approach. He drags over an upside-down milk crate and sits a few feet from the lounger, now at Charlotte's level.

"Are you okay?" he asks, his eyes imploring.

Charlotte looks down at her body, worried she might have hurt herself just now. "I'm fine," she says, rubbing her arm.

"From earlier. You passed out on the porch." Darryl's eyes are wide and intense, making her uneasy. She finds herself looking away, but something draws her in. She searches his face and is met with overwhelming sadness. Charlotte knows the feeling of loss all too well. And she can see it on him like a sign he wears around his neck.

"I do that sometimes," she whispers.

"Pass out on porches?" He laughs, and Charlotte catches a glimpse of the young baseball player she saw in the photo at the pub. The cute boy without a care in the world.

There's something familiar in his smile. Perhaps reading about him through Lark's point of view has made her feel some sort of kinship. Her fingers hover by her mouth. "I faint sometimes. Low blood pressure."

He nods. "So, you're better now." He is tapping his fingers on the crate in a tense rhythm. Charlotte recalls Lark's from journal that he's a drummer.

"Yes, and thank you. For catching me?" She tries to stand, but her knees still feel weak, and she collapses into the chair, hearing her mother's voice in her head. *You should eat something. Raise your blood sugar.* "I think I just need to eat."

Darryl scans the room and then jumps from the crate with urgency. Charlotte follows him with her eyes and is surprised when he reveals a crate acting as a pantry. His place is well-stocked with food.

"Cereal? Instant noodles? Fruit rollup? I have Little Debbie brownies, too."

Charlotte raises her eyebrows, surprised at the offer. There is a teenager stuck in this man's body. It's almost as if he stopped aging the day his sister died.

"What kind of cereal?"

"Fruity-O's," he announces.

This further proves her point, but sugar should help.

"Okay. I guess I'll take a bowl." It's been years since she tasted children's cereal, but she finds comfort in his offer.

Darryl carries over a plastic bowl full to the brim of rainbow loops and carefully places it on the armrest. "I don't have milk. Sorry."

Charlotte glances out the half-moon windows above the garage door. There is still daylight, and she allows her shoulders to relax slightly.

She pops a Fruity-O into her mouth. It tastes like synthetic lime. Darryl reclaims his position on the crate, his eyes intently watching her.

"You're Charlotte. The new owner?"

She narrows her eyes and drops a cluster of Fruity-O's back into the bowl. She notes how he extends the first syllable of her name, almost as if he might stop there and call her by her mother's nickname for her.

"I swung by the pub to check that you were okay ... and to apologize for, you know ... everything. I'm Darryl. But you probably figured that out."

She catches herself wondering what he might look like if he cut his hair; he's attractive, she can admit that. She shakes off the thought. "It's a small town, I'm discovering."

He laughs. "You could say that." Darryl's smile fades, and he stands at attention. "Someone's here." He rushes to the door and closes it, securing the lock.

Is he trying to keep someone out or her in? She ditches the bowl and climbs out of the chair.

"Shhhh," Darryl utters softly, closing the gap between them. She doesn't retreat and instead mimics his stillness. Her heart beats heavily, steady as a metronome.

A piercing sound rings out, echoing through the garage, and Charlotte startles, accidentally grazing Darryl's hand.

"Darryl, I know you're in there."

The voice is punctuated by three more bangs on the garage door.

"You realize you're trespassing on private property."

She recognizes the voice. It's Armstrong.

With each bang, Charlotte cowers, feeling both responsible and anxious about what will happen if Armstrong finds a way in.

"Come on, we can do this the easy way or the hard way."

Charlotte glances up at Darryl, who stands more than a foot taller than her. He remains frozen in position, his left eyebrow twitching slightly. She can't tell whether he is calm or if he's as scared as she is. Will she get in trouble for being in here? What will Armstrong say when he finds the two of them hanging out, eating cereal two days after she called the cops on Darryl?

"Consider this your final warning. I'm coming back tonight, and I'm prying this door open. Hell, I'll burn the whole garage down if I have to."

There is one last urgent bang on the door and then Charlotte hears Armstrong mutter *deadbeat* under his breath before he erupts into a wild laugh. She follows the fading laughter as he trudges down the driveway.

Charlotte shuffles toward the chair. "That was intense."

"Armstrong's an intense person."

She wonders if Armstrong will return with a lighter and kerosene tonight. If so, she doesn't want to be here to witness it. It's obvious now that Armstrong will do anything to get rid of Darryl and won't stop until he's gone. It's more than a history, they have. It's bad blood. And while on paper she knows she should trust the cop, she feels calmer in Darryl's presence than Armstrong's.

"I didn't mean for this to happen," she says, partly to Darryl but also to herself. "When I called the police ..." She recalls the glow of the garage the night she found Darryl squatting. The flicker of light that for a second seemed ghostly. "I was freaked out." Now that she knows it was Darryl, the eerie feeling of the house fades.

"It's my problem, not yours. I'll figure it out."

Charlotte shoves her hands in her pockets. She still can't believe she touched his hand seconds ago. Her finger slides along the edge of Landry's Junk Removal card, and she realizes what she needs to do.

"Stay in the house tonight. Bring anything you want in there." She hands him the key to the front door. "I was planning on leaving the door open for you tonight anyway, so you could claim anything you wanted that you'd left behind."

Darryl removes his toque to scratch his head. His greasy hair falls over his eyes.

"You can take a shower too," she says and then looks down at her feet, worried she's offended him.

"I smell that bad, eh?" He laughs and returns the hat to his head. "I may just take you up on that. Just so I can get some of Bird's—my sister's—things."

Lark's nickname sounds fitting, coming from his mouth. Charlotte wants to ask about Lark. She wants to hear what happened to her from the person who mattered to her most. She bites her lip. "Your cat! I have your cat at the inn."

"Tux. Yeah, I may have seen you leave with the kitty crate the other night. Thank you for watching her."

"Tux?"

"Short for Tuxedo. She's had a few different names. My mom finds it hard to stick with one. Anyway, the cat seems to like Tux."

"Tux, it is then. She's been nice company."

"Hang with her for a while if you like. I'm more of a dog person."

Charlotte studies his crooked smile and then forces her gaze to the back door. "I guess I'll leave you to it. I'm staying at the inn until tomorrow afternoon."

Darryl walks Charlotte to the door and unlocks the deadbolt.

The sun is setting now, and the lower half of the sky looks like it's caught fire. Precise strokes of fluorescent oranges and yellows paint over the dark clouds.

Charlotte eases down the driveway, careful not to slip. When she arrives at the sidewalk, she glances back to the garage. Darryl, standing beside it, offers a wave, and she returns it awkwardly. She isn't sure what transpired in that garage or why she felt at ease in his presence. It's almost as if Lark was guiding her new friend to Darryl.

Shouldn't Charlotte have wanted to run away from him? Flee the scene and call the cops? He's an intruder. He's an outsider.

Then again, Charlotte feels like an outsider most of the time.

A rumble in the pit of her stomach reminds her dinner is nearing and she recalls the offer from Armstrong for a date that evening. Perhaps if she can suffer through it, she can keep the pyromaniac from returning to her house tonight. She owes it to Darryl.

She opens her message app.

Still on for dinner tonight?

Duh! Pick you up at 7.

When Charlotte arrives at the pub, her face and hands are numb, but everything else buzzes with warmth. She sits at the bar and orders a hot toddy from Merle.

"Feeling adventurous today?" He slides over the glass mug.

"Optimistic, perhaps." She sips the drink and a burning tingle slides down her throat.

This evening, the Christmas lights strung along the bar appear a little brighter. Charlotte doesn't think about calling her parents to vent about her day or scribbling tomorrow's tasks in her notebook. Instead, she sips on her beverage and sheepishly wonders if Lark has written more about Darryl in the notebook.

Chapter Nineteen

LARK

January 29, 2006

I'm so full of moussaka I don't think I'll ever eat again. Mrs. Poulios kept dishing it out, and I don't know if it was nerves or me wanting to please both her and Dani, but I ate like four helpings. After dinner, Dani and I sat in the den, and I undid the top button on my jeans to ease the tightness in my stomach, but that did nothing to shield me from the pain of Dani's next comment.

"I know I've been a bit MIA lately, and I'm sorry about that. Really. But I do think it's good for us to hang with other people. I dunno. I guess I just need to surround myself with positive people right now, you know?"

It ripped my insides out. Absolutely gutted me. Listen, I know I'm not cheerleader material, but neither is Dani and it's unfair that she told me this with a flip of her hand like it was an afterthought and not the reason for replacing our friendship. In that moment, I wished I had never opened up to her about the ache in my heart most days, about the fact that I can feel so off, like I'm floundering in a waterbed, flailing my limbs, trying to grab hold of something steady. If I had known she'd use it as a reason to swap me for the Tangerines, I'd have never confessed it.

Brittany, the girl with resting bitch face. Brittany, the girl who once convinced a room full of pre-teens to hide their pads and tampons from a girl who had bled through white jeans at a party.

This is the positivity Dani is seeking. The positivity I lack.

February 1, 2006

Would you rather be invisible or be noticed by the wrong person? I posed that to you tonight over deep-fried pickles and lemon-lime soda at the pub, and you looked at me with that cut-the-shit attitude and asked, "Why, who noticed you?" We both burst into laughter, and I almost choked on the damn pickle.

I can never have these philosophical chats with you because you can't humour me with an answer. You're always hell-bent on finding out the reason I'm asking it. I muttered something about how you are challenged when it comes to intellectual conversations (which you are), and you flashed your golden retriever smile and stole a pickle off my plate. That was the end of it—well, for you.

Sometimes, I wish I could be in that head of yours, dreaming of baseball and your

next punk show.

I wonder if you ever feel down like I do. It's like an itch I can't scratch. I can never be satisfied—there's just this niggling feeling that something isn't right. But like, all the time. I wonder if you inherited your laissez-faire attitude from Mom or Dad. It's getting harder to remember him, and Mom feels like she's pulling farther away the older we get—I'm not sure I know her at all anymore. I'm not sure she knows herself. Half the time she's out and when she is here, I catch her staring off into space like her mind is somewhere else. This was what, our third dinner without her this week? I get it, she's in love with Jake, and he has his own kids-free house, but come on, doesn't he want to get to know us better? Doesn't *she* want him to?

Don't get me wrong, I love our dinners—though you do need to work on your macaroni-to-milk ratio. It was like soup last time. Maybe I'll make us Hamburger Helper tomorrow, and I'll share the real reason I asked you that question tonight.

I'll work up the nerve to tell you about *him*. I can't even write his name—like if I do it will make it more real.

Darryl, he's been watching me so intensely that I requested a locker change. I already ignored his last two advances, but he doesn't seem to be getting the hint I'm not interested, and his notes are getting more aggressive. His last one, which he slipped into my locker sometime between first and third period yesterday, really freaked me out. He said he is scaring himself with how much he thinks of me and what he wants to do to me. Is that supposed to be a turn-on?

Everyone thinks the guy is vanilla. But I've seen something different in his eyes. I saw it the night of your show—the way he gripped my arm when I walked by without saying hi. He has a darkness, Darryl. Something you haven't noticed.

Maybe I should take a lesson from you in being more direct and just tell him that he and I will never be a thing.

I just hope it doesn't set him off.

Chapter Twenty

CHARLOTTE

Charlotte closes the journal with a thud and pushes it to the other side of the bed like it's a bad dream she wants to wake up from. Tux moves from her cozy spot in between Charlotte's legs and settles on top of the book.

"You don't want me to read this anymore, do you? I'm not sure I do either."

So far, every entry has been addressed to Darryl. In the news report, Darryl mentioned that Lark kept a lot to herself, but she knew she could come to him if she had a problem. Was the journal Lark's attempt to reveal what was going on in her life?

Who was she afraid to name—even in her private diary?

Charlotte could keep reading the journal—the truth is likely written somewhere in cursive within the 300-page book. But the guilt of exposing its contents swells with each page she turns. With every new entry she reads, her heart beats like it wants to escape her chest. She's not sure she can handle the anxiety.

Charlotte checks the time on her phone—seven o'clock. Armstrong will be here soon, and she can use the distraction—and some food. She hasn't eaten dinner yet, and the hot toddy swirls in her empty stomach.

As she pulls on her boots, a knock on the door interrupts her.

"You're under arrest." Outside the door, Armstrong breaks into laughter. "Charlotte, it's me, Kyle. Ready for our date?"

Charlotte squeezes her eyes shut. Perhaps he'll just leave. She shoos Tux off the journal and hides it under her pillow. Then, she takes a breath before unhooking the lock. When she opens the door, Armstrong leans against the door frame, his blonde hair perfectly coiffed.

Maybe she can do a bit of her own detective work tonight. Find out from Armstrong, who was friendly with Lark in high school. Charlotte retrieves her purse from the desk. "So, what's the plan? Downstairs for some food?" She pets Tux, who weaves between her legs.

Armstrong presents his arm for her to hold. "You'll see," he says with a raised eyebrow.

———————— ◆ ————————

While the pub would have been preferable, Charlotte allows her shoulders to relax when Armstrong leads her a few blocks down Main Street to a steakhouse not far from the Angel. When he opens the door for her, he pauses.

"Wait, you're not one of those vegetarians, are you?"

Charlotte shakes her head and steps through the doorway. The restaurant is warmly lit with pendant lamps and tea-light candles. The host leads them to a red leather booth with a dark wood table and presents a wine list and two menus. The establishment appears expensive for Anville, and Charlotte eyes the other customers who are dressed far nicer than the guests who frequent the Angel pub. She glances down at her salt-stained boots and her tapered jeans with the ripped knee. She shrugs off her parka, revealing a burgundy fleece sweater that she sewed a felt reindeer onto. It was more fitting next to Marie's poinsettia sweater this afternoon.

Armstrong sits across from her with a pristine posture and dressed in an olive-green button-down. He consults the wine list, then peers at her through narrowed eyes. "I'm thinking you're a rosé gal?"

"Californian cab sauv if I'm having steak."

Armstrong howls and smacks his knee. "Girl knows her wine." Then he slides the wine list her way. "You choose, we'll get a bottle."

Following twenty minutes of small talk about Armstrong's fishing trips—last summer he caught a fifteen-pound Walleye that hangs on the wall of his apartment—Charlotte gives in to her temptation. She cocks her head to the side.

"So, you grew up in Anville?"

"Born and raised."

"What was that like? I grew up in the city. I can't imagine knowing everyone in town."

He juts out his jaw and tilts his head to the side with an exaggerated thinking face. "You know what? I loved it. Anville High served the best chicken tenders."

Charlotte scoffs. "Come on, what was it really like? You were a jock, weren't you?"

He shrugs. "I guess. I played baseball, football, soccer. Hockey, obviously."

"Merle mentioned Darryl was on your baseball team."

"Every summer. He wasn't so bad when he was younger. We were actually tight. He got a bit weird with his punk music, though. That whole family was a tad off."

Charlotte casually sips her wine. "Darryl's? Did you know the sister?"

"Yeah, I knew Lark. She was two grades below. Quiet. Mysterious. Sort of like you." He smirks. "But she could be moody. I guess that's obvious, considering ..."

Charlotte clenches her fist under the table. She feels protective of Lark—like she's her close friend and this douche is talking behind her back. She clears her throat. "Moody?"

"She was bookish. A ballerina. Wore dark colours." Then he grins. "No reindeer sweaters."

"A ballerina? Did you ever see her dance?"

"Once or twice." He gulps his wine. "So, what's your thing? Are you a sporty girl?"

"God, no. I guess I'm bookish, too."

He grimaces. "Oops. Foot in mouth."

"It's fine," she says, picking at her bread.

"There's nothing wrong with being bookish. Lark was ... she was a bit of a loner. Preferred it that way, I think."

"No boyfriends?" She glances down at her bread, wondering if she's asking too many questions.

"Nah, not Lark."

"Really?"

He leans in closer and whispers, "She was a cutter."

It takes everything in Charlotte to prevent a look of disgust from creeping across her face. Armstrong assumes he knew Lark from her choice of recreational activities and the clothes she wore. Then, he exposes her secrets to Charlotte—a stranger.

Armstrong shakes his head. "Forget I said that. That was dumb of me."

The server brings over their salads, presenting the mixed greens with a flourish.

Charlotte nudges a crouton with her fork. "Do you think Darryl is dangerous? Should I be worried?"

"Nah, he's fine. We had it out once, and let's just say I got the last hit in." With an eyebrow raised, he butters his roll. "It's time he moves on from everything."

Charlotte slides to the edge of her seat. "What was your fight about? Who got to be the pitcher?" She laughs, but it comes out forced.

"Something like that."

The server returns for a quality check on the salads, and after that, Charlotte has a hard time directing the conversation back to Darryl and Lark. Armstrong spends the meal sharing cop stories—how he was once called to the scene where a burglar had gotten stuck in a doggy door.

"Have you ever had to use your gun?" Charlotte asks, genuinely curious.

"Nope. But my partner has. Officer Landry. He's been on the force for close to thirty years, though. Spent some time in Toronto, too. He's seen some messed up stuff. He was actually the first to the scene when Lark, you know ..." Armstrong stabs his final piece of steak.

"What about you? Where were you that night?"

The steak rolls around in his mouth. "I wasn't on the force yet." He laughs. "I was in grade twelve."

"Right." She allows her shoulders to slump forward. It's after nine, and the investigation has proven fruitless. Armstrong was admittedly a jock, and he and Lark didn't run in the same circles. She lets out a yawn, but Armstrong doesn't seem fazed.

"So, I checked times for the Empire. There are a couple of showings at ten, so we'll have to kill some time," he says.

"Oh, I don't know if I'm up for a movie tonight. Rain check?" she asks.

Armstrong's smile fades. "Really? Come on, don't be lame."

"It's been a long day."

He slouches against the backrest and fiddles with his phone. "Laaaame," he whines.

"I'm sorry, I was up early running errands. Another time, though."

Armstrong looks up from his phone. "Okay, fine, but humour me with another half hour. I have a surprise for you."

Chapter Twenty-One

CHARLOTTE

Armstrong approaches the passenger door of his truck, which is illegally parked beside a fire hydrant. "This is me."

Charlotte remains on the sidewalk, agonizing over where he plans to take her. "We're driving?" she asks, chewing on the inside of her lip.

He opens the door wide. "I'll have you back by ten, Scout's Honour."

Her feet stay firmly planted on the cement while her entire body shivers from the damp night.

"Come on, it'll be worth it," he coaxes.

She steals a glance behind her at the lively pub just a few feet away. She imagines Tux cuddled up on the pillow, softly purring as she guards Lark's journal. A voice in Charlotte's head orders her to walk the few steps to the pub, to seek solace in her cozy room. But some external force, like a cattle prod poking her back, forces her to follow Armstrong. Maybe he knows more than he's letting on, and she should keep an eye on him; she should make sure he doesn't return to light the garage on fire.

She sucks in a sharp breath as she climbs into the passenger seat of the pick-up truck, shuddering when Armstrong slams the door. A rock song blares over the radio, and he scrambles to lower the volume. "Whoops. Forgot I had it that loud. What do you want to listen to? Something festive?"

He scans the radio until he comes across "O Holy Night." The carol is hauntingly eerie as it underscores Armstrong's lead foot. Charlotte clutches the armrest, tensing her stomach muscles to suppress the anxious fluttering in her core.

She focuses on the road ahead, taking note of the streets they turn on. "Want to tell me where we're going?" she asks, her voice serious and pointed.

He laughs. "Where's the fun in that? You gotta live a little." Then, he steps on the gas pedal harder.

The neighbourhood streets are narrow, the snowbanks creeping onto the asphalt and leaving little room for two cars to pass each other. Luckily, there aren't many vehicles on the road. Charlotte squints as they near a stop sign, and Armstrong maintains his speed. When she opens them again, they are through the intersection, the red octagon shrinking in her sideview mirror.

"Slow down," she says through clenched teeth.

"It's not like I'm gonna get pulled over."

"I mean it." Charlotte closes her eyes tight.

"Don't worry, these streets are always empty this time of night."

It is only when Charlotte throws her hands in front of her face, a whimper escaping her lips, that Armstrong takes her advice and lowers his speed to ten over the limit.

"Sorry," he says, slouching. "I didn't mean to scare you."

Charlotte opens her eyes. She glances out her window and recognizes the park with its outdoor skating rink illuminated by the surrounding trees draped with twinkle lights. Perhaps this is the surprise he alluded to.

"Our next date idea," Armstrong says, nodding to the rink as they pass.

They continue down the road, headed in the direction of her parents' home. *Shit.*

"What time was the next film at?" she asks, her eyes flitting past familiar houses. "I think I'm getting a second wind." As they approach her house, she stiffens in her seat. The four-square and accompanying garage stand in darkness, providing no evidence that Darryl is inside.

Armstrong edges onto the driveway and cuts the engine.

"What are we doing?" Charlotte asks, unable to utter more.

Armstrong turns to face her, wearing a wild grin. "I'm gonna pry open the garage door. We're gonna catch the bastard."

"Shouldn't you do this on duty? And with your partner?"

His smile fades. "I thought you'd want to see if you were right."

Charlotte knows she is right. She gave that testimony to Armstrong the night she discovered Darryl. It's not about that, she realizes. He wants to show off in front of her like he's some kind of knight.

"What if he's in there? Then what?" she asks.

Armstrong reaches over Charlotte, opening the glove compartment to reveal a handgun. "Don't worry. He's not gonna do anything."

She shakes her head, astounded by what is unfolding before her. "No. Let's go back to the pub. I'll buy the next round," she pleads, a metallic taste in her mouth.

Why in the hell would Armstrong bring her here after their date? If he thought this act would impress her, he was wrong.

"Don't be scared. It's just for show," he says, wagging the gun.

"I'm serious. This is a bad idea. Let's do something—anything else."

"The night is young," he says, his eyebrows dancing.

"I'm waiting in the truck."

"Suit yourself." He slides out without another word, gun in one hand and a lock pick in the other. He presses the door closed so as not to make a sound.

Charlotte watches as he creeps up the driveway toward the garage, and she wills it to be empty, hoping Darryl has moved its contents into her living room. She gave him her word. She told him he would have the night to go through the boxes, take a shower, and sleep under an actual roof. But the way this is transpiring could be read as a trap Charlotte set up from the beginning. She releases her seatbelt and leans forward, her forearms folded on the dashboard. Armstrong stands in front of the garage, fiddling with the door handle.

A warm light glows in the living room like a firefly igniting, drawing her attention to the house. Her heart flutters, and she inhales a deep breath. Darryl is safe in the house. He's likely turned on one of the kerosene lamps he was using in the garage, presumably to avoid switching on the main light. Her eyes dart from Armstrong to the front window and back. She watches Armstrong's frame as he works.

She needs to tip Darryl off or Armstrong will find him squatting in her house, and the damn cop can't be trusted with his handgun. She counts down from ten and then in one swift movement, escapes the confines of the truck, slamming the door with a jarring thud.

Armstrong jerks his head toward the sound and brings his finger to his mouth in an exaggerated motion. Once again, Charlotte scans the living room, waiting for the light to extinguish. If Darryl were to glance out the window, he'd see the truck. Armstrong motions her over, and she complies, wanting to keep him near the garage where he doesn't have a view of the living room.

"You changed your mind," he says, jamming the metal pick in the keyhole repeatedly.

"You know there's a back door," Charlotte says, shifting her weight from side to side, her nerves and the cold air compelling her to keep moving.

Armstrong pauses, a curious look on his face, and then he smiles, his confidence returning. "This will be more dramatic. And I've already got it." He slides the pick back into his back pocket. "Turn your flashlight on your phone. When I open the door, I want you to shine it into the garage." He readies his gun.

Charlotte clenches her jaw even though she trusts Darryl is in the house. She abides and presses the flashlight app on her phone, holding the device above her head with a shaking hand.

Armstrong cranks the handle and pulls it toward him, backing up so the metal door can lift open. Charlotte flashes the light into the blackness, exposing the bare walls and floor. She expels an extended breath along with the anxiety that has been brewing beneath her breastbone. It's hard to believe that five hours ago, she was sitting in the fully furnished garage eating cereal. Darryl has worked efficiently. Everything save a few garbage bags has presumably been transported into her house.

Armstrong rushes forward, still holding up the gun like he's a TV cop called to a murder scene. He kicks at one of the bags, and it topples over, the sound of cans and bottles crashing against the cement floor.

"I think you're right. He was here. I didn't want to worry you, but I swung by this afternoon, and I heard noises from inside the garage." He turns to face her, standing at attention like a G.I Joe. "Looks like I scared him away."

"He's moved on then." Charlotte shrugs. "Took his stuff and found another place to crash."

"Looks like it. Unless …" He nods toward the house. "Have you changed the locks yet? Maybe he does still have a key."

Charlotte shakes her head and then freezes, betrayed by her quick reflexes.

Armstrong raises his eyebrows. "Want to go exploring?" His wild smile returns along with Charlotte's uneasiness.

Her voice raises an octave. "No, I have to get back. I can't leave Tux too long. And I don't even have my key on me."

"You named the cat? I like it. Alright, I'll take you back to the Angel. Just let me have a quick look in the window." He trudges through the snowy yard that leads to the back door.

Charlotte doesn't have time to think. She needs to warn Darryl before Armstrong notices the light in the living room. She runs straight for the garage door, throwing her shoulder into the metal with an ear-splitting bang. When Armstrong spins around, Charlotte lies next to the garage.

"Charlotte?"

She rolls onto her side, the snow dampening her jeans.

"Shit, are you okay?"

"I slipped on some ice." She searches his eyes for confirmation that the display fooled him.

He rushes over to her and extends a hand. "Are you hurt?" He guides her up to a seated position.

"I'm fine." Charlotte brushes the snow from her jeans. "Can you take me home now?"

Armstrong moves closer and sweeps the hair out of her face. His hand hovers next to her chin. "Fuck, I'm in trouble," he says before closing his eyes and leaning in.

It takes a moment for Charlotte to realize what is happening but when she feels Armstrong's wet lips on her own, she pulls away. "I ... um—"

"You want to take things slow; I get it."

Charlotte scrambles to her feet, and Armstrong follows. It was brief, but she could taste the peppermint on Armstrong's breath as if he was planning for the kiss.

"Let's get you home," he says, linking his arm through hers and leading her down the driveway toward the parked truck.

Charlotte keeps her focus on her steps until they near the porch. The front window is no longer aglow. She drops her arm from Armstrong's and hurries to the passenger door.

As they back out of the driveway, the sheer curtain dances.

Darryl is watching.

Chapter Twenty-Two

CHARLOTTE

Charlotte lies on her stomach on the bed at the inn, staring at the blank page beneath her nose. She has swapped Lark's diary for her own notebook to curb her curiosity and calm her nerves. Her incessant to-do lists have taken a back seat over the last few days, and Charlotte realizes it's because of Lark's confessions. The truth is, she hasn't had someone confide in her like this since high school, the fact that Lark isn't really confessing to *her* notwithstanding.

Pen in hand, Charlotte commits to a list of tasks to complete over the next twenty-four hours.

-Pack
-Offer cheque to Merle and Cindy
-Meet the locksmith at the house
-Order dumpster

None of these directives involves indulging in Lark's diary. Even though it's all Charlotte can think about, she needs to stop. The guilt is growing like an infection in her bloodstream.

She stares down at her phone screen, and the latest text she received just a minute ago. At least Armstrong has an android phone that won't reveal she's read his texts:

Sent Thursday at 10:33 PM: *You okay? You kinda rushed out of the truck.*

Sent Thursday at 10:46 PM: *Goodnight, beautiful. Get some rest!*

Sent Friday at 10:00 AM: *Morning – sleep okay? Last night was fun. Let's lock in that skating date.*

Sent Friday at 12:45 PM: *I hope I didn't annoy you with the surprise …*

Sent Friday at 2:00 PM: *If you want some company while you deal with all the Peters' junk, let me know!*

She exits their one-sided conversation and instead shoots a text to her parents, responding to a series of photos they sent her of the beach clean-up they volunteered at yesterday.

Look at you go! Dad – don't forget to wear sunscreen. P.S – I might need to come home for a few days.

She follows with a lie about a dentist appointment—anything to get some time away from Armstrong and the temptation of the diary.

In the photos, her father has adopted a red hue, which is accentuated by the white T-shirt he wears, The Florida Aquarium logo proudly on display. Her mother is perfectly sun-kissed with a smattering of golden-brown freckles gracing her cheeks and shoulders. They really are living their best lives. It is then that Charlotte realizes they haven't had a conversation of more than ten minutes since she arrived in Anville. So much has happened in the short week that she's barely had time to arrange for the contractors to start their work. She's barely had time to miss her parents, but now as she swipes through the carousel of photos, she feels an ache in her chest like she's lost another part of herself.

She sends a final text before resuming her packing: *Never mind, it's fine. Let's plan for a video chat soon.*

Charlotte slides her notebook into the bag and scans the room for any forgotten items. Lark's diary is already safely stowed with her laptop in the side compartment. She hasn't decided what she'll do with it. She could surrender it to Darryl. Lark had intended the entries for him after all. But then she would have to admit that she took it in the first place, and she fears what he might think of her for invading his sister's privacy.

It's also possible he's already on a bus halfway across town, but she hopes she hasn't missed him. She doesn't feel like their business is finished quite yet. She had told him to take his time going through the boxes and that she wouldn't be back until late afternoon.

She digs her nails into her palms leaving purple crescent moons on her flesh. What if he asks about last night? He likely saw her from the front window as she left with Armstrong. She can only hope he didn't witness the unexpected kiss. How did she let that happen?

—— ◆ ——

Charlotte glides along the sidewalk deep in thought, occasionally trudging through a foot of snow that a resident hasn't bothered to shovel. By the time she arrives in the driveway and catches a glimpse of the large dumpster, it is three in the afternoon. Darryl must have ordered it—something she can cross off her to-do list. The locksmith will arrive at four to change the locks. As she climbs the porch steps, the screen door swings open, nudged by Darryl who is balancing two crates in his arms.

"Oh, hi. I'm almost done," he says, his green irises taking on a golden hue in the sunlight.

Charlotte notices that the skin around his eyes is red. He's either just enjoyed a blunt or digging through his sister's memories was too much.

They find themselves trapped in an awkward dance, each moving in the same direction until he gives up and places the crates down, laughing it off.

Charlotte climbs the last step, joining him on the porch. "How'd it go? Did you have enough time to get through everything?" She meets his gaze for a moment and then finds a spot on the brick wall to focus her attention on, the eye contact feeling too intimate.

"I did, thank you again. Hope you don't mind the dumpster. They'll pick it up on Tuesday." He motions to a few boxes stacked neatly on the porch. "I'm taking the rest of this stuff with me."

"That works." Charlotte kicks her boot against the step to release snow that has gotten stuck in her treads. "I guess I'll head inside while you finish up."

Darryl nods and bends down to pick up the crates he's abandoned.

"Lift with your knees," Charlotte says making her way toward the door and then rescinds into the house, embarrassed by how much she sounds like her dad.

Inside feels emptier than when she first moved in, the stacks of crates reduced to only two in the corner of the living room. Charlotte hangs her coat on the newel post and meanders across the room. She discreetly peeks into the contents of the remaining boxes and recalls a few items—the teddy bear and jewellery box—both with presumed sentimental value. She catches sight of an Anville High yearbook, and as if being guided by an unknown force, she removes it from the box and tucks it into the fireplace. Something else of Lark's that draws her—another inexplicable pull.

The sheer curtain of the front window sways in the warm wind escaping the register below. Charlotte pulls the curtain open, revealing an unobstructed view of the driveway, where Armstrong's truck sat last night.

She is about to consult the back door and determine whether Darryl would have had a line of sight of the kiss when the screen door swings shut with a bang.

Charlotte releases the curtain and allows her hand to fall to her hip. "Need any help?"

"I'm all good. My friend is swinging by soon to pick me up and then I'll be on my way."

Gone. Out of her life for good. She should feel relieved by this. She can finally focus on getting the house in order and then return to her old life in the city.

"Where's Tux?" he asks.

"Oh, Merle offered to drive her and my bag back before the dinner rush. Is that okay? He shouldn't take long."

"No worries. Unless ... do you want to keep her?"

"Keep your cat?"

"She's my mom's, and the place she's at doesn't allow pets. You'd be doing me a solid if you did. The apartment I'm staying in isn't exactly pet-friendly."

"Absolutely, yes. I'd love to keep her." Tux's company has made Charlotte's stay in Anville bearable, and she can't imagine sleeping in this house without her feline friend.

Darryl crosses the room to the crates. "Lifting with my knees," he says with a laugh as he picks up a box.

Charlotte smiles, scrunching up her nose.

Once he has moved both boxes to the door and it is clear there is nothing left to do but wait for his ride, he shrugs. "Thanks again, for letting me sort everything out."

"For sure. No worries."

There isn't food in the fridge to offer or even a couch to sit on, but she doesn't want to see him go right away.

"You've found a place, okay?"

"A buddy of mine has a basement apartment he's offered up."

"In town?"

"Not too far." Darryl leans against the banister. "Hey, you didn't notice a leather notebook at all when you moved in, did you?"

Charlotte clenches her jaw. "A notebook? I don't think so. Was it important?"

"It was my sister's. I was hoping I'd be able to track it down in her things."

Charlotte nods. "If you give me your number, I can let you know if I come across it." She's surprised by her boldness. She can't recall the last time she asked a guy for his number. Of course, this is purely tactical, and she hopes he views it that way.

"Yeah, for sure. That would be great, if it turns up."

Charlotte passes her phone over and is reminded of the last time a guy programmed his number into her phone. Darryl types in his number and then pauses, his eyebrows pinching together. "Text from Kyle ... sorry, didn't mean to look." He passes the phone back and retrieves his own phone from his pocket, busying himself.

Are you alive?! Make it back to your place? Let me know if you need a hand.

If Charlotte doesn't respond soon, she suspects Armstrong will show up on her doorstep, garbage bags in hand.

Yes, made it home. Thanks for the offer, but I'm out running errands.

The wind picks up outside, rattling the screen door.

"This house," Darryl begins and then clears his throat. "You feel everything. When it thunders, the walls shake," he laughs. "Lark used to refuse to sleep in her own room during a thunderstorm. Even when she was sixteen."

"I'm so sorry. About your sister."

Darryl nods, his gaze falling to the floor. The wind subsides, and an eerie silence fills the space. Charlotte searches her mind for something to break it. Thankfully, a car door slams outside, and they both look up at the door.

"That's my ride. Thanks again," he says as he pushes open the screen door and waves to his friend climbing out of the truck. "Everything on the porch is coming. Just got a couple more boxes in here." He turns toward Charlotte. "I'll see you around, maybe."

"Yeah, I'll look for that book of your sister's. Let you know if I find it."

Charlotte watches Darryl and his friend lift the last of his possessions into the cab of the truck. If she ever wants to see him again, she'll have to give up the one thing that has been keeping her mind off her own problems.

She'll have to give up the diary. She'll have to say goodbye to Lark.

And she's not sure she's ready to do that.

Chapter Twenty-Three

LARK

February 2, 2006

The box dye was labelled *Blueberry*, but it was basically black. I stained the bathroom sink and one of the hand towels in the process.

I love it. It's not a huge change from my dark brown hair, but it makes me feel like a lead character in a graphic novel. I don't think Miss Lindsay will approve. Exams are coming up, and the slight blue shimmer is hardly a ballerina colour.

I wonder what Dani will think of it. She needs positivity right now. Translation? She needs predictable blondes. I think you'll dig it. I look a little punk rock, so maybe you'll want me to do some more backup at your shows.

I wonder if Mom will be pissed. Probably more so that I chose box dye over going to her salon. She'll get all nostalgic and reminisce about how I used to let her French braid my hair after my baths so I'd have crimpy waves. Then she'll complain that I don't let her near it anymore. She'll take advantage of the moment to once again criticize my use of the iron to straighten my hair. How it's killing it, one strand at a time.

I already know Jake tolerates it. I ran into him at the pub. He mumbled something like, "That colour suits you." So, I'm sure he'll convince Mom it's not that bad—definitely not grounding material.

———— •✦• ————

February 4, 2006

I think there is a moment in our lives when we are no longer children. When we realize that our lives aren't like those perfect pictures in the *Little Golden Books* series. They are puzzles and sometimes the pieces go missing. They get lost under your futon, and a week later, you figure they've been sucked up by the vacuum.

Lately, I've been feeling like I'm losing more and more of those pieces. I have these moments where I forget entire parts of myself. Am I someone who enjoys poetry? Do I prefer sweet or savoury? Do I even like ballet?

Or maybe it's that I'm starting to believe what others think of me. The image they've sketched. There are rumours going around. You've maybe heard them, too.

Lark's a goth now, have you seen the new hair?

Did you see the cuts up her arm?

Why is she always alone?

And then there's the other rumour that made my stomach do summersaults like I was pushed off a ten-story building when I first heard it. The one I can't bear to write.

I know who's been spreading them. The timing is too convenient—right after I reject him, telling him it will never happen between us, I hear the whispers in the hallway like a Greek chorus. And the Tangerines (and practically everyone in the school) are all too eager to play a game of broken telephone.

I know what you'd say if I told you: *Screw everyone. They are bored with their lives. They are looking for a target, for someone else to skewer, so they don't have to face their own bullshit.*

I don't think Mom's reputation helps the situation. If any other girl in the school was targeted, their moms would step in—use their influence at book club or with the parent-teacher association to shut it down. Instead, Mom is a bit of an outsider herself. She's known for bouncing from one thing (*cough*, man) to another. I wouldn't be surprised if the other mothers joined right in, confirming the rumours and adding their own spin.

Remember my first sleepover party when Mom was going through the spiritual phase and bought my friends and me a psychic to tell our fortunes? Camille couldn't fall asleep because the clairvoyant told her that her mom's cancer would return after remission. And then, the next morning Mom's boyfriend at the time—Moustache Murph, remember?—attempted pancakes (while in his boxers). He only made things worse when he failed to cook them long enough, the insides still soupy, and Giordanna threw up all over the kitchen table. Five out of six girls' mothers ended up calling the house to complain about the event. I never hosted a sleepover again, except with Dani.

Everyone else at school has normal lives. Dinner at six each night that isn't nuked in the microwave. Someone to remind them to do their homework, to drive them to their activities. Sleepovers with makeovers and junk food. No psychics or undercooked pancakes. No mother in spandex testing out her latest workout fad, her vision boards of the ideal female body guarding our fridge so she doesn't snack.

Sometimes, I wonder if a little part of them is right about me. If I'm a little off.

Maybe we both are because of her.

Chapter Twenty-Four

CHARLOTTE

C harlotte is disciplined over the next couple of days busying herself with the renovations and swapping progress photos of the hardwood staining upstairs for her parents' poolside selfies. She hasn't allowed herself to read a single entry from Lark's diary. Not since her imagination got the better of her and she dreamt a harrowing scene of Lark swinging from a noose among the oak tree's branches, maggots squirming through her empty eye sockets.

After tucking the journal away in the primary bedroom closet, sealed within a cardboard box along with the new hallway light fixtures, Charlotte's been less tempted to open it. Instead, she's distracted herself by writing practical renovation to-do lists and the scribbled notes on the bed evidence.

-Call with kitchen contractor

-Buy Christmas presents for Mom, Dad, maybe Merle and Cindy?

-~~Bleach bathtub~~
-~~Order paint~~
-Install doorbell cam

The afternoon sun melts the snow on the roof and the water escapes in rushes down the eavestrough. Charlotte, still in her pyjamas, lies on her side while propped on an elbow, consulting the renovation binder. She is ordering the kitchen paint—Benjamin Moore's colour of the year, *October Mist*—when her phone notifies her of an incoming video call.

"I'm still not sure I understand," Sheryl says, her face mere inches from the iPad. "You're going to keep the cat?"

Jared appears in the background, slathering a generous amount of sunscreen onto his arms. "Why not? I think it's good for her to have some company."

Charlotte scratches the oily fur behind Tux's ears. "Don't worry; I'm going to take her with me when I'm done."

"And the son—he got rid of the junk in the living room? I'll be complaining to the realtor. The closing date was weeks ago. There's no excuse," Sheryl says, her lips pursed.

"It's fine, Mom. They're picking up the dumpster tomorrow."

"It's not fine. We should have let you come home when you asked. Jared, can we cancel today's showing? Char, just come home. We can change our plans for Christmas. Let's sort this all out together."

Charlotte rubs the goosebumps on her arm. This is her out. She can escape Anville and get as far away from Armstrong as possible—and the diary, which has been consuming her mind.

Jared's head dips, along with Charlotte's stomach. Her parents deserve this time to focus on themselves. For once, she doesn't want them to drop everything for her.

She clears her throat. "Just enjoy the Florida weather, and don't worry about me."

Her father's eyes widen. "Char, they've got a Christmas tree in the courtyard. It looks just like Rockefeller, only instead of the skating rink, we are dipping our feet in a pool."

"Sounds festive. Is that what you'll do Christmas day?" It's time she accepts she'll be spending Christmas alone for the first time in thirty-two years.

Sheryl assumes an exaggerated pout. "Maybe we can watch *The Polar Express* while we FaceTime? We could all order Swiss Chalet!"

"Yeah, maybe."

"It will be our first Christmas away from you," she says as if it wasn't their idea to leave before the holiday.

Jared hums the Jeopardy theme song in the background, leaving the tune on a cliffhanger note.

"Okay, sweetie, we've got to run, but I'm so glad we made the time for a real chat. I can't believe it's already been a week. Call us again tomorrow if you'd like."

Charlotte lets the iPad fall to her bed and reaches for the Anville High yearbook. She scans the messages written to a fifteen-year-old Lark, when she was in her first year of high school—only a year before her suicide.

First one to sign! We're going to have a blast this summer, Birdie. Can't wait to get up to some trouble with you J –Dani

This year was fun! Loved getting to know you in math. Have a great summer and see you next year –Lisa S

Have a great summer! Hope to see you around! –Jenna

Most of the messages are generic greetings from girlfriends, recounting the good times in Ms. Oulette's French class and anticipating summer vacation at their cottages. The pages are made up of curvy penmanship in varied colours of ink and candid group shots done up in a scrapbook aesthetic, bordered with faux tape.

A sadness weighs heavy in Charlotte's chest as she thinks about her own high school experience before the night everything was stolen from her. She distracts herself by flipping to the blank pages at the back of the book, where a few more messages live. She skims the text and finds a note from Darryl.

Bird, you survived your first year! I know this year had its ups and downs, but I hope you know how proud I am of you. Here's to taking it easy this summer and binging cherry popsicles.

Next, Charlotte scans the tiles of portraits, all with blue gradient backgrounds. She finds the juniors first and spots Kyle among the A's, looking pretty much unchanged from the other night. He is voted most likely to be a sports agent, which is emphasized by his chosen quote: *"You miss 100% of the shots you don't take." – Wayne Gretzky.*

Charlotte huffs. This motto seems to be Armstrong's mantra in life, taken too far. Persistence is one word for it, but controlling and obsessive also come to mind.

On the next page, Charlotte finds Darryl. His dark hair reaches below his chin, his swooping bangs meeting his green eyes. His smile is breezy, and Charlotte feels the familiar pull toward him like they are bound by a string. *Interesting*—his classmates voted him most likely to be a doctor.

"Doctor?" she asks aloud to Tux, curled up next to her in the fetal position. She considers a seventeen-year-old honour student, Darryl, becoming the thirty-four-year-old she just evicted from her garage. The dichotomy astounds her, but of course, Charlotte can gather the reason for this change. She rifles through the book until she finds the freshman portraits.

Lark Peters sits tall with a toothy grin, her long, dark hair straightened and parted on the side. Her eyes are wide and bright, and there is no evidence that they are a façade. Charlotte swallows a lump that has formed in her throat as she wonders what Lark would look like today.

She considers the boys in Lark's grade. Any of them could be *the* guy, but they all hide behind awkward smiles, looking even younger than the grade nine girls. Charlotte is scanning the remaining students with last names that begin with V-Z when she comes across a group shot. The cursive caption reads, *Students hanging in the courtyard: Sarah Russell, Dani Poulios, Lark Peters, Kyle Armstrong, and Xander Campbell.* Lark sits on the stone steps of the school with a shy smile, between a brunette with ringlet curls whom Charlotte assumes to be Dani, and Kyle. Kyle grins enthusiastically in his forest-green Aeropostale polo. And next to the photo, he has written a message:

Who's that attractive couple in the middle? Admit it, Lark – we look real good together. Don't be a stranger this summer. P.S. don't tell your brother I have a crush on you. –KA

Cold tingles creep up Charlotte's arm, making her skin horripilate. She reads the message again, this time hearing Armstrong's booming voice in her head. She stares at his portrait, searching his eyes for the darkness Lark wrote about. The repeated texts he's sent Charlotte now take on a creepier tone. She plays out a scene in her mind. Armstrong grabs Lark by the arm after she unintentionally ignores him, pulling her close and digging his fingertips into her flesh.

The more Charlotte gets to know him, the more he seems like someone who could have done those things. His behaviour is aggressive and, at times, erratic.

She falls back on the bed and rubs her sternum with the pad of her thumb. Has she unintentionally involved herself with Lark's stalker? Is she his next conquest? A knock at the door sends a flurry of tingles through her core. She peers out her bedroom window and spots a squad car in the driveway behind the dumpster that has yet to be picked up.

Charlotte spots the man in uniform from the stairs. She opens the door a crack and is relieved to discover Officer Landry on the stoop. At least it's official police business.

"Ms. Boyd. Have I caught you at an okay time?" he asks, and Charlotte suspects his question has to do with her loungewear at four in the afternoon.

"Sure. What can I do for you?"

Landry is a stocky man with wide shoulders. His thirty years as a cop seem to have taken a toll on him. His grey hair and beard are wiry, and his sombre face is creased with deep lines, each with a story, she suspects.

"Just doing a patrol and wanted to check-in. Have you had any more trouble in the garage?"

"Nope. Garage is all clear, and I've gotten rid of the Peters' stuff."

He turns around, eying the dumpster. "Huh." He grunts. "You didn't use Landry's Junk Removal."

"Oh. No, I didn't." She feels her cheeks grow hot and breaks eye contact with the officer. Darryl had ordered the dumpster, not her. Even still, did it matter whether she used Landry's referral? He seems perturbed that she proceeded with another company.

"It would have saved you the cost. How much did they charge you for the dumpster?"

Charlotte plays with a hangnail on her thumb. His questioning presents itself as an interrogation. "I lost the card you gave me, so just went with the first company on Google. It's no big deal though; I'm honestly just glad to be done with it all."

He nods. "Let me guess, they aren't picking it up for a few days either. My cousin has a twenty-four-hour turnaround." He shrugs as her guilt grows.

Small towns. Everybody supports each other's businesses. And everybody knows each other's business.

"It's fine, really," she says.

"Okay, well if you do see Darryl lurking around your property again, please reach out. We treat these matters very seriously, especially when it involves those with priors."

Charlotte ignores his last remark. It feels inappropriate, like he wants her to ask about Darryl's criminal record. "Thank you, but I think it's been taken care of."

Landry bows his head and then turns to leave. On his way down the stairs, he scans the contents of the dumpster. When he reaches the bottom, he circles back to face her.

"Ms. Boyd."

Charlotte pushes the screen door open. "Yep?"

"Darryl Peters isn't someone you want to get mixed up with."

"So I've heard."

Chapter Twenty-Five

CHARLOTTE

Did you mean to take this with you? Not sure if it's important but you're welcome to swing by if so.

Charlotte stares at the unanswered text she sent to Darryl shortly after Officer Landry left her stoop. She considers adding to it and reframing the invite. She places the phone down on a temporary TV table that was marked *free* and that she dragged over from a neighbour's house yesterday. It will have to do until the coastal-style bench her mother picked in refurbished white arrives.

She follows the text with a photo of the yearbook, which appears grainy because of the dim lighting of the living room.

Darryl probably thinks it's strange she is only now texting about the yearbook. It's not like it could have been hidden among her belongings. The place is practically bare. And why is she asking him to come over? The invitation seems both intimate and random.

She frees her hands from her lap and types another message: *I'm thinking of swinging by the pub tonight. I can bring it there if it's easier?*

After a moment, her thumbs continue tapping: *Or I can get rid of it if it's not important?*

As she stares at her three unread messages, she feels almost as desperate as Armstrong, who still hasn't gotten the hint that her lack of response is a lack of interest. Though, his last message, which arrived a few moments ago, had been brief:

Heard you got through all their stuff on your own.

Clearly, he had been talking to Officer Landry.

Charlotte takes a break from staring at her phone to install a new doorbell camera at the front of the house—an added security measure following the new locks. When she's satisfied with the doorbell test, she retreats into the house and climbs the stairs to the freshly cleaned bathroom.

She generously sprays a lemon air freshener to mask the bleach, which has made the entire second floor reek like a public pool. She cracks open the window an inch and breathes in the icy air while she waits for the bath to fill with hot water.

Charlotte places her phone on the floor, where she's laid down a towel, and peels out of her clothes, letting them collect in a pile. She dips a toe in, only to discover the bath is lukewarm. The water heater in the basement is on the list of appliances to replace.

With her hair secured in a bun on the top of her head, Charlotte allows herself to sink deep into the tub, the water rising to her chin. Below the surface, tiny bubbles cover every hair on her body. Feeling inspired by Lark, she allows her arms to float through various ballet positions in a port de bras, and the hairs resemble snow-covered coniferous trees blowing in the wind.

She releases her hair from the elastic and submerges herself. She remains underwater until she can no longer hold her breath, and then she flaps her arms at her sides, finally connecting with the tub walls and clawing herself back to a seated position. When she reaches the surface, she gasps for air and wipes the water from her eyes. The body's survival instincts always kick in—at least for Charlotte.

She allows her mind to wander to another member of the Peters' clan. The silence is a reminder that he still hasn't responded to her texts. Sheepishly, she gives her right hand permission to explore between her legs, leaning back against the tub's wall and welcoming the warm ache. It feels wrong—she doesn't even know him—but maybe that is part of the appeal. With her eyes closed, she conjures the image from the yearbook and Darryl's kind smile and then imagines his tall and sturdy frame—his muscles engaging as he heaves the snow and hauls crates from the house to the porch. She remembers the feeling in her core when she grazed his hand and what might have happened if the touch didn't stop there.

Her heartbeat quickens, matching the tempo of her fingers, and she comes quickly, faster than she'd hoped. She allows herself to slide beneath the water. The orgasm renders her embarrassed, guilty, so she busies her hands, scrubbing her body with a loofah sponge.

The connection she feels toward Darryl is undeniable; she attempts to reconcile why. Is it the image Lark presented in her diary of her optimistic and protective big brother? Or perhaps it stems from the fact that Darryl, like her, has experienced a loss so profound he's misplaced a part of himself. She wonders if it's still inside somewhere.

Charlotte tries not to think about the person she was before seventeen—the charismatic, confident, yet naïve girl. Her parents are the only people who can remind her, and they know better than to do that. But there are moments when Charlotte will come face to face with an emblem of her former life—she'll run into a parent of one of the girls, or she'll be tagged in an old photo from the gymnastics club.

There's also a part of her that perceives Armstrong and Landry's warnings as a sort of dare; going against the grain might actually cure her. Or perhaps she's just attracted to the danger of it all.

Before she can give it further thought, she receives a notification. Reaching for her phone over the side of the tub, she drips water along her towel and onto the screen.

Appreciate you checking. Meant to pack that up, so if you don't mind hanging onto it, I can be at the house in an hour. Does that work?

Her breath quickens.

He's coming to the house, and she's not sure whether that excites or frightens her.

Chapter Twenty-Six

CHARLOTTE

In approximately ten minutes, Darryl Peters should arrive to retrieve the yearbook. Charlotte took the time to blow dry her hair after the bath and applied modest make-up. She isn't certain if she'll invite him in for a slice of pizza and a thrown-together garden salad or if she'll simply pass over the hardcover of memories and watch him leave—this time likely for good.

When her newly installed doorbell cam elicits a shrill chime on her phone, she is in the middle of cutting a tomato. He's early. The doorbell itself follows, repeating the chime once more in real life. She rushes to the door, the juice from the knife running down her hand.

Darryl stands before her, blowing into his hands for warmth. "Cold one tonight."

Charlotte pulls the door open. "Come in. I'll go grab the book."

Darryl's eyes are wide when he steps into the foyer. "Do you always answer the door holding a knife?"

Running back to the kitchen, she calls, "Only since I found a guy living in my garage." She giggles at her joke to ease the tension. "I was making a salad to go with my pizza. You hungry? I ordered way too much." Her boldness surprises her, remnants of her personality before the accident—before she recoiled into herself, trying to take up less room in the world.

Darryl glances toward the screen door. "My buddy actually dropped me off."

Sure enough, a truck idles in the driveway, its headlights shining through the doorway.

Charlotte hadn't considered that, but it makes sense. Darryl didn't have a car three days ago, so why would he now?

"I'll just grab you the book then." She places the knife on the cutting board and washes her hands at the sink.

"Just hang tight a sec," Darryl says and then disappears out the front door. He returns a minute later as the truck eases out of the driveway.

"Xander will swing back a bit later to get me. I'm starving. Where'd you order from?"

She bites her lip. "Luigi's?" she says with hesitation, seeking approval.

"Good choice."

She places the box on the coffee table along with two plates. "They had a spicy sausage and honey feature that sounded good."

Tux darts down the stairs and heads straight for the couch. She weaves between Darryl's legs, and he reaches down to properly greet her. Charlotte carries over forks and the salad bowl, then sits on the opposite side of the couch. As she sinks into the plush cushion, she finds Darryl has removed his coat along with his toque. His dark waves have been chopped to the chin and now frame his face. His thick brows highlight his eyes. The haircut suits him.

She grabs two slices and then nudges the box his way. "New hair?" she asks.

Darryl runs his hand through the flow. "Yeah, part of the rooming agreement with Xander. He wants me to work on self-care," he says with a laugh. He takes a bite and motions with the pizza. "Not bad."

It is only when Darryl has finished his second slice that Charlotte offers him a drink, her hostess skills out of practice. "I have beer, wine, water?"

"Water's good."

She returns with his water and red wine in a Frosty the Snowman mug for herself. "You're cool if I drink?"

"Oh yeah, go for it. I'm just not much of a drinker."

The graphic story of his father's death makes its way to Charlotte's mind. She would never dare drink and drive even before her accident, so she understands if Darryl has made this vow. She wonders if his dad was the one at fault and if there were others involved.

Charlotte flips open her laptop. "Music?"

Darryl nods with a mouthful of pizza. She uses the opportunity to dive into the back catalogue of the artists she enjoyed in high school—the same artists whose CDs were found in one of the milk crates.

He perks up at the second song. "Broken Social Scene, right? 'Stars and Sons.' Great tune. I haven't heard this in ages."

"Sorry, I don't have a TV or much entertainment. Still getting every-thing sorted. My parents are going for *coastal chic*. They are in Florida as we speak." She takes a bite of her second slice. "How about your new place? Settling in?"

"I am. It's closer to work, so that's good."

As Darryl taps the beat of the chorus, Charlotte probes him on what he does for work. He explains the collection of odd jobs—general maintenance at a nearby community centre, golf course landscaping in the summer, and until his truck went kaput, he had been doing contract snow plowing. "Exciting stuff," he says. "How about you? Let me guess, something in fashion."

A shrill laugh escapes her throat. He must think she's far more interesting than she is. She glances down at her plate, her crusts staring back at her. "There's not much worth sharing. I've had mostly temp jobs. I'm taking some time off to help with my parents' renovations."

Darryl nods, his face showing no judgment.

"Why'd you change your mind about being a doctor?" Charlotte asks before realizing she's just exposed that she went snooping in the yearbook.

Darryl cocks his head to the side, and a smirk stretches across his face. "Were you reading my yearbook?"

Her eyes grow wide as she struggles to backpedal. "Um ... I might have glanced at it briefly. In my defence, I don't have a TV until next week and only got internet yesterday."

He rises to clear their plates, and she uses the time to retrieve the book.

"I always liked sciences in high school, especially bio. The human body is fascinating." He turns on the tap and rinses their plates. "I applied to kinesiology and health sciences programs, but it just didn't make sense to go to school after everything. I needed to be home with my mom." He returns to the couch. "I'm not sure I could have handled all the schooling anyway."

She places the book on the coffee table in front of him and then clears the pizza box and what's left of the salad.

"This is actually Lark's," he says as he flips through its pages. "Wow. She looks so young here." He points out her portrait, and Charlotte pretends it's the first time she's seen it.

"She's beautiful," she says.

Darryl smiles. "She's a spitting image of our mom."

Charlotte hesitates before asking her next question. "How is she? Your mom. I heard she's had some health issues."

"Dementia. It was a long time coming, really. She hasn't been herself since Lark."

Darryl continues skimming through the book, and Charlotte excuses herself to the washroom, giving him the time and space to digest it all. When she returns, he is fixated on the page featuring the group shot of Armstrong and Lark. He shakes his head and sighs.

"Everything okay?" Charlotte asks, approaching the couch with soft, careful steps.

He looks up from the book. "This is none of my business, but if the Kyle who texted you the other day is Kyle Armstrong ..." he pauses as if to word his next thought delicately. "Sorry, I just don't like the way he treats women."

She raises her eyebrows, prompting him to elaborate.

"He wasn't great to my sister. And I'd hate for him to do that to you."

Charlotte nods and joins him on the couch. "There's nothing going on between us. I agreed to one date. I should have just said no. Anyway, he's not my type."

"Yeah," he says, and his energy depletes. "He wasn't Lark's type either."

Charlotte is about to ask more about their relationship—what exactly he did to her—

when a car horn beeps outside.

"That'll be Xander." Darryl rises. "Thanks for dinner."

Charlotte rises and follows him to the door. "See you around?"

Darryl opens the front door and steps into the night. "I'd like that," he says with a smile. "Night, Charlotte."

Then, he jogs past the dumpster and down the driveway where his friend's truck idles.

Charlotte watches as Xander pulls out of the driveway and offers a wave from the doorway. She is closing the door when another truck approaches, slowing as it nears her house. She doesn't wait to find out who it is and instead closes the door, locking it behind her.

———— • ♦ • ————

Later that night, while lying in bed, Charlotte replays the evening. She turns onto her side and runs her fingers along Tux's curled spine. The cat's ear twitches, but she remains asleep. Charlotte glances down at her phone and the text Darryl sent once he arrived back at his place:

Thanks again for tonight. You have good taste in music. And pizza.

Charlotte types out her response and reads it a few times before committing.

Just wait until you discover my taste in movies.

She is sixteen again. The warm surge in her core has replaced the usual tension in her chest. She feels calm, her body heavy and like she could drift off to sleep in seconds. Her eyelids begin to flutter, her breathing slowing until her phone rings out, the doorbell camera app warning her of movement outside. Charlotte scrambles to a seated position, and Tux, disturbed by the abrupt movement, leaps off the mattress and darts across the room.

Her heart is a bass drum reverberating behind her ribs. She opens the app to consult the camera as she struggles to catch her breath. Her eyes focus on the scene presented—the view of the front yard and driveway from her porch. There isn't a car in the driveway that she can see, though the dumpster composes most of the view. The dumpster. That's when she notices movement from within. Someone is in the dumpster, poking around. Charlotte enlarges the picture, but it's no use. With the current angle, she can only see above the culprit's shoulders, and this person is wearing a hat, which makes it hard to decipher any facial features.

She gives herself an internal pep talk and then makes her way to the other side of the room. She flicks on her bedroom light to scare off the perpetrator. Her eyes remain focused on the footage of the driveway, and she follows as the intruder hoists themselves out of the dumpster with what appears to be a book in hand.

Her wide eyes track the lurker on video as they run down the driveway, nearly slipping on the ice. She continues to watch the choppy image until the person disappears from the frame.

Charlotte hugs her knees to her chest.

She can't help but wonder whether it was Lark's diary they were after. Eager for reassurance, she clambers down the hallway to her parents' closet and finds the journal safe in its hiding spot.

Chapter Twenty-Seven

LARK

February 5, 2006

The rumours have calmed down thanks to Todd breaking up with Brittany. She apparently hooked up with some college guy when she went to visit Windsor for a campus tour last weekend. How's that for positivity, Dani?

Speaking of which, Dani has asked me to go see *Little Miss Sunshine* with her this weekend. Part of me wants to flake on her. Why should I always jump at the chance to hang out with her? I know for a fact she didn't come to my defence when I was the talk of the school last week.

I happened to be in the corner stall in the second-floor girls' washroom when she and the Tangerines were sneaking a Captain Black cigar, passing it back and forth, each lip-glossed mouth taking a turn. One of them, Candace maybe, had finished telling the version she'd heard, that a student walked in on me cutting my wrist with a pair of scissors in the dark room after photography class, the red of my blood masked by the lighting of the small room.

I knew it was Brittany who spoke next, her raspy voice a dead giveaway. "That was the second time. The first happened around the holidays. I noticed her cut on New Year's Eve. It was obviously a cry for attention. No one forced her to wear a tank top."

Dani must have taken a drag of the tiny cigar then because she broke into a coughing fit, and I could see her convulsing through the crack of the stall door.

"Shit, Dani, someone will hear you," Brittany said.

I sat, motionless on the toilet seat, straining to hear any word come out of Dani. *I know what really happened and it's not like that. You don't understand Lark like I do. You have no idea what you're talking about.* But she didn't say a thing. Their sneakers scuffed along the hexagon tile and then the door swung open, and they were gone, leaving me with the scent of cherry tobacco.

I hate thinking about power dynamics, but I know she holds all the control in our relationship. I'm like a puppy, following her around and coming back to lick her hand after being kicked.

But I can't just cut her out. For more than one reason.

———————— · ✦ · ————————

February 7, 2006

You missed quite possibly the weirdest night that has ever taken place at our house. I walked in the door, expecting to enter an empty home where I could work on my *Oryx and Crake* essay and there was Mom, cooking in the kitchen. And no, this wasn't like the time when she decided she would work her way through Oprah's personal chef Rosie Daley's cookbook, which, as you'll remember, resulted in the mushy sweet potato pie and burned corn chowder.

She was cooking dinner for Jake. And me (but let's be honest, probably more so for Jake).

The meal wasn't half bad. Pork tenderloin—his favourite apparently—and little roasted potatoes and green beans (not from the can)! This was the first time I think I've had a conversation with Jake that lasted longer than the usual niceties:

"How's school going?"

"Fine. How's work?"

"Good. Looks like rain."

"Looks like it."

He was still quiet, but he did show some interest, asking about the talent show and whether your band would be playing, and what song I had chosen for my dance routine. And Mom was like June-Fuck-ing-Cleaver. Dishing up second helpings and asking me all about my day. *Mom—would you like to hear about today? Or perhaps my year, as this is the first you've inquired about me in months.* I gave her a superficial answer—*school was fine, thanks,* and I·let the fact that she called me Lisa slide. I guess Aunt Lisa was on her mind.

She and Jake cleaned up after dinner to an album by some country singer named Dierks Bentley (did you know Mom likes country now?), and I decided to work on my essay in the living room. Once the country album ran its course, Mom put on her tried and true *Best of Rod Stewart* album. She made us all dance to "Young Turks," and she looked the happiest I've seen her in years. Stoic Jake even smiled and taught me some line dance he'd learned when he was stationed out west.

If you had been there, it would have felt like the closest thing we've had to a functioning family. Mom mentioned doing it again this weekend. Jake offered to cook this time.

I'll believe it when I see it, though.

Chapter Twenty–Eight

CHARLOTTE

The high-pitched rev of a drill competes with the Latin pop booming in the kitchen. With the kitchen renovation now fully underway, Charlotte feels compelled to escape her bubble and venture into town—if only to ease her headache briefly. She leaves Tux nestled in her unmade bed, fresh food and water by the closet, the litter box positioned on the other side of the room.

Marius, the contractor, arrived at seven in the morning with the rest of the crew to begin day three of the kitchen renovations. She consults with him on the day's plan before bundling up for the frigid December air.

A new dumpster has taken the place of Darryl's and is half full already with the kitchen's previous green ceramic countertop and white-painted wooden cabinets. The peach laminate flooring will be stripped today, along with the dated appliances. Luckily, the new floor plan is similar, so the plumbing can remain as is, but they will add an island feature in the middle of the room, presumably where the kitchen table once stood, complete with a wine fridge.

With her hands shoved deep in the pockets of her parka and her eyes on her feet, Charlotte takes hurried steps in the direction of Main Street. She has a haircut scheduled for noon and hopes to find a modest Christmas gift for Merle and Cindy—preferably at a place that gift wraps so she can deliver it on this outing. Christmas is a couple of days away.

There have been no additional nighttime visits from the unidentified lurker since the incident two nights ago. Charlotte is thankful she installed the doorbell camera when she did and has since ordered another camera to be positioned at the back of the house. She avoided telling her parents about it during their last FaceTime, knowing it would only worry them. Sheryl still hasn't gotten over the garage.

When she turns the corner onto Main Street, the town's clock tower indicates she has five minutes before her haircut. She pulls down her hood and steps into the quiet salon where Darlene, Darryl and Lark's mother, used to work.

"Hi there, come on in and grab a seat," a young woman says as she completes the finishing touches on her client's new do.

Charlotte removes her coat, hanging it on the provided coat rack, and sits on the sapphire-blue, suede loveseat near the coffee table scattered with magazines. She is perusing a holiday-themed *House & Home* when the stylist calls for her. "Charlotte? I'm Daniella, your stylist. What are we looking to do today?"

Charlotte joins her at the mirror, recognizing how familiar she looks. "A couple of inches off. Mainly the dead ends," Charlotte says.

"Some face-framing?" Daniella asks, her head tilted to the side.

"I like what you have." Charlotte notes the woman's dark brown layers that curl toward her nose and cascade down her shoulders. After she says it, though, she realizes the style won't look the same on her pin-straight hair.

"Right on. Let's do it," Daniella says as she leads Charlotte to the sinks at the back of the salon next to a planter of palm fronds.

Charlotte attempts to clear her mind, inviting the fresh scent of the coconut shampoo and invigorating scalp massage to distract her, but the truth is, she has been consumed by the thought of someone scouring for Lark's journal in the dumpster.

She's ashamed to admit that her mind first went to Darryl, having recently discussed the missing diary with him. But then she realized that wouldn't make sense. He had already gone through the items in detail, throwing out what he no longer wanted. A text from him confirmed he was at his apartment at the time of the incident. In response to Charlotte's text about *The Life Aquatic* being her favourite movie, he had sent her a photo of his Wes Anderson Blu-ray collection nestled in one of his milk crates.

Armstrong quickly came to mind after that. He knew Lark wrote in a journal. He had divulged that on the "date," when he spoke of Lark's moodiness. He was eager to help Charlotte sort through the Peters' possessions—she has the six text messages on her phone to prove that. And it's possible he saw the dumpster if he drove by her house. Officer Landry might have mentioned it too after his house call, but was likely still sour that she didn't choose his family's business.

Charlotte is convinced more than ever that Armstrong was Lark's stalker. There must be something in the diary he doesn't want to be exposed but consuming Lark's words makes Charlotte's stomach spasm and her heart pump in overdrive.

"Okay, let's get you over to my station," Daniella says and guides Charlotte to a chair and mirror near the front of the salon. Daniella's station is plastered with stickers—affirmations in pastel pinks, blues, and mauves. *I am fierce. I am worthy. I am brave. I am me.* It's unclear whether the messages are meant for her or her clients, but Charlotte sinks a little lower in her chair, contemplating if this woman can spot Charlotte's lack of self-worth.

Charlotte watches Daniella inquisitively as she sprays a detangler and proceeds to comb through Charlotte's knotted hair. Daniella must resemble a celebrity, but Charlotte can't put her finger on who.

"Do you have plans later today?" the stylist asks, pulling Charlotte's hair taut with one hand and carefully trimming it with the other. "Because I could style it with an iron if you want. Do some soft waves?"

"Um, no plans, but sure, if you have time."

"You got it. You're my last appointment until school lets out," she says, continuing with the trim. Strawberry blonde chunks fall to the floor. "Visiting for the holidays?"

"Not exactly. My parents are new to the neighbourhood, and I'm helping them with some renovations."

"Oh, that's sweet of you. Where did they buy?" she asks.

"Over near Victoria Park." Charlotte makes eye contact in the mirror with Daniella, who raises an eyebrow.

"Not the Peters' old house?" Daniella asks.

"That's the one."

"Oh, shit."

That's when the realization hits Charlotte like a Mack truck. Daniella is Dani, Lark's former best friend. She's been the topic of discussion in nearly every entry. She sat next to her in the yearbook's group shot with Armstrong. She's suppressed her ringlet curls, so Charlotte failed to recognize her.

Daniella goes quiet after that, finishing up the trim, and then she swivels Charlotte's chair so that they are face to face. "Time for your layers."

When Charlotte's hair has been gathered in front of her eyes, she works up the courage to probe. "Didn't Mrs. Peters work at this salon?"

Daniella pauses the task at hand, and her voice escapes with caution. "She did, but before my time here."

"Did you know her kids?"

"I went to school with them both." She spins Charlotte around to face the mirror. "Happy with the length?" she asks, changing the subject.

Charlotte nods. "I am, thanks." She chews her inner cheek before continuing. "It's so tragic what happened."

Daniella's smile fades, and she offers one quick nod and then moves to a neighbouring station to retrieve a blow dryer.

"I imagine that would have been really hard on her classmates."

Daniella plods back, her pristinely white sneakers scuffing along the floor. She plugs in the dryer and then sets it down on the counter with a thud. "I don't mean to be a jerk, but Lark was a friend. And this isn't something I want to rehash today."

Charlotte's cheeks burn, and a lump in her throat swells. She hadn't meant to upset Daniella. She only wanted another perspective on what happened between Lark and Armstrong.

"Of course, I'm sorry. I shouldn't have brought it up."

Daniella shakes out her shoulders and head as if to reset the conversation. "All good. Let's get your hair dried, and then I'll make it look cute."

Charlotte and Daniella are quiet for the remainder of the appointment, allowing the radio to count down to the week's Billboard number-one song. It isn't until Charlotte is paying at the counter that Daniella's demeanour softens. Charlotte considers the timing, seconds before the card reader prompts her for a tip.

"Sorry about earlier. It's been years, but it still feels very fresh when it gets brought up."

"Please, don't apologize. That's completely understandable. I shouldn't have said anything." Charlotte selects the option for a twenty percent tip on the keypad, her way of smoothing things over.

Daniella is staring off into the distance now and doesn't notice when the reader spits out the receipt. "She was doing so much better. It came out of nowhere."

Chapter Twenty-Nine

CHARLOTTE

Charlotte glides her hand over her smooth tresses as she stands in line at the gift shop. "Time to wine down" reads the miniature marquee sign that she chose for Merle and Cindy's Christmas gift. Charlotte's intention is for the couple to list their rotating drinks specials on the sign and display it at the bar. She places it on the counter next to the cash register. "Any chance I can get this gift wrapped?"

Sandra, indicated by her pewter nametag, holds up three rolls of wrapping paper. "You betcha. Which do you like better?"

Charlotte chooses the red and green plaid pattern and scans the turnstile of greeting cards, settling on a cartoon penguin wearing skis with a simple holiday message.

Sandra meticulously fastens the gift wrap in place, pausing only once to push the bridge of her glasses up her nose. "Such a cute gift. Who's it for?"

"Just a friend," Charlotte says. It still comes as a surprise how sociable, at times nosey, the residents of Anville can be.

"They make for great photos on the Facebook," she says, as if she's just learned of the social app.

Charlotte imagines boomer Merle posing by the sign for the Angel Pub's Facebook page and she chuckles at the thought. "For sure," she says, so as not to be rude and then weaves through the glass display cases of ice wine chocolates, stuffed animals, and Christmas tree ornaments toward the exit.

The sidewalk is livelier now that school has let out, and the teenagers rush past her, en route to their part-time jobs at retail stores and restaurants in the area. Charlotte glances up at the shop windows and feels winded at the sight of a gymnastics logo on one of the doors. *We're hiring! Seeking an experienced gymnast to coach our ten to twelve-year-old competitive team.* She tosses her head. At one time, that would have been her ideal job, one step closer to opening her own gymnastics club, but now she can't step inside a gym without having visceral flashbacks.

As Charlotte walks the rest of the way to the Angel Pub, her fresh waves whipping in front of her face and losing their form, her mind returns to Dani's detached gaze and the words that sounded similar to Darryl's in the news report. *She was doing so much better. It came out of nowhere.* Darryl had said that the act didn't make sense. That it probably never would. But does it ever make sense?

She takes swift steps, recalling her own mother's words when Charlotte had woken up at the hospital following her accident. When Charlotte was eighteen, her car collided with a telephone pole, and she suffered a concussion, a dislocated shoulder, and a broken clavicle. Only seconds before the crash, she had veered left, allowing the passenger seat to absorb the brunt of it. And while the doctors had said Charlotte was incredibly lucky, that the crash would have been much worse had she hit the pole on the driver's side, Sheryl had questions for her daughter.

"Tell me it was an accident, Char. Surely, you didn't mean to ..." She left Charlotte to fill in the blank, unable to finish her own words.

"What if I did?"

Sheryl had looked so frightened, her eyes frantically flitting over Charlotte. And while the scene wasn't all that different from Charlotte's first car accident—the one where she was lucky enough to be positioned in the middle of the back seat of her friend Chloe's Taurus—this time, her mother's gaze was different. Relief had been replaced with distress. Unlike the first accident, this wasn't just an act of God, Sheryl's only daughter nearly escaping death from a terrible accident. There was a chance that Charlotte had attempted to end her own life, and that prospect was more than Sheryl could bear.

"What do we do next?" Sheryl had asked Charlotte, her hand on the hospital bracelet secured on Charlotte's wrist.

Charlotte finally looked her mother in the eye. "You're the parent," she'd said. "You tell me."

Charlotte hops over a snow mound where this stretch of the sidewalk's snowfall had been cleared to. She might understand more than anyone how those closest to us aren't always aware of everything going on inside our heads. Or if they are, they're afraid to admit it.

She tosses away the memory with a literal shake of her head and, clutching the parcel, continues her walk toward the Angel Pub.

— • ◆ • —

"You didn't need to get us a gift," Merle says, placing the sign on the bar counter.

"You hate it."

"Quite the opposite. Now, we seem trendy. We'll attract the hipster tourists," Merle says, using air quotes for the word hipster. "Anyway, it's time to *wine* down. What can I get you?"

Charlotte eyes the novelty clock above the bar. The long hand reaches the Roman numeral twelve, intercepting the embrace of two porcelain cherubs. The small hand is positioned at the four.

"I suppose I could have a small glass of wine. House white, please." Charlotte will aim to be back at the house by six to see off Marius and the crew.

"Coming right up," Merle says, retreating to fetch the wine.

Charlotte scans her last text message exchange with Darryl from earlier in the day. There are a few texts back and forth recounting lines from *The Life Aquatic*. Charlotte had confessed to having a celebrity crush on Jeff Goldblum. Darryl had said he wasn't surprised that *Jurassic Park* had been a favourite flick of Lark's—and it wasn't only for the dinosaurs.

Now, there is nothing left to do but respond to Darryl's last message. The one where he proposed that they watch *The Life Aquatic* together.

Cindy appears at the bar with a plate of food. "Just the person I was hoping to see." She places the sampler plate in front of Charlotte. "Our holiday dinner special. Turkey, apple stuffing, and my aunt's mashed potato recipe straight from Limerick." She passes the fork to Charlotte. "Give 'er a try."

Charlotte scoops a generous helping of the potatoes onto her fork, but Cindy raises her hand. "No, no, best to get a taste of everything in your first bite."

The savoury comfort food is better than Charlotte imagined. It transports her to the Christmas dinners at her maternal grandmother's, where salt and butter were used generously. She immediately takes a second bite. "This is delicious, Cindy."

When Charlotte is done with the plate, nearly licked clean, Cindy clears it onto a cocktail tray. "We're serving it all week."

"Available for take-out?"

"For you, absolutely."

Charlotte pulls up the text thread between her and Darryl.

Let's do it, she types. *What are you doing Christmas Eve?*

She stares at the text, waiting to see if he's read it. She's just invited Darryl on a date, and on a holiday, which feels weightier.

Merle returns with a stemless glass of golden wine. "Merry almost Christmas."

Charlotte raises her glass to him and then tilts it to her mouth, inviting the oaky chardonnay to slide over her tongue.

"And a nearly happy New Year," someone chimes in from behind her.

Charlotte swivels in her chair, by now recognizing the boisterous voice all too well.

Armstrong claims the open seat next to her. "I'll take a glass, too, Merle. What she's having." He flashes a sideways smile and shuffles his stool closer to Charlotte. "How have you been, city girl?"

Charlotte stiffens in her seat and places the wine glass down on the beer-stained and peeling coaster. "Fine, thanks." She eyes Merle as he pours a glass for the uniformed officer.

"You've been busy?"

Charlotte picks at the coaster, ripping off bits of cardboard and rolling them between her thumb and forefinger. "Renos are underway. Lots to do before the holidays."

Armstrong peers at her with narrowed eyes as if he is using X-ray vision to see through her. He shakes his head. "I'm glad you took care of the Peters' stuff. Good to get that junk out of the house. You know, a fresh start and all."

She nods and sips her wine.

Merle returns with Armstrong's glass, and Charlotte notices he's poured a couple of ounces less than what he poured for her. Perhaps Merle is trying to monitor the officer's day drinking.

Armstrong accepts the drink, oblivious to the missing ounces. "I was game to help you. Not gonna lie, I wanted to see what that family was hoarding."

"Mostly old appliances. Some CDs and movies. Yearbooks."

Armstrong raises an eyebrow. She suspects she's caught his attention with the mention of the yearbook. It's hard to say for sure whether Armstrong would remember the message he wrote to Lark, whether he remembers admitting his crush all those years ago. But he shifts in his chair, and his eyes dart toward the floor.

Charlotte doesn't mind watching him squirm a little. She gulps the last of her wine and

makes a move for her wallet.

Merle waves her off. "Consider that my Christmas gift."

"Want a ride home?" Armstrong asks as he scrambles to his feet to join her.

She is already walking toward the exit, and without turning around, she says, "Nope, I'm good. You've got your wine to finish."

Before she can make it to the door, she is pulled back by her wrist. Charlotte spins around to find Armstrong gripping her arm, her skin burning beneath his grasp. His face softens as he loosens his hold, and a smile emerges.

"What's the rush? I'll buy you another round."

She rubs the tender skin on her wrist. "Don't touch me," she says, her voice strong and assertive.

Armstrong raises his arms above his head. "Whoa, now. Calm down."

Merle, who has deserted his bar, appears. "Is there a problem here?"

"Not with me," Armstrong says, backing up, his hands still above his head. "City girl's a bit jumpy. I'm not gonna mug you." He takes his seat at the bar and gulps his wine. "In Anville, when someone offers you a ride, you usually say thanks."

Merle places his hand on Charlotte's shoulder. "Are you okay?"

Charlotte nods and continues to the exit.

She walks briskly down the sidewalk, playing witness to the setting sun. The wrought iron light posts are now aglow, and with the garland crawling up them, it's as though she's been thrust into a Charles Dickens story.

She shoots a glance behind her, confirming Armstrong has not followed her. That was the darkness Lark had described—the way he grabbed her arm and the fierce look in his eyes before he played it off as nothing more than a friendly offer.

Charlotte is convinced Armstrong was the one rummaging in the dumpster, and she's determined to find out what in Lark's diary he's afraid of getting out.

Chapter Thirty

LARK

February 9, 2006

So, the movie was a bit of a ploy. We did go see it, and the cast was perfection, but Dani only invited me to ask for a favour. She wants me to work at her summer camp on Lake Rosseau. It turns out Brittany accepted a job there but is now bailing to go to Europe with her nana. Enter Lark, the runner-up. Brittany was supposed to be an extra belayer for the rock-climbing wall (yes, the camp has a rock-climbing wall). Talk about a ritzy camp.

Anyway, I guess the camp director was impressed to hear about my dance background. If I get the job, they'll work dance into the programming, and I'll teach it daily in addition to bunking up with twelve-year-olds in something called a yurt.

Dani's already landed me an interview in two days. Why can't I ever say no to her? Is she trying to mend our friendship? I don't know. Maybe it isn't such a bad idea to get away from Anville and *him*. He's not going to drive all the way to Muskoka.

I guess I'll give it a try. But what the hell is a yurt?

———————— · ◆ · ————————

February 11, 2006

The job interview went terribly. There is no way I got it. And honestly, I'm not sure I even wanted it. Camp counsellor? Me? The only reason I even considered it is because it would mean a summer with Dani and without the Tangerines.

"Tell me about the craziest thing you've ever done?" That was the question Chad, the camp director, posed as we sat across from each other in a booth at Sunshine Café. He had ordered a coffee and made a point of telling me he normally drinks his coffee black, that he likes to taste the beans, but that it's best to mask diners' instant coffee with cream and sugar. Pretentious jerk. I ordered mine black to make a point.

The patch on his navy leather jacket showed he belongs to the Health Sciences program at Queen's University and is expected to graduate later this spring. The only nice car in the parking lot, a bright blue Camaro with an obnoxious black stripe on the hood, was likely an early graduation present from his parents. He's one of *those* (insert eye roll).

Chad probably expected me to answer his trivial question with "sky-diving" or something sexy like, "This one time, I made out with my best friend because we were bored." Because intimacy between two women could only exist for a guy's pleasure, right? I'm sure Chad thinks so. I told him that I once wished on a pinecone to see if it would come true. Everyone wishes on stars or pennies or precisely at 11:11. So, when I was thirteen, I picked up a decrepit pinecone in our backyard, and I made a wish. It hasn't come true yet.

Anyway, after he heard that story, Chad twisted his face like the cream in his coffee had expired.

I'm not expecting a call for a second interview.

When I got home, I went out back with my Polaroid camera and took photos of the oak tree. You know how I love bare trees in the winter. Their naked branches expose their true selves. Not hiding behind lush leaves or navy letterman jackets.

I thought about when we used to take the sled down the hill, and you'd try to steer us into the tree to freak me out. I thought about the hammock that Dad fastened that one summer and sat in every weekend with a beer and Jerry Howarth announcing the Blue Jays play-by-play on the portable radio. I thought about the initials I carved into the trunk last fall—the proclamation I have yet to admit out loud to anyone.

I thought about all the moments I have yet to experience.

I stayed out there until you came home and asked what I was doing outside in the negative temperature. I muttered something about photography class. I should have just said that I was exactly where I wanted to be. A place where I feel safe. A place where I feel understood.

When I stand underneath that tree, I feel like there's hope for me.

Chapter Thirty-One

CHARLOTTE

Looking at the oak tree in the backyard from the washroom window, Charlotte realizes it's taken on a new meaning after reading Lark's latest diary entry. She now recognizes the contradiction—it is both a place of life and solace, as well as death and decay. The setting where Lark took her last breath is also responsible for many joyful ones. Charlotte feels differently now when she peers at its sturdy trunk, its symmetrical branches like rungs on a ladder, twigs like children's fingers reaching for the clouds. She is no longer scared of it. Instead, she is captivated by its beauty.

She feels more connected to Lark than she ever has as she clutches the Polaroids that were taped inside the page alongside the entry. Stripped of its leafy décor, she is reminded that the oak tree Lark photographed is the same one standing fifteen yards outside her window.

With her index finger, she glides through the window's condensation, leaving behind Lark's initials. Once she's dressed, she'll need to venture out to the yard, where she expects to find Lark's proclamation carved in the tree. Did Lark have a secret crush she was afraid to admit to her friends and family? Something she could only confess within the tree's crevices?

Charlotte considers what compelled Lark to choose the tree on that fateful day in May. How did she lose the hope she had once found among its branches? Charlotte instinctively brings her hand to her neck and then shivers, an icy sensation travelling down her spine. Unless. She bites her bottom lip so hard that she almost draws blood.

Unless Lark didn't choose.

A series of chimes build to a crescendo, and Charlotte is pulled from the thought. She consults her phone, discovering her parents' request for a video call. Charlotte secures her robe tight and accepts it with a smile.

"Merry Christmas Eve," her parents say in attempted unison, Jared lagging slightly.

"Same to you. What are your plans for the day?" Charlotte asks.

Sheryl takes the lead, positioning her phone so her face is centred on the screen and only a third of Jared's face is in view. "We've already been to a holiday brunch at the golf club. Going to take it easy by the pool for the rest of the day, and then there's a dinner—"

"And dance," Jared pops into the frame.

"Right, and dance this evening. Did you just wake up?" Sheryl thrusts her head forward as if to magnify the screen.

"No, I just got out of the shower."

Jared chuckles. "Oh, lazy day for you. It's nearly two."

"Yeah, on a holiday, so ..."

"He's just teasing you," Sheryl says. "She's sensitive," she adds at a lower volume, likely intended for only Jared. "What are your plans? Holiday movies and baking?"

Charlotte is reminded of the Boyd's Christmas Eves over the years, which typically involved Charlotte's film pick—*Home Alone* or *It's a Wonderful Life* depending on whether she was in the mood to laugh or cry, and her mom nearby in the kitchen, baking last minute goodies like chocolate macaroons or shortbread with jelly drops. They often ordered Chinese takeout, adding some variety to the turkey dinner marathon of the holiday season.

"I've got an order in at the pub for their dinner special and a date with Bill Murray."

"A date with who?" Jared asks. He turns to Sheryl. "Who'd she say she has a date with?"

Charlotte cuts in before her dad gets carried away. "The actor Bill Murray. It was a joke. I'm going to watch *The Life Aquatic*."

"That's not very festive," Sheryl says.

Charlotte shrugs. "I'm not feeling very festive this year."

Her parents go quiet, shooting each other sideways glances.

"It's all good. We'll make up for it next year," Charlotte says.

Further silence prompts Charlotte to consider that their holidays may never look the same. If Charlotte wants to spend the season with her parents, she'll likely need to fly to Florida, which doesn't scream Christmas.

"Of course," Sheryl says. "Of course, we'll make up for it next year. And we have our FaceTime tomorrow."

Charlotte nods. She considers divulging about Darryl and her movie night but hesitates. She'll wait until there's something worth mentioning.

Sheryl rushes her off the phone with an explanation that if they don't venture to the pool soon, they won't find open chairs. "Love you, babes. Talk tomorrow."

"Love you."

And then her parents disappear.

Charlotte unwraps her towelled hair, allowing the wet strands to fall to her shoulders. Darryl will be at the house in under two hours with their takeout order from the pub. She's set up her bedroom as a movie-viewing space, leaning pillows from the living room couch against the wall behind her bed, her laptop set up on the night table like a TV. The main floor is off-limits with the renovations, so this is the best option, though she now realizes how intimate it is. She suspects it might feel like a typical night in a college dormitory, though she doesn't know for sure, having only attended a commuter school. Tonight, she does not plan to drink. And there will be no hooking up with Darryl Peters. They will watch the film, eat their meals, and she'll inquire about Armstrong.

That is all, she tells herself. Nothing more.

Chapter Thirty-Two

CHARLOTTE

Charlotte and Darryl sit on opposite ends of her bed, Tux nestled between them and the laptop centred in front. Charlotte has kept the light on for a more casual vibe, but it is harder to see the small screen with the glare. She makes small talk in between bites of the Angel Pub's turkey special, which is perched on her lap in a takeout container.

"How's work?" she asks.

Darryl finishes chewing a bite of turkey and then places his plastic fork down. "Can't complain. I got my truck back from the shop, so I've picked up some jobs."

"Just in time." The snowfall has reached record amounts for December. Charlotte is still sore from yesterday's attempted shovel, but she is pleased it will be a white Christmas. "Do you plow driveways, too? I should get you to do mine; I only got halfway." Charlotte glances out the window where feather-like flakes parachute to the ground.

"That hill can be a pain. I'll plow it before I leave tonight." He stirs gravy into his mashed potatoes, inviting the starch to absorb it all.

"It's good, eh?" Charlotte asks.

"Very." He chews his bite. "They think a lot of you. Merle and Cindy."

Charlotte reddens. "Oh, I don't know. They probably just feel sorry for me because I'm by myself." After she says it, she realizes that Darryl is also alone and has been for a while.

Darryl meets Charlotte's eye. "It's more than that. You've made an impression. Merle even gave me a father's warning about coming here tonight."

Charlotte laughs it off, but they, too, have made an impression on her, especially with her parents out of the country. "What did he say? Did he reveal a shotgun behind the bar counter?"

Darryl shakes his head. "He said you're special." He keeps his eyes focused on his potatoes. "And not to fuck this up."

Feeling suddenly warm, Charlotte rolls up the sleeves of her sweater. What exactly is *this*?

"Lark and I used to spend a lot of time at the pub. At least two dinners a week. And she would sometimes go before her dance rehearsals and do her homework there."

"They are nice people. They really make you feel like you're family."

Darryl nods. "That's exactly it. And they never had kids, so I think they like being the pseudo aunt and uncle of the neighbourhood, you know? That's what it was like with Lark. Merle treated her like a daughter."

Charlotte isn't surprised to hear that. It didn't take him long to open up to her. Ever since that first night, he was nothing but warm, offering the room at the inn and going out of his way to make her feel at home.

He even seems to understand her trepidations toward Armstrong and was quick to come to her aid when the cop crossed the line the other day.

The film continues to play in the background. Darryl and Charlotte occasionally take breaks to laugh or comment but then quickly return to their conversation. In the middle of Darryl's story about setting a bunch of frogs free during a grade twelve biology class, Charlotte gets the courage to ask again about his previous plan to practice medicine.

"Do you ever think about going back to school?"

"No. I think I'm too old for that dream."

"You're not that much older than me, and I'm still trying to figure out what my dream is."

Darryl opens his lips as if to speak but then hesitates, something seemingly holding him back. He scratches his head. "Sometimes I think about nursing. Maybe working in eldercare? I could see myself working somewhere like my mom's residence."

"Do you visit her often?"

"Going there tomorrow for Christmas. I try to get there at least once a week, but it was tough when I didn't have the truck."

Charlotte can't imagine the responsibility of taking care of a parent. It's always been Sheryl and Jared who have provided for her, not the other way around. Yet, before her, sits a young man who has been acting as a caregiver for years.

"I think you should do it," she says, scooping up the last bite of potatoes.

Darryl eyes her curiously, his dark brows furrowed.

"Nursing. I think you should go back to school. What do you have to lose?"

He lets out a long sigh. "Maybe." Then, his warm smile stretches across his face. "Where were you fifteen years ago?"

She considers the answer. Fifteen years ago, she was recovering from her second car accident. She was barely sleeping, living at home with her parents and deferring college admission.

She shrugs. "It's not too late." She rises to clear their takeout containers, Tux following her like a trusted sidekick. "Something to drink?"

"Water's good."

When Charlotte returns, she flicks off the light and sits closer to the laptop, and as a result, closer to Darryl.

She stitches her brows together, studying him.

"What? I have gravy on my face, don't I?" he asks.

"Yes."

He paws at his mouth with a napkin.

"I'm kidding. I was just thinking of asking you a question."

"Shoot."

"Is the reason you don't drink because of ..."

"Ah, you've heard about my dad." He tosses the napkin down. "That's part of it."

Charlotte tucks her foot underneath her, getting more comfortable.

"He had quite a lot in his system that night. Luckily, there wasn't another car involved, so no one else got hurt."

"Except for his family."

"Right." He nods. "I wasn't always sober, though, only the last five years."

She leans in, curious as to what prompted the change.

"I don't love the person I become when I'm drunk."

Before Charlotte can ask a follow-up question, he continues his thought. "Okay, my turn."

She tenses her shoulders, bracing for his question.

"When we first met, you fainted."

Charlotte bites her thumbnail. Where is he going with this?

"And you said that happens to you a lot."

"What's the question?"

"Why does that happen to you?"

She shrugs. "No one can figure out what's wrong with me."

"What are your symptoms?"

Charlotte lets out a laugh. "Am I talking to Dr. Peters now?"

"Humour me."

"There's the fainting, which you had the pleasure of witnessing. Heart palpitations. Chest tightness. I don't know. Probably just low blood pressure." She dismisses the thought with a wave of her hand.

They continue to chat throughout the movie, swapping stories from high school and bonding over shared music and literature. By the time the end credits roll, David Bowie's "Queen Bitch" underscoring the main character, Steve Zissou's strut, Darryl and Charlotte have closed the gap between them.

Darryl's hand is precariously close to Charlotte's leg. And he might also be thinking this, she realizes, as both of their gazes focus on the area. She continues to watch as his finger flutters, ever so slightly brushing her knee. Their eyes meet at that moment, and the entire room blurs in the background. Before Charlotte can talk herself out of it, she is leaning in, those green eyes like magnets. A warm pulse travels through her core as she moves closer, mere inches from his mouth ... until a chime from Darryl's phone interrupts like a wave pushing their boats off course.

"Everything okay?" Charlotte asks, composing herself.

"Yeah," Darryl says, his eyes planted on his phone. "It's a job. The town is looking for help clearing some of the rural roads tonight. They're offering time and a half."

Charlotte isn't ready for the night to end. She hasn't even had a chance to ask about Armstrong and Lark.

"Want to come? Join me in the truck?" he asks.

As much as she'd like to continue their evening, the fear of driving in a snowstorm supersedes her desire. "That's okay."

"I'll let you turn on the flashing blue lights."

She shakes her head with a laugh. "I'm good. But you go ahead."

His smile fades, but he nods. "I'll still plow your driveway before I go."

Charlotte raises her eyebrows. "Cocoa."

"Cocoa?"

She rises and scoops Tux up in her arms. She had picked up a jar of homemade cocoa from the bakery. She had planned to serve it after their dinner. "Yeah, I'll make you a thermos of cocoa before you go."

He laughs. "I haven't had hot cocoa since I was a kid. That sounds nice."

———————— • ✦ • ————————

With her own thermos in hand, Charlotte watches as Darryl maneuvers the truck back and forth to clear the laneway, erasing the snow like chalk on a blackboard. When he's done, he pulls onto the side of the road and steps out of the car.

"There you have it," he calls.

"Thank you!" she yells back with a wave. "Stay safe out there." She turns to head inside, where she plans to finish her drink while watching one of the cheesy holiday romances advertised on every streaming platform since November. A few more steps toward the door, and something hits her back. She spins around to find Darryl still standing by the truck, holding what she assumes is his second snowball.

"Very funny," she says, deserting her thermos on the porch and scooping a handful of wet snow. It clumps together in her hands. She runs down the steps and hurls it as far as she can. It barely finds his foot.

"You asked for it." He smiles as he winds up, and then the snowball sails toward her and

nails her in the right shoulder.

"Are we having a snowball fight?" she calls out.

Snow soars through the air, hitting her other shoulder.

"Looks like it." Darryl laughs.

She grabs more snow and runs toward him to minimize the distance. She finally makes contact, the snowball brushing his left leg. She chuckles at the absurdity of it all. Her hands cramp from the cold, so she warms them between her thighs.

He retaliates with a hit to the stomach.

"How is this fair? You were a freaking pitcher in high school." She is hunched over now, laughing hysterically. She never imagined their date ending with a snowball fight, yet at the same time, it feels only natural it would. Both of their youths were cut short, after all, and this might be their second chance.

"I'll stop on one condition," he says, tossing a snowball in the air and catching it. "Come with me tonight. I'm not ready for this night to end."

She twists her mouth, biting on the inside of her cheek. She isn't ready for the night to end, either. She retrieves her thermos, bringing the nozzle to her mouth to mask her smile.

Darryl closes the gap, travelling up the path towards Charlotte, smoothing the snowball in his hands.

A beam of light breaks through the quiet darkness. A truck turns into Charlotte's freshly cleared driveway. The door swings open, and Armstrong steps out, the truck still running. He is wearing street clothes, so she guesses he's off duty. A bewildered look takes over his face when he notices Darryl.

"Are you kidding me? What the hell are you doing back here?" he asks, homing in on Darryl.

Charlotte rushes toward them, worried a fight might break out. "He's here for me," she says. She stands next to Darryl, choosing sides. "I invited him over."

Armstrong's mouth falls open. "Are you kidding?"

Charlotte picks at the sticker on her thermos.

"First, you call the police on him and now you're going out with the guy?" Armstrong cackles frenetically. "You're crazier than I thought."

"Watch it," Darryl says, and it comes across like a practiced warning. He remains calm and stoic next to Charlotte.

Armstrong steps closer. "We both seem to like crazy, eh Peters?"

Charlotte registers the comment. She assumes Armstrong is referring to her, but something about the statement makes her wonder if this isn't the first time they've liked the same girl.

"Let's go," Charlotte says to Darryl, moving to the passenger door of his truck.

Darryl follows her lead and joins her in the cabin. Charlotte watches Armstrong from the sideview mirror. He kicks at his tire before returning to his truck.

When Charlotte can no longer see Armstrong's truck in the mirror, she refocuses her eyes on the road ahead, and her stomach sinks at the thought of driving in a snowstorm. What has she agreed to?

The two remain quiet as Darryl plows through the storm. He drives cautiously, his eyes maintained on the road, but it doesn't stop Charlotte's palms from sweating. A light fastened to the roof of the truck emits a pulsing blue glow on the snowy road ahead of them. The wipers keep up with the pace of the snowfall, and the plow scrapes along the road, producing a gentle vibration in the cab.

She wipes her palms on her pants and uses her words as a distraction. "Sorry about that. He's practically stalking me," Charlotte says.

Darryl glances her way. "Do you mean that?" he asks with a waver in his voice.

"He keeps texting me and showing up places where I am. Maybe I'm reading into it," she says, unsure if the accusation went too far.

"I hardly think him showing up at your house is a coincidence. The reason I asked was he did the same thing to my sister back in high school."

And there it is. Charlotte finally has her proof, though she's known it in her gut for a while.

"What happened?"

"He wouldn't leave her alone, even after she made it clear she wasn't interested."

"How did she get him to stop?"

Darryl shoots a glance her way. "She didn't."

Charlotte considers the comment, her throat suddenly dry. Armstrong was still harassing her up until her death.

With her thermos in both hands, Charlotte listens to Darryl's story, noting the pained look on his face as he confesses what's been haunting him these last sixteen years.

"The week before Lark ..." Darryl struggles to finish the sentence and pauses to clear his throat. "The week before, she wasn't herself. She didn't outright tell me what was going on, but something was weighing heavy on her. She said she was in trouble. It was obvious she was afraid of something. Of someone. Of course, I knew it was him."

"How did you know?" Charlotte asks.

Darryl glances at his rear-view mirror as if he is confirming they're alone. "He had been writing her these intense notes. I saw one in her locker once. He'd also creep around our house. One night, I saw him in the backyard. I think he was spying on her."

"Her window faces the yard," Charlotte says. She thinks of the purple room overlooking the backyard. If Armstrong made a habit of lurking around the Peters' property, she's even more convinced he had been the one scouring the dumpster.

"I should have done more. I should have protected her."

Charlotte reaches across the centre console, placing her hand on his arm.

"I think about it every day. What if I got home earlier? What if I could have stopped it?"

"It's not your fault," she says, and then she sees something out of the corner of her eye, glowing white. "Darryl!" she shouts.

Darryl swerves to miss a deer and slows the truck to a stop on the shoulder of the opposite side of the road. Charlotte tries to catch her breath, gasping for air.

"I'm so sorry. She darted out. I didn't see her," Darryl says.

Charlotte undoes her seatbelt and heaves open the door. Her heart rate is too high. She needs to slow it.

Darryl cuts the engine and then he's out of the truck, following her. "Charlotte, come back. It's too dark on the road."

Charlotte continues the opposite way, hurrying along the cleared path that Darryl recently plowed, her treads slipping on the black ice.

"Charlotte, it's dangerous. Cars won't see you. Please, come back."

Her hands shake and she shoves them in her pockets to hide them. "I can't."

He jogs toward her, placing his hand on her shoulder when he gets close enough. "Are you hurt?"

"I don't know," she says. She feels numb all over.

He is in front of her now, his eyes searching her. "We weren't going very fast," he says to himself. "Did you hit your head when I braked? Was it the seatbelt? Did it tighten up?"

"No." She rubs her hands together, trying to bring the feeling back to her fingers, which tingle with every movement.

"What hurts?"

She bends over, allowing her head to fall between her knees. The movement compels Darryl to crouch by her side. "You don't have to get back in the truck, okay? But I'm going to call an ambulance." He fumbles in his pocket for his phone. "You might be in shock."

She shakes her head, still hunched over. "No, don't. Please, no ambulance."

"Let me help you back to the truck, then. Maybe you need to sit."

She nods and allows him to guide her along the shoulder of the road back to the truck. He helps her into the passenger's side and then takes his seat beside her. He turns on the ignition, but she protests. "Please, I don't want to drive anywhere."

The hazards come to life with a click of a button, the amber glow reflecting in the snow ahead. "No problem. We can stay here a while, but let's keep warm."

After a few moments of focused breathing, matching the rhythm of the windshield wipers, Charlotte lifts her head. "I'm sorry. I shouldn't have come with you."

Darryl angles his body toward her, inviting her to offer more of an explanation. She could close him off like she normally does. Make up an excuse and never call him again. It's a pattern she has perfected.

She looks into his eyes and sees a softness. Darryl wants to help if she'll let him.

Chapter Thirty-Three

CHARLOTTE

C harlotte fiddles with the barcode, still stuck on the bottom of the thermos. "When I was a kid, I used to joke about how God created me in a rush. I'm double-jointed." She demonstrates a trick, touching her thumb to her wrist. "I would tell my friends I didn't expect to live long because my joints felt thrown together." Charlotte wasn't raised in a religious family; it was more of an expression to account for her body's weirdness.

"It served its purpose, though. I trained in gymnastics, and my flexibility was my strength. I trained at the same gym almost every day from age eight until seventeen. Always with the same group of girls." They were Charlotte's best friends, her family. It is a feeling she suspects Lark could relate to. Maybe even Darryl with his bandmates. She shoots him a glance to confirm he is following, and he offers a nod.

"One weekend in February, we were driving to Ohio for a competition. My friend Chloe had just gotten her full license, and we wanted to take one car together, us girls. Our parents didn't mind the break either. So, Chloe, Madison, Erica, and I drove Chloe's Taurus across the border. We stopped for dinner at a highway diner, and by the time we were back on the road, full of tuna melts and cherry crullers, the sun had gone down. Chloe was a good driver—she did everything right, but it didn't matter."

Darryl covers his mouth with his hand.

"We were in the right lane, and a car was coming up quickly behind us. Chloe sped up, not wanting to piss off the driver, but they just continued to tailgate us. I yelled at her to slow down, that they could pass us if they wanted to. So, she did, and the car clipped us as they passed. We spun out and hit a twelve-wheeler head-on."

Charlotte pauses, fighting back the lump that has formed in her throat. "I lost three of my best friends that night. The man driving the truck had a heart attack and ended up passing away at the hospital. The driver who clipped us blew point fifteen over the legal alcohol limit. He was absolutely fine, with only a scratch on his car. Not only did I survive the accident, but I was untouched by some miracle. Or maybe a curse."

Darryl reaches for Charlotte's hand. She hasn't spoken about her friends, hasn't uttered their names in years. She doesn't tug her hand away. Instead, she leans in, pulling his arm into a hug and resting her head on his shoulder. He lets her stay there for a while. His earthy smell and the sound of his controlled breath calm her.

She looks up at him. "Sometimes, I think I'm just waiting for my turn."

He kisses the top of her head. "I get it."

She nods, believing he does understand.

He strokes her hair. "Living can feel like a sort of betrayal."

A warm rush replaces the sinking feeling in her stomach. When they lock eyes again, Charlotte doesn't want to hesitate for even a second. She doesn't want to hold back.

It is time to start living.

The kiss is soft but quickly turns urgent, Darryl's arms pulling her closer. Charlotte's hands find his hair, and their tongues begin to explore each other. The centre console keeps them at bay, and Charlotte kneels in her seat to get closer until one quick siren screams in the night.

Darryl retreats, sitting up straighter in his seat. He eyes the rearview mirror. Charlotte turns in her seat, craning her neck, and spots a police car pulling up on the right side of the road.

"Shit," Darryl mutters.

"Do you think it's Armstrong?" Charlotte asks. They are pulled over on the wrong side of the road, the four-way flashers giving their location away.

The police officer steps out of the car.

"It's Landry," Darryl says, and he clenches his jaw, tensing the muscles in his neck.

"Is that bad?" Charlotte asks.

Officer Landry saunters across the road toward them, smacking a flashlight in his hand in a slow, methodical fashion. When he arrives at the truck, he uses the flashlight to tap Charlotte's window. She consults Darryl before lowering it. "Officer?"

Officer Landry flashes his light into the truck, first at Darryl and then at Charlotte. "Ms. Boyd, I didn't expect to see you here. Is everything okay?"

Darryl speaks first. "I'm plowing roads tonight. Charlotte joined for the ride. We had some trouble; a deer ran out on the road. We were just catching our breath before heading back out."

"I was talking to Ms. Boyd."

Charlotte nods. "Everything Darryl said is right. I was a bit shaken up and just needed a minute."

"You're pulled over on the wrong side of the road."

Darryl scoffs. "We literally just swerved to miss a deer—we aren't having a picnic."

Charlotte sinks in her seat. Surely, the officer had been too far away to notice their make-out session.

"Best you move on now. I don't need to tell *you* of all people the dangers of the road."

"Yes, sir," Darryl says, his eyes on the dashboard ahead of him. "Anything else?"

Landry shakes his head and then eyes Charlotte. "You're a bit of a non-conformist,

aren't you?"

Charlotte lets out a forced laugh, unsure of the meaning behind his comment.

"Well, you're on your own then." He turns away. "Have a good night."

Darryl and Charlotte sit in silence as they wait for Officer Landry to return to his car. It's only after the officer makes a U-turn and is heading in the opposite direction that Darryl replaces the four ways with the blue light and merges onto the road. "I take it Landry offered you some advice about me."

"A bit. Strangely enough, he didn't offer any advice on his creep of a partner."

"Landry's never been my biggest fan. I don't have many friends at the station. I was a pain in the ass for them when Lark passed."

Charlotte shifts in her seat.

"For quite a few years, I'd come to them with questions. Things that didn't add up."

"You aren't convinced it was a suicide."

He shrugs. "I know that seems silly. That grief made me want to believe that, but there were things that pointed in another direction."

"So, foul play then?"

"Lark had bruises on her arms as if someone had grabbed her. They found drugs in her system. Valium. I don't even know where she could have gotten that. My mom barely kept Aspirin in the house. And honestly, I know Lark, and she would've come to me first. I truly believe that."

"Did they do an autopsy?"

He shakes his head. "They did the blood test, but after that, my mom didn't want to do the autopsy. She didn't like the thought of them doing that to her little girl. I probably should have pushed for it, but at the time, I just wanted to help her through it."

"Do you think Armstrong had something to do with it?"

He shrugs. "He was terrorizing her. Stalking her every move, leaving threatening notes, spreading disgusting lies. He wanted to ruin her after she rejected him."

Charlotte's throat tightens, and she swallows to relieve it. If Armstrong was dangerous as a teenager, what is he capable of now as an adult and a member of the police force? She thinks about his excitement when he had planned to ambush Darryl in her garage. How he laughed anytime he sensed Charlotte's discomfort. He seeks violence—in fact, he seems to get high off it.

"How do we prove it?" she asks.

"We find Lark's diary."

Chapter Thirty-Four

LARK

February 13, 2006

My room now matches the overgrown lilac bush at the side of the house. Mom had painted three out of the four walls of my bedroom by the time I got home from school. I could hear Rod Stewart's raspy tenor and thumping and stomping upstairs. When I arrived in my doorway, Mom was dancing to "Maggie May," rolling purple paint in large W's.

She never asked if I wanted my room painted, if I wanted the teal I chose only last year covered up.

"You're just a little girl." That was her response when I asked what she was doing. Darryl, it was so strange. It looked like she had left the room, her eyes glassy and distant, like her mind was lost in a memory. After a few moments, she shook her head and apologized. Then, she ran to the laundry room to clean up the brushes. Once showered, she returned sheepishly and said, "Purple was always your favourite colour when you were little. Might have had something to do with Barney the dinosaur."

I stared at the three pale purple walls, wondering what compelled her to do it. Then, I pulled the paint can and roller out of the laundry room and finished the fourth wall myself.

An hour later, sweat seeping through my T-shirt, I had finally finished.

Then, Jake showed up at my bedroom door. You can imagine my shock to see him standing there with two bottles of beer in hand. "Your mom mentioned you were redecorating," he said, passing me one of the beers. "Thought you might need a refreshment."

I stared at the lager before accepting it, wondering if it was some kind of trick. He clinked his bottle to mine when I finally did.

"It looks nice," he said, nodding at the nearest wall.

I took a small sip of the beer. He likely knew it wasn't my first but, again, I was worried he was testing me in the way those in authority do.

"I'm making mac and cheese for dinner. When does your brother usually get home?"

I told him his guess was as good as mine. I'm not mad, but you have been going to Xander's more and more often. Unless there's a girl you aren't telling me about? Merle is going to start putting me to work serving tables with how often I show up at the pub.

I still can't believe Jake cooked dinner—staying true to his promise from earlier in the week. I guess this is what making an effort looks like. I wonder if Jake has noticed something's off with Mom—if he knew *she* decided to redecorate my room. I get the sense he did. The beer and the dinner—are they his way of apologizing for her?

I give him one more month, tops, before he breaks up with her.

It's too bad because his mac and cheese was pretty good.

Chapter Thirty-Five

CHARLOTTE

At sunset, the purple walls Darlene chose have an iridescent quality. Charlotte sits cross-legged on the floor of Lark's room, the renovation binder open in her lap. It is Christmas Day, yet she has decided to familiarize herself with next week's renovations. She reads her mother's instructions for the upcoming transformation:

-Get rid of the ugly cough medicine purple! Replace with Benjamin Moore's Barren Plain.

-Another horrible popcorn ceiling feature! Why? Anyway, remove that.

-Closet door is to be replaced with bypass doors like all bedrooms. Talk to the closet guy about adding an organizer. It's small, but I think it can work.

-You can choose the furniture as this will be your room when you stay! Nothing too loud though. Keep in mind the aesthetic of the rest of the house.

Charlotte runs her finger over the words *your room*. At least she is being considered in this new life her parents are building—as long as she's not too loud.

Charlotte no longer fears Lark's bedroom as she did when she first arrived in Anville. She now feels a responsibility as she scans the space Lark once called home. She will do right by Lark. She will help Darryl uncover the truth, but she needs to be smart about it. Darryl can't find out that she's been holding the diary this whole time. It will ruin the trust they've built.

Driving her home last night, Darryl had said he realized it was next to impossible they'd find Lark's diary. He had gone through the items they'd kept from her room many times. Lark's hiding spot—the *Alice in Wonderland* VHS case—was effective. And, although he had hoped he'd find it when Charlotte gave him another chance to dig through the crates, he was met with disappointment.

Charlotte understands she needs to get the diary into Darryl's hands, but she can't admit she stole it and kept it from him.

She'll need to stage a hiding spot in Lark's room. One that they can discover when the renovations take place, which are planned to begin in four days. Then, she can leave it up to Darryl to search its pages for the truth.

Charlotte opens the closet door with a creak, and Tux rushes in to explore the cramped space. Above Charlotte is a light bulb, a string dangling beneath it. She pulls the string to bring it to life and scans her surroundings, searching for an inconsistency she can take advantage of—a surreptitious shelf, a loose floorboard—but there's nothing but a single rod, much like a ballet barre, with a couple of wire hangers swaying. Charlotte advances to turn off the light when she notices it. A hatch door leads to the attic. It is the only part of the ceiling not covered in glow-in-the-dark star stickers.

At five foot two, Charlotte is unable to reach the door, so she re-trieves a step stool and positions it beneath the hatch. She shakes out her shoulders, preparing for the task that she can't believe she is undertaking. She is willingly opening the attic of a 20th-century home. One that has a haunting past. Two weeks ago, she wouldn't even dare step into this room, especially since Charlotte's nightmares where Lark has a starring role.

Charlotte carefully lifts the ceiling hatch a couple of inches, then she drops it back down and shudders. Maybe she can just tell Darryl she went exploring and found it there. But wouldn't that be suspicious? They spend the night talking about how they need to find the diary, and she magically discovers it in the attic the next day. No, Darryl must discover it. She lifts the access panel and slides it to the left side, creating a gap in the ceiling above her. When she shines her phone's flashlight into the attic, the A-frame ceiling comes into view. The walls are coated in fibreglass insulation, reminiscent of pink cotton candy. There isn't enough space to stand, only crawl, but Charlotte isn't going to climb inside. She just needs to place the journal on the floor above, within view for when Darryl opens the hatch. She tucks the journal under her armpit and steps higher on the stool, then she places the moleskin notebook on a beam above, nudging it so it is just out of reach. She replaces the piece of drywall and expels a slow breath.

Goodbye, Lark.

A thump at the back of the house startles her, and she nearly tumbles off the ladder.

Charlotte peeks out Lark's window. The oak tree is in view, but the back door is obscured. She examines the rest of the yard. There is no one in sight. It sounded as though someone knocked on the door, but why would anyone come to the back? On her phone, she consults the front door camera. Nothing has been left on the porch, and the driveway remains empty. Perhaps it is a delivery of one of her recent orders. It could be the package of LED lightbulbs she purchased a few days ago; however, a Christmas Day delivery seems unlikely.

She waits a minute, switching her focus repeatedly from the phone to the window, searching for further movement. When there is none, she ventures downstairs.

She peeks out the front door first. She cleared the stoop and stairs last night when she got home. There is a dusting of snow that has accumulated since, but that shouldn't have deterred someone from using the front entrance. No footprints. No attempted delivery.

Charlotte opens the back door to reveal a small cardboard box that has been deserted on the stoop. Charlotte doesn't dawdle at the backdoor, fearing the person who delivered it might be close by, watching. She picks up the nondescript box, retreats inside, and locks the door behind her. She plods across the construction-papered kitchen floor, wading through the half-finished reno jobs, and carries the box at arm's length to her room.

For a moment, she considers something of malice might be nestled within the box. She recalls a former boss at one of her temp jobs insisting she, the receptionist, open an envelope addressed to him because it lacked a return address. It ended up being a resume to work for the firm, free of anthrax or whatever else he thought was hidden inside.

She stabs the box with a nail file, slitting it open where it had been taped.

Cookies. Ginger molasses cookies according to the card, which reads: *Merry Christmas, Charlotte. Hope you like ginger molasses.*

There is no salutation, but Charlotte knows they are from Armstrong based on the postscript at the bottom of the card assuring her there is no chocolate in them and an added winking emoji. She tosses them in the garbage and Googles whether Valium can be baked into food. After falling down an internet rabbit hole of the effects of diazepam and other benzodiazepines, she sets up her room for her movie date with her parents. She's looking forward to seeing them but part of her wishes she was spending the holiday with Darryl. She has a few minutes before her parents will join on video, likely in adorable matching Christmas sweaters. She opens her message thread with Darryl and types: *Hope everything is/was good at your mom's.*

Darryl responds right away. *Still here and all is well. Very festive, actually. I'm wearing one of those paper crowns you get in Christmas crackers.*

Charlotte loves those silly crowns even though they always fall down her forehead. Her phone dings again before she can ask him to send a selfie.

I told her about you. Now she wants to meet you.

Charlotte can't help but smile, though she is curious about how truthful he is being. She isn't sure his mom is lucid enough to have a conversation, though she's never known someone with dementia.

Tell her I'd like to meet her, too.

Her phone chimes again.

What are you doing New Year's Day?

Looks like she'll soon find out.

Chapter Thirty-Six

CHARLOTTE

Four nights ago, after hiding the diary, Charlotte dreamt that Lark was trapped in the attic, pounding on the hatch door, pleading for Charlotte to let her out. Ever since then, Charlotte has avoided walking by the room.

She will have Darryl discover the diary this week, and perhaps then she won't feel entirely consumed by Lark and her story. Between Lark's confessions and the kiss with Darryl, the Peters are dominating Charlotte's every thought.

Charlotte stretches out on the couch, far away from Lark's room, cozying up by her laptop with an assorted platter of potstickers. This is her plan for the evening, Charlotte's New Year's Eve tradition, until she receives an unexpected text from Dani.

Charlotte, hi! It's Daniella from Snips (your stylist). I hope you don't mind me texting you. Got your number from your booking. I wanted to invite you to the Angel Pub. I know you're new in town, so I thought you might not have New Year's Eve plans.

Charlotte stares at the paragraph of text that takes up half the phone screen. She brushes a crumb off her snowman pyjama pants. The thought of swapping them for jeans and journeying across town to the busy pub is daunting. Especially since she could risk running into Armstrong at his local watering hole. At the same time, she is intrigued to see who Dani has become and wouldn't mind learning more about what happened between her and Lark.

You're so sweet. Not gonna lie, I'm in my pjs and eating mozzarella sticks.

The soggy, rubbery appetizer sticks to Charlotte's teeth as she bites into it. The microwave calls to her, announcing her second round of munchies has finished defrosting, and she plods over to the counter, her slipper socks scuffing along the unfinished floor. She retrieves the piping-hot plate and transfers the weight from one hand to the other as she dashes back to the couch, where another message awaits her.

Something tells me the Angel's mozza sticks are better. It's just me and a few friends. We are aiming for 10 p.m. and would love to see you there.

Charlotte tosses the phone to the other side of the couch and turns onto her side so her laptop screen is in view. She's never had a problem bailing on this holiday before, so why does she feel tempted to participate now? Dani is practically a stranger, even though she's been a common character in Lark's diary. It's not like Dani gave ample notice with this last-minute invite. Plus, Charlotte has a busy day ahead of her, having agreed to accompany Darryl to visit his mom tomorrow. So, it's settled then. She'll stay right here on the couch. Safe in her bubble.

But what if she went for an hour or two? After her hair appointment, she thought she'd ruined any chance of connecting with Dani. Yet, here she is, reaching out to Charlotte. If Charlotte declines, she may not get this chance again.

She unravels her hair from her bun, tousling it a few times. She uses the selfie mode on her phone, studying her reflection. It could be worse. She licks the corner of her mouth where a smear of marinara stains her skin.

Dani and her friends will be at the pub in an hour, which would give Charlotte plenty of time to throw on a tinge of make-up and trek over. At the very least, she could use the occasion to say hi to Merle and Cindy.

She spots Tux by the fridge, grazing on her kibble. "What do you think, Tux, should I ring in the New Year with Dani and the Tangerines?"

The cat ignores her and continues to munch.

What happened to you and Lark, Dani? What was so special about you that Lark couldn't let you go?

With her hands on her knees, Charlotte pushes herself to a standing position. Tonight, Charlotte will break tradition if it means finding out more answers.

— ◆ —

When Charlotte arrives at the pub, she is introduced to three friends of Dani's, none of whom are named Brittany, and none of whom have orange-tinted skin. Gary, Jade, and Courtney are only in town for the weekend. They are friends from Dani's hair styling program, emphasized by their trendy tresses. Charlotte tucks her hair behind her ears as if that will hide the fact that she air-dried it this morning, and the strands are limp and stringy.

Courtney's jet-black hair is bluntly cut to her chin, the edges razor sharp. She chews on her paper straw, which will soon be too soggy to function properly. "Last New Year's, we went to a country bar in Barrie, Jade's hometown. It was a riot. Are you a fan of country?"

Charlotte shifts in her seat. She hates country music, but she isn't going to admit that here. "Sure. Taylor Swift and Miley."

Jade pulls her intricate braids to one side of her shoulder. She leans in and whispers, "I'm not a fan either."

Courtney peels a piece off her straw. "We're doing my hometown next year. I'm not far from here."

"Niagara Falls," Gary cuts in with a raised eyebrow, the only hair on his head. "It's going to be a scene."

Dani apologizes for the tiresome pub and the lack of young patrons, but the group takes turns convincing her they are enjoying their night. Jade spots the jukebox at the back of the room and stands up, pushing her chair back with a squeak.

"Do you think it needs coins to work?"

Charlotte scans the bar. "Just ask the bartender, Merle. He'll hook you up with some change."

Jade pulls Gary by the arm, forcing him to follow her to the bar, and Courtney trails behind them.

Dani, who has embraced her ringlet curls tonight, puckers her lips. "I thought you just moved here. How do you know Merle?"

Charlotte shrugs. "It's kind of a long story, but I had to stay in a room upstairs for a few nights."

WHAT SHE LEFT BEHIND

Charlotte sneaks a glance at Merle, who is chatting up his customers. His arms move wildly as he tells a story to the group, and they laugh in response. Her eye catches the marquee sign she gifted him and Cindy, and she notes it's been updated for the occasion: *Happy New Year, You Filthy Animals!*

At the back of the pub, the friends have selected a song from the late nineties. Len's "Steal My Sunshine" plays with its familiar opening beat, and Sharon Costanzo's vocal fry sends Charlotte back to her early teens.

"This is a blast from the past," she says, gesturing towards the jukebox.

Dani nods, her gaze on her friends who have formed a semi-circle around the machine. "Tell me about it." She turns back to Charlotte, eying her inquisitively. "I'm glad you decided to come."

"Me too." Charlotte holds up a mozzarella stick. "You were right, these are much better."

"I really didn't like the way I reacted during your appointment. It was completely unprofessional. I'm sorry. I think I was just caught off guard."

Charlotte had been debating how to mention Lark again. "It's okay, Dani. I never should have brought it up."

Dani parts her lips and tosses her head in bewilderment.

"Are you okay?"

"It's just—you called me Dani."

Charlotte inhales a sharp breath. Not once has Dani introduced herself as that. She has always called herself Daniella. What if Lark was the only person who called her that nickname?

"Right. Of course. I have a friend named Daniella who goes by Dani. Habit."

"It's fine. It's just been a while since I've heard it." She raises her pint to Charlotte. "Anyway, cheers to making new friends in a town where there are only familiar faces."

Charlotte clinks her glass to Dani's. She considers Dani's choice to stay in Anville after high school. With a universal profession, she could have chosen to settle anywhere. "Cheers. Thanks for the invite."

Dani extends her arm, her sweater inching up, exposing her wrist. Charlotte can't help but notice the raised scar, two inches long, that creeps up her forearm. Dani sets her pint down with a thud and pulls her sleeve down. "They're playing my song," she says, rising from her chair and she flees the table while a song Charlotte has never heard before rings out.

Charlotte swigs the last of her peach cider, swishing the tart drink around in her mouth. The scar looked like an old wound. Deep enough to be raised like Braille once it had healed. Perhaps Lark wasn't the only one with a habit of self-harm.

The bar becomes livelier as they near midnight, and if Charlotte weren't friendly with Merle, she would have to wait an hour for her next drink. As soon as he spots her at the end of the counter, he makes eye contact, gesturing to the cider tap. Charlotte nods and receives a fresh pint within seconds.

"Made some new friends, I see," Merle says, passing her the drink.

"Daniella cut my hair last week. She took pity on me and invited me out."

"Between you and me ..." Merle leans in, and she anticipates that what he is about to say is hearsay. "Daniella doesn't have a lot of friends in town. Most young people want to leave Anville for Toronto. So, don't think of it as her taking pity on you. I'm sure she wants to get to know someone else her age."

Charlotte drags her finger down the glass, wiping off the condensation. She glances toward Dani and her friends, whose dancing now matches the slower-paced ballad they've selected, taking on an interpretive dance quality. Charlotte watches as Dani laughs with her friends, her arms floating above her head.

"Any idea why she stayed?"

"Your guess is as good as mine," he says, and then he turns away to serve the next customer.

Charlotte is walking toward her new friends when she spots Armstrong at a table nestled in the back corner of the pub. It is too late to turn away without being noticed. He raises his eyebrows and holds up his pint in a toast, but his face remains stoic, his mouth etched in a straight line.

She offers a slight nod and continues toward the group. When he rises from his seat and disappears into the crowd that has formed on the dance floor, Charlotte excuses herself to the washroom.

She slides the lock into place and collapses on the toilet seat of the cramped stall. Of course, he would be here. And she came anyway, driven by her curiosity. Her obsession. She wouldn't put it past Armstrong to enter the women's washroom, so she stiffens when she hears the door swing open.

"Charlotte?" a woman's voice calls out. "Are you okay?"

Dani's white sneakers stop in front of Charlotte's stall.

"Yeah, I'm fine. Mozza sticks didn't sit well." It is the only thing she can think of to explain why she ran away in the middle of the song.

When Charlotte leaves the comfort of the stall, Dani is waiting at the full-length mirror, examining photobooth strips taped around it. She appears peaked, her olive skin tone muted.

"I didn't know they had a photo booth here," Charlotte says, joining Dani at the wall.

"They don't anymore. Cindy got rid of it when people started hooking up inside it."

Charlotte grimaces and continues to scan the photos that border her reflection. People of all ages pose in the high-contrast black-and-white images.

Dani runs her finger along one. "We took this one on the last day of grade nine."

The strip of photos features a young Dani and Lark in varying poses: uninhibited smiles, their tongues sticking out, the girls offering peace signs, and Lark kissing Dani's cheek. Charlotte hovers nearby, waiting for Dani to elaborate.

"I love these photos. Things were simpler then," she says, and Charlotte watches as Dani rubs at her scar beneath her sleeve, perhaps unknowingly.

"You should take it home."

Dani reaches for the strip and frees it from the wall, the blue sticky tack now the only evidence the photo was ever there. She tucks it into her purse. "It's almost midnight. We should get back." Dani reaches for Charlotte's hand, and she complies, following Dani out of the washroom in linked arms.

When Gary spots them, he pulls them into a hug. "Okay, so I was lying earlier when I said the night was as fun as last year's New Year's Eve."

Dani swats his arm.

"You didn't let me finish." He looks around the room, gesturing to the impromptu dance-off they started, where locals are showing off an assortment of moves. Cindy and a few women demonstrate a simple line dance, a young couple slow dance as if they are the only ones in the room, and a father sways with his young daughter on his shoulders, likely up past her bedtime. "Tonight has actually been awesome," Gary says as he looks around the room. "Anville can party."

During the next song, Merle abandons his station at the bar to twirl Charlotte around in a swing dance, daring her to loosen up. Just as her reserved smile begins to grow into a laugh, the regulars heckle him to fetch them another drink. Dani approaches, a questionable look on her face.

"You and Merle seem close," she says, but before Charlotte can utter a word, Merle climbs onto a chair and calls out to the packed bar.

"Alright, everyone, it's almost time for the countdown. Someone, pull the plug on the jukebox."

Gary obliges and follows the act with a dramatic bow. The dance floor cheers in response, filling the silence in the machine's wake. Charlotte scans the crowded pub for Armstrong. She wants to be as far away from him as possible when the crowd sings Happy New Year and everyone scrambles to find the nearest person to kiss.

Merle leads the group in a countdown, shouting, "Ten…"

The pub lights go dim.

"Nine…" the crowd joins in.

Charlotte spots Armstrong at the bar.

"Eight…"

Armstrong locks eyes with her, then slings back his shot.

"Seven…"

He wipes his mouth on his sleeve.

"Six..."

Charlotte's heart pulsates.

"Five..."

Armstrong is swallowed by the crowd.

"Four..."

Charlotte squeezes her way in between Dani and Gary.

"Three..."

She can hear her heartbeat in her ears.

"Two..."

The room is closing in, the air thick and sticky like molasses.

"One..."

Everything goes black.

Chapter Thirty-Seven

CHARLOTTE

The bubbles from the lemon-lime soda burn Charlotte's throat when she sips the straw. Merle pats her back. "That's one way to ring in the New Year. How are you feeling, champ?"

Her head throbs, but a far greater pain screams at her. She rotates her left ankle and winces. "Shit. I think it's broken." She lifts the hem of her jeans and carefully removes her boot. She should have worn sneakers. Her outer anklebone is nowhere to be found, the surrounding ligaments swollen to the size of a tennis ball.

Merle crouches in front of her chair and cradles her foot in his hands. "Probably just a sprain." After a moment, he lowers it to the floor. "I'll grab you some frozen peas."

Charlotte leans back in the chair and closes her eyes. If only there were an icepack for her ego. She must have fainted in the middle of the dance floor just as the bar yelled, "Happy New Year," "Auld Lang Syne" cued up to follow. Dani and her friends would have seen and wondered what the hell was going on with her. Maybe they'd chalk it up to her drinking too much, even though she only had two pints.

At least she avoided a run-in with Armstrong.

She scans the room she's never stepped foot in before. Not much larger than a utility closet, the pub's office has a small desk, a filing cabinet, and inventory stacked neatly against the wall. It smells of stale beer and she wonders how often alcohol has seeped into the maroon carpet. She feels around for her purse and finds it hanging on the back of her chair.

Four text messages greet her, all with interactive fireworks prompted by their New Year's wishes.

Dani: I feel so bad that I jetted but the crew was getting tired. I hope you feel better. Remind me to never order the mozza sticks haha. Happy New Year!

Darryl: Happy New Year! Hope your night in was good. I barely made it to midnight. If I swing by at 11 am tomorrow, does that work for you?

Mom: Happy New Year, Char! Love Mom and Dad xoxo

Armstrong: What happened to you? Merle said you fainted?! Too much to drink? I'll hang around for a bit in case you want a ride home. P.S. Happy New Year.

Charlotte props her foot on a case of Bud Light. She may need to rethink her main mode of transportation if her ankle is sprained. She'll have to learn the bus schedule, but what if she faints on a crowded bus ride? Her ankle will likely be prone to injuries in the future, too. Her mind spirals like a spinning top when she thinks of what this ailment could lead to.

She opens a search tab and types in, *how to heal a sprained ankle* but before she can dig into the results, Merle returns, holding a half-empty bag of frozen peas.

"Ice and keeping it elevated is the best thing for it. I see you've already got the elevation down. Here's your ice." He passes her the bag of peas, which are secured with an elastic band.

"I'm sorry if I caused a scene." She presses the bag to her foot, allowing it to mould to the shape of her ankle.

"Are you kidding? It was perfect timing. A good excuse to kick everyone out."

"Did everyone leave, then?" She worries Armstrong might be the exception and pictures him hovering by the bar like a coyote growling for scraps.

"All gone, and I'm glad. They would have been asking for liquor until three in the morning. Speaking of which, can I pour you another drink? Or have you had enough for the night?"

"This," she begins, gesturing to the fountain drink, "is all I need. And, the number for a cab if you have it." It's her only option for getting home, even though the thought of it makes her buzz with uneasiness.

"There's a room upstairs with your name on it if you'd rather stay the night."

Charlotte strums her fingers on the armrest. Her own bed is calling her, but at this point, she'd do anything to avoid getting in a car. "You have a free room on New Year's Eve? Tonight's gotta be one of your busiest nights."

Merle shakes his head. "We left them all vacant. Cindy didn't want to clean up puke and soiled sheets after the biggest drinking night of the year."

"I don't blame her. You can tell Cindy—"

"Tell me what?" Cindy appears in the doorway, her face sullen and her speech monotonous. She must be exhausted after the busy night.

"I'm thinking of taking Merle up on his offer to stay the night."

Cindy shoots him a glance.

"Unless it puts you out," Charlotte says, lowering her foot from the beer case and straightening her posture. She suddenly feels like she shouldn't be in this room.

"It's fine, stay. Merle, a word?"

Charlotte can almost feel the heat radiating off Cindy's ruddy face. Charlotte averts her eyes from the unspoken tension until they have left the room, and their voices become a dim murmur. She is eyeing a retro Dow Brewery poster on the corkboard above the desk when she notices another photobooth strip partially hidden behind it. She narrows her eyes, straining to focus. There are two people in the monochrome images, a man and a woman, but she can't decipher who they are from where she sits.

She pushes herself to a standing position and hops toward the desk on her good foot. She is lifting the corner of the faded poster when Merle re-enters the room.

"Need something?"

Charlotte slaps the desk in front of her to steady herself. Perhaps she got up too quickly. Pushed herself. She lifts one hand to her head and feels the blood rushing through the veins in her temple. "No, I was just putting pressure on it." She uses the table in front to guide her away from the corkboard.

Merle rushes toward her and leads her back to the chair. "Here, let me help you. It might be a few days before you can walk on it." Cinnamon gum wafts from his breath.

Following fifteen minutes of icing—Merle's orders—he helps her climb the steep stairs that lead to her room for the night. Cindy is nowhere to be seen, and Charlotte tells herself she will make up her bed tomorrow and tidy the room, so there isn't much for Cindy to clean. The first time Charlotte breaks tradition on New Year's Eve, she's left with a sprained ankle and a sour taste in her mouth. She hopes Cindy isn't annoyed with her for long. And she hopes Dani will see her again.

She suspects Dani knows more about Lark's death than she's letting on.

Chapter Thirty-Eight

CHARLOTTE

Descending stairs with crutches requires a precision Charlotte hasn't practiced since her days of balancing on a beam. She maintains eye contact with the steps, carefully centring the rubber feet on the carpet below her before lowering herself to the stair. She pauses halfway down, brushing her hair out of her face.

Darryl greets her at the bottom of the staircase, his eyebrows drawn together.

She shrugs. "I only had two pints, I swear."

Merle pokes his head around the corner. "I blame myself. I made her dance with me for a song. I should have known she wouldn't be able to keep up." He laughs at his joke and then hurries up the stairs to help her the rest of the way down. "How are the crutches working out?"

"They're a bit tall for me, but they'll work until I can get to a doctor."

Darryl busies himself, moving various obstacles out of Charlotte's path to the exit. The attention unnerves her. Here in Anville, she is the shiny new toy. Dani's latest best friend, Merle and Cindy's daughter they never had, Armstrong's obsession, and Darryl's—well, they haven't exactly talked about what they are. What will happen when the novelty wears off, and they all realize she isn't so shiny, but rather, tarnished?

Darryl tucks a chair beneath a table, kicks an empty beer box under the bar, and when they make it to the front of the pub, he holds the door open for her to hobble out of.

"I parked close."

Charlotte nods, but her face scrunches up at the idea of driving the thirty minutes to Darlene's long-term care facility.

"And I can just drive you home. I don't expect you to come to my mom's anymore."

Hmm. An easy out. One he won't take offence to. But Charlotte doesn't want to disappoint him. While a visit to a facility for dementia patients is hardly on her bucket list, whenever she spends time with Darryl, she is surprised at how much closer they get and how their relationship progresses. She's also curious to meet Darlene, the eccentric woman in the pages of Lark's diary.

"How about a quick stop at the house first? So, I can feed Tux." What she really wants is to change out of her bar clothes, which are damp with sweat, and wash off yesterday's mascara.

"You sure?" he asks, helping her into the passenger's seat.

Charlotte hands him her crutches and fastens her seatbelt.

———— • ✦ • ————

The J. George Evans Centre, named after a doctor or perhaps a founding donor, sits on a hill off the Queen Elizabeth Highway, overlooking

Lake Ontario. The facility recently underwent a major renovation with appliance upgrades and a dining room that rivals a private golf club. The grounds are well-manicured with perennial gardens of ornamental grasses and native pollinators. Charlotte knows this despite the snow covering the grounds because she researched the facility as soon as Darryl told her the name. Like perusing a restaurant's menu in advance, Charlotte aimed to take any element of surprise out of her day, and so, she had checked the address and driving route and swiped through gallery images as if she was considering sending a loved one to the residence. She learned this is where wealthy families send ailing relatives, and it explains why there was barely any money left from the sale of the house for Darryl's personal use. It also explains why he was squatting in Charlotte's garage.

Charlotte relaxes her shoulders when Darryl jerks the gear into park. They've arrived in one piece, but a new dread takes hold of her chest. She is meeting Darryl's mother. She doesn't know what to expect. Darryl's explanations of his mother's condition have been brief.

"You've told her I'm coming?" she asks, gripping her crutches with intensity after he helps her out of the truck.

"Yeah, last week. She likes having visitors."

Charlotte nods. "And she knows you?" She clears her throat. "Like, she remembers who you are?"

Darryl shrugs. "Some days she does. Other days, I don't think she knows herself."

"I'll follow your lead, then."

Darryl squeezes Charlotte's shoulder and then scans the empty parking lot. The wind is cold and damp, sending a frigidness deep into Charlotte's bones.

Darryl remains close to Charlotte's side as she shuffles along the stone pathway; all the while, she wonders how he will introduce her to Darlene. Charlotte pauses at one of the many wooden benches, deserted due to the cold weather. The two-storey, red-brick building ahead has an oversized A-frame entrance and a discrete pewter sign that reminds them where they are. The glass doors are accented by winter urns with birch branches, juniper, and silver fir. But Charlotte realizes that despite appearances, this isn't a spa or hotel. It is a facility for people who are no longer capable of caring for themselves, and she finds that both depressing and unnerving.

Darryl is on a first-name basis with the nursing staff, and he exchanges holiday greetings before asking Mavis how his mother is feeling this afternoon and if it's still a good day for a visit. Charlotte hovers at the check-in counter behind a poinsettia arrangement and outstretches her leg. This was a mistake. She's not ready to meet Darlene. She turns toward the exit. Perhaps she can wait in the lobby until he's finished with his visit.

"You'll be pleased to know she participated in the group session on Monday." Mavis hands two visitor passes to Darryl. "Art therapy. She seemed to enjoy it."

Darryl slides his pass on. "I'm not surprised. She was always the creative type."

Charlotte bows her head, allowing Darryl to hang her pass around her neck. She releases her hair from its grasp.

Mavis leads them to the resident wing, a narrow corridor spattered with doors, the odd one wearing a festive wreath. Charlotte is conscious of her movements as she hobbles down the hallway, her crutches squeaking on the linoleum. Her sweaty palms slip on the foam handles, and she pauses for a moment, wiping them one at a time on her jeans before resuming her laboured steps.

Mavis knocks softly on the threshold and pokes her head in before opening the door wide enough for Darryl and Charlotte to enter the modest room, a slightly homier hospital room. "Someone will bring her by shortly."

Darryl directs Charlotte to the small card table by the window. He retrieves a children's puzzle from his backpack and spills the primary colours onto the wood surface. It takes everything in Charlotte's power not to construct the picture, as the wheel of the school bus begs to find its other half.

"I read an article on puzzles helping with memory," he says, spreading the pieces out and turning over the rogue ones that fell cardboard side up. "Thought we'd give 'er a go."

Charlotte nods, but she can't help but focus on the fact that there are only two chairs at the card table. She occupies the one, her crutches leaning close by against the neutral wall. The other is meant for Darlene. She hopes Darryl will remain close to lead the conversation.

Darlene's room resembles the featured images on the website, but in person, it feels more sombre. The bed is made up neatly with a green and purple knitted throw folded at the foot, not much different than the one Darryl was using on the garage cot. A stuffed blue bunny shares a seat with a teddy on the chair to the right of the door. A few photos sit atop a shelf. Lark and Darryl as kids, wearing fluorescent green and pink swimwear and snapback hats to match. Darryl's high school graduation photo. Lark's, of course, is missing. Even with these flourishes, the room feels sterile, melancholy.

Charlotte is staring out the window when the scuffing of slippers on the tile redirects her attention to the doorway.

Darlene shuffles into the room, arm in arm with one of the staff. Her green eyes widen when she spots her guests, and it's hard to know for sure, but her crooked expression appears joyful. She holds Darryl's stare, perhaps in recognition, as the nurse guides her to the card table.

"Happy New Year, Mom," Darryl says, and he touches her elbow, helping her into the seat. "This is my friend, Charlotte, that I told you about."

Charlotte reaches her hand slowly across the table. She hovers over a puzzle piece and then retreats when Darlene doesn't return the handshake. Darlene grinds her teeth, a tic which Charlotte finds off-putting, almost menacing. She does her best not to stare and instead meets Darryl's eyes. "It's so nice to meet you."

Darlene remains quiet but alert, and Darryl directs her to the puzzle, helping her find the edge pieces. He speaks about his job clearing roads and the record snowfalls this December. He jokes about his lacklustre New Year's Eve, how he attempted to watch *Dick Clark's Rockin' New Year's Eve* and fell asleep on the couch, waking up only moments before the ball dropped.

Darlene doesn't speak but follows the conversation with her eyes, nodding occasionally. When the puzzle is complete, mostly by Darryl's hand, he asks his mother if she'd like him to brush her hair. She nods, and he moves to a drawer by her bed, where he retrieves a soft bristle brush. As Darryl meticulously combs her greying hair, Charlotte shares a modified story of her sprained ankle, leaving out Armstrong and blaming it on a trip over the jukebox cord.

Darlene nods her head, the teeth grinding intensifying, and she reaches her hand out to Charlotte who obliges, meeting her halfway. Darlene holds Charlotte's hand for the remainder of the visit and when Darryl advises they should be on their way, Darlene squeezes harder, like she doesn't want to let go.

After Darlene and Darryl hug goodbye, Darlene reaches for Charlotte, pulling her in for an embrace.

"Always so beautiful, Lark," Darlene says in an almost whisper.

Charlotte jerks away, taken aback by the mistake, but she is unable to pry her wrist from Darlene's rigid grasp. The woman's jaw is tense, the chattering pronounced, and her deep-set eyes vacant. Charlotte considers correcting her. She finally loosens her grip.

"I'm so sorry," Darlene whispers, wringing her hands.

Charlotte glances at Darryl to confirm whether he's heard, but he is already out in the hallway, chatting with another staff member.

"I should have been there for you," Darlene adds.

Charlotte joins Darryl in the hallway, and just like that, the visit is over.

"She loved you," Darryl says with a jovial grin when they are back in the lobby, signing out. Charlotte thought she made a good impression, too, but it's possible Darlene thought Charlotte was Lark the entire visit. Charlotte inspects the red skin around her wrist. Either way, Darlene must have trusted her enough to take her hand.

When they are seated in the truck, Charlotte asks, "Is she always that quiet?"

On the drive home, Darryl explains how the doctor switched up his mother's medications when she moved into the facility due to some aggressive behaviour she was developing in the later stages of the disease. The catalyst for her move was the day she mistook the paper boy for an intruder when he opened the screen door to tuck the weekly inside. She chased him away with Darryl's baseball bat, and later that day, Darryl called the centre.

"Her medication calms her. It helps ease some of her frustration." He lets out a sigh. "But it also took away her spirit. I'm lucky if I get a *hello* now."

Charlotte bites her lip. She had thought it might have been her presence today that discouraged Darlene from speaking. That maybe she was shy.

"What's in the envelope?" Charlotte asks.

Darryl drops his right hand from the wheel and retrieves the manila envelope from the centre console. He passes it to Charlotte. "Be my guest."

She hesitates and then raises her eyebrow.

"It's usually just flyers for their upcoming events. A Valentine's dance or a Mother's Day tea is my bet."

Charlotte edges her house key into the small opening and drags it across for a clean rip. She sifts through the contents of the envelope and holds up a flyer with a snowman, "Winter Carnaval on February fourth."

Darryl smiles. "You in?"

"Sure. It says they'll be serving snow cones."

She continues to read aloud the notices—modified visitor hours for the spring, the opening of the renovated recreational room, a profile on a new staff member—when she stumbles upon a piece of artwork that makes her heart pulsate.

The watercolour painting is a mess of blues and greys, the colours fighting for space.

Charlotte rubs her finger over the centre of the page, and the black leaves a stain. Darlene must have used a pastel crayon to draw what Charlotte interprets to be a tree, its branches jagged and naked. The only warm colour she used is the red acrylic that makes up the tree's roots, running off the page like viscous blood.

"What is it?" Darryl asks, his eyes maintained on the road.

Charlotte holds up the Darlene Peters original and clears her throat.

Chapter Thirty-Nine

CHARLOTTE

Back at the house, Darryl has barely uttered a word since he picked up the painting to study it. He turns it over, eying the text Charlotte read aloud to him in the truck:

Patient: Darlene Peters

Activity: Art therapy group session one

Date: December 28, 2022

He tosses the page on Charlotte's coffee table and rests his head against steepled fingers. "I used to think her disease might be a blessing in disguise."

"What do you mean?" Charlotte inches closer to Darryl on the couch, which is still covered with a low thread count sheet to protect it from the construction dust.

"It's hard to explain," he says.

"Try me."

In the dim glow of the pillar candles that grace the coffee table and fireplace mantle, Charlotte and Darryl's shadows loom like twisted creatures.

"I thought it was her body's way of helping her forget what happened. So she wouldn't have to live with it." He traces the charcoal tree with his forefinger. "But maybe she does remember it deep down. Maybe it's a pain that will never leave us."

Charlotte allows her fingers to sweep up his arm, stopping at his shoulder, where she gives it a squeeze. "I don't know. The mind is complex."

He shakes his head. "I think I'll call them tomorrow. Ask them to find her another group activity to do." He gestures toward the drawing. "This can't be good, right? Stirring up these feelings?"

Charlotte shrugs. "It might be cathartic for her. It's a form of therapy."

He nods his head a few times as though he's considering the gravity of her words. "What about you?" he asks, narrowing his eyes.

"What about me?" Charlotte dips her pinky in the wax that pools atop the ivory candle, unfazed by the initial sharp heat.

"Did you do any therapy after your accident?"

She lifts her hand, allowing the wax to harden around her nail and considers her words carefully. "I had physio to do, so no, I didn't really have time."

The first accident left Charlotte unscathed. Had she already mentioned that to Darryl? It was the second collision two months later, her head-on crash with a hydro pole that fractured her clavicle and dislocated her shoulder. Sheryl and Jared were eager to get Charlotte back in physical shape. They had assumed she'd return to gymnastics, as if that could ever happen. Jared left work early every day to ensure she made her appointments at the clinic, and Sheryl set up a space at the house dedicated to Charlotte's shoulder exercises, which she taped to the wall of the den. But neither of them—no one in her family—had encouraged her to seek therapy, and she hadn't sought it out either.

"Do you think it would have helped?" he asks, then he shakes his head as if to renounce the question, his loose waves falling away from his face.

Charlotte sighs and removes the wax casing, tossing it onto the coffee table. At that stage of her life, therapy probably would have helped. It might have allowed her to shed some of the guilt. It might have helped her come to terms with the fact that she was the only one who survived and that there was no logical reason for that. It might have even prevented her second accident. She wasn't in a good place that night. She should have gone to sleep instead of venturing out for a drive to clear her mind.

But there's no point in thinking about it now. It's done. She fixed that part of herself. She's suppressed those dark thoughts. Buried them far, far away like her three best friends.

Like a reflex, she rubs her chest.

"Sorry, didn't mean to pry," Darryl says. "I was just thinking it might be something I'd like to try. I never did, either. Better late than never, right?"

Charlotte stares into the flame of the nearest candle, its light distorting. She doesn't realize she is crying until Darryl moves closer, stammering that he's sorry; he didn't mean to upset her. She hides her face behind her hands, and her cries turn into sobs, her body convulsing. "I'm sorry. I don't know why—"

Before she can finish the words, he pulls her in close to him, and from behind, he wraps his arms around her like a harness. Charlotte succumbs to his touch, her hands finding his fingers intertwined across her ribcage.

Her moans erupt from deep within her abdomen, and the vibrations pass from her body to his, like he is absorbing some of her pain. She believes there is no judgment from Darryl. The warmth of his body against hers grants her permission to release her sobs.

Maybe it was seeing him and his mom today, knowing it should be different; there should be three of them celebrating the new year with party favours and sausage rolls. Maybe it was the loneliness of Darlene's bedroom, its cookie-cutter floorplan, and the underlying scent of lemon cleaning spray. Or perhaps it was Darryl's questions about her past which forced her to think of that dreaded day and the friends who left her alone on Earth. Whatever the reason, it's liberating to release the emotions, and she feels safe doing it in his arms.

Darryl calms her with measured hushes, his fingers strumming hers at the same tempo. When her whimpers subside to shaky breaths, he drops his chin to her shoulder, and the warmth of his breath on her skin brings the hair on her neck to attention. She releases the tension that has been consuming her, allowing her shoulders to relax and her body to collapse into his. His mouth moves closer, his breathing audible. He kisses her neck lightly, his lips barely grazing her skin. Charlotte's breath catches in her throat, and he pauses.

She unlocks his clasped hands, releasing herself from his grasp and turns toward him, their faces mere inches from each other. His eyes search hers, and he bites his bottom lip where a lip ring once punctured, the skin now flecked with a small, purple scar. Before Darryl can apologize, she closes the gap and returns the kiss with urgency, biting the same flesh he was seconds ago.

The next few moments rush past Charlotte, who is in a whimsical daze. It's finally happening, and she welcomes the tingles which travel throughout her core and into her extremities the more he kisses her. The more his hands explore her body. She still can't explain the carnal need to be near him, but she doesn't want to resist it for another day.

She pushes him against the couch, satisfied with her boldness, and she straddles him, disregarding her injured ankle. As she sits atop him, her legs on either side, she rocks her hips methodically, feeling him grow beneath his jeans. He lets out a hushed moan, and she gains her power, pushing harder against him.

His hands travel through her waves, down her spine, and return to the front, hovering near her sternum. Holding her stare, he undoes her buttons one at a time, his fingers trembling against her skin. She shrugs off her blouse and tosses it to the floor. His eyes zero in on the iridescent scar that travels from her shoulder to her collarbone, impossible to miss.

"It's from the accident," she says as if he requires an explanation for her flawed skin.

He plants a series of kisses along the scar and then another, tender, lingering on her lips. When he finally pulls away, their eyes fluttering open, he smiles. "Fuck, you're beautiful."

She twists her mouth and looks away, embarrassed by the attention. "Aren't

you going to join me?" she asks, gesturing towards his shirt.

Darryl pulls his T-shirt over his head, adding it to the pile. His chest is a magnet, reeling her in, and she remains in his arms for a moment, not wanting to leave its warmth.

They shed their clothes like they are ridding their emotional baggage, then exchange glances at each other's naked bodies. When they fall to the couch, Darryl positions himself on top. He begins with a fervent kiss, which reveals his hunger, and Charlotte suspects it has been a while since he, too, has allowed someone in.

His kisses travel down her body, hovering at her breasts as he explores her curves. She arches her back when he crosses her naval. Her breath quickens when his tongue finds her inner thigh. She runs her hands through his hair, and he meets her eyes before burying his head between her legs. Charlotte encourages the act, instinctively lifting her pelvis toward him as his tongue encircles her. He licks. Slow at it first, allowing the pleasure to build with an underlying ache. She focuses on the dull throb at the precipice of ecstasy. Could this fill the void? Or is it a warning? Like with everything good in her life, something bad waits around the corner, lurking.

When Charlotte's body tenses, when she claws at the white sheet beneath her, Darryl laps her up like he's thirsty for her, and her moans grow louder. She whimpers his name as she orgasms, the tingles enveloping her entire body in jolts.

Darryl rises to a seated position, his boyish grin widening, and Charlotte must have every part of him. She pulls him toward her.

"You sure?" he asks.

"I want all of you," Charlotte says, her voice breathy.

Darryl fumbles in his wallet, retrieving a condom. Once it's secured, Charlotte welcomes him into her warmth.

Darryl lowers himself, melting into her, the weight of him providing a security she hasn't felt in so long. He moves slowly at first, gauging her response. As she wraps her legs around him, he thrusts deeper and deeper into her, the warmth surging through her abdomen until she can no longer suppress her moans. Darryl accepts this as permission, and he, too, finds ecstasy, his body tensing as he fills her.

They both collapse, their sweaty bodies defeated but still pulsing. Lying on her side, Charlotte watches Darryl's breath rise and fall. She plants a kiss on his cheek before snuggling into his chest, where she fits like one of his puzzle pieces.

Chapter Forty

CHARLOTTE

Charlotte wakes to Darryl's jade eyes staring at her, and for a moment, she believes she is wrapped up in a dream, the light of dawn hazy.

"Morning," he says. His naked back is pressed against the wall, and Charlotte realizes she is taking up most of the queen-sized bed, her limbs sprawled.

She pushes herself to a seated position and shuffles toward her side of the mattress. "Sorry. I'm used to sleeping solo."

Darryl's black and white baseball T-shirt hangs off her like a nightgown, miles too big. The clothing is faded and worn, the fabric pilling. It smells like him. An odour she finds both comforting and sensual, equal parts piquant cologne and earthy cannabis. She considers keeping it captive beneath her pillow, holding it close when she touches herself.

At some point in the night, they had awoken downstairs, stiff and cold, the candles still aglow and the wax spilling over. That's when they decided to make their way to her bed. Darryl carried Charlotte because of her injury, and she had joked that they were newlyweds, having just consummated marriage.

Now, as they sit in bed together, their lack of clothing and a ripe soreness between Charlotte's legs are reminders of what transpired the night before.

Tux paws at the door, and Charlotte makes her way limping. She sits down, defeated. "Do you mind?" They left Charlotte's crutches leaning against the couch.

"No, of course not." Darryl throws off the sheets and plods across the hardwood, wearing only boxer briefs. Charlotte watches the muscles in his back tensing as he stops to stretch at the door. Tux rushes past him, joining Charlotte on the bed.

"I guess we know who she belongs to," he says.

As Charlotte scratches behind Tux's ears, she catches herself staring at Darryl's body and the trail of hair that extends from his naval. It is no longer left to her imagination.

"I've taken your shirt hostage," she says.

"That you have." His smirk tells her he doesn't mind, and she is thankful they are being playful with each other rather than awkward. "Can I have it back?" he asks, raising an eyebrow.

"Right now?"

"Yeah, I really need it back." He approaches, wearing a devilish grin. "It's my only shirt."

"I don't think so. I like how it looks on me."

He rushes toward her, and she rolls onto her stomach, taking cover. She squeals as he tickles her, his fingers finding her ribs beneath the shirt. He undresses her and covers her in kisses.

After they make love for the second time, he perches on his elbow. The sun is higher in the sky and bathes the room in warmth. "I don't have to work today."

"No? Done enough plowing for one day?" Charlotte breaks into a cackle.

"That was good. How long have you been waiting to say that?"

She shrugs, a smile tugging at the corner of her mouth. "About as long as I've been waiting for this to happen between us."

He runs his fingers between the valley of her breasts. "Just clearing some snow," he says. "Your breasts can be the snowbanks." He drives a makeshift truck from one to the other.

She swats at his hand. "Stop it, loser. You don't have to work today. No more talk of snow removal."

He lies his head on her shoulder. "Got any jobs for me to do around here?"

It is the perfect segue for Charlotte to ask Darryl to check on the insulation in the attic so he can discover Lark's diary. *Lark*. She had completely forgotten about her. She doesn't want this moment with Darryl to end quite yet. She shrugs. "I'm sure I can find a use for you. I'll let you stay for the day. Do you have a daily rate?"

"You'll *let* me stay?" He is laughing fiercely, his chest vibrating. "Hey, this was my room a month ago."

He points out how the bedroom has changed. Her mirror leans where a poster of the band Blink 182 once hung. The bed has been moved from the north wall to the south. His single mattress sat atop a slatted wood base whereas she sprang for the queen with an oversized headboard.

"I guess it's kinda weird being here," she says.

"A little."

"I thought of a job for you."

"Shoot."

"You'll need to go into the attic. Or at least poke your head inside." She tucks her lips inside her mouth.

"Scared of the attic, are we?"

"Too short to reach the latch door."

Darryl's eyes widen at the realization of what she is asking. She suspects he knows what this means; he'll need to access the attic from Lark's room. "Ah, right. The door's in Bird's closet. Sure, no problem. Are you worried something got in through the roof?"

Charlotte grimaces. "No, should I be?"

He shrugs. "Wouldn't be the first time. We had a family of raccoons make themselves at home once. Lark had to bunk with me for a while."

She explains how the contractors had asked her what type of insulation was used in the house, prompting him to pull his shirt and jeans on. Charlotte follows suit, swapping Darryl's shirt for leggings and a sweater. He helps her down the hallway until they arrive at the purple room. Darryl opens the door slowly, and the air feels cool, the room not yet touched by sunlight. He hesitates, and she wonders when the last time was that he ventured into his late sister's bedroom. Darryl turns toward the stairs without a word. Charlotte leans against the doorframe for support, wondering if she hit a nerve.

Darryl returns moments later with Charlotte's crutches and a step stool. "I'm tall, but not that tall," he says and proceeds to set up the stool in the closet. "I'm pretty sure we have fibreglass insulation. But let's check it out."

Charlotte holds her breath as Darryl removes the latch door. She'll have to feign surprise, pretending like she wasn't the one who hid Lark's diary above them. After a moment, he steps down. "Yep, it's fibreglass. Want me to snap a picture so they can see it?"

Charlotte nods. She needs him to spot the journal. He steps back onto the stool, and she hovers closely, trying to peer into the darkness. "Done." He texts her the photo.

Charlotte will need to discover the diary herself. She consults the photo, scrunching up her face. "Don't take this personally, but I'm going to retake it. It's a little dark." Darryl helps her up onto the stool. She feels around the floor of the attic, but she doesn't encounter the journal. She shines her flashlight above and slowly turns 360 degrees.

The diary is nowhere to be found.

"You okay up there?" Darryl asks.

She snaps a quick photo and pretends to study it. "Yours is better after all."

Even on steady ground, Charlotte's body seems to be off-balance, like she is sinking through the floorboards. If the diary isn't in the attic where she planted it, who took it?

Chapter Forty-One

CHARLOTTE

To-Do:

 -Find Lark's diary

Charlotte scribbled the task in her notebook as soon as Darryl left Monday morning to clear the roads for Anville residents commuting to Niagara Falls. She retraces the sentence in red ink, emphasizing its importance.

Cozying up next to Darryl the last two nights, Charlotte slept better than she ever has in the house. Normally, unsettled by the walls that creak and moan as if they have secrets to share, when she lay next to Darryl, she immediately felt calm, her mind going quiet.

With Darryl gone and the contractors expected within the hour, Charlotte returns to Lark's bedroom with a flashlight in hand for a thorough inspection. She enters the room quickly before she can talk herself out of the task. Standing on the footstool on her good leg within the confines of the closet, Charlotte grows lightheaded. The air is stuffy, and the purple walls appear to be closing in. She squeezes her eyes shut, but that only makes her sway back and forth, leaving her balance at risk.

"Please, please, please," she utters before opening the hatch door. She shines the light into the attic. "Where are you?" she asks, running her hand along the perimeter of the opening. The wooden slats are rough, and a small piece of wood pierces into her finger. "Shit." She pulls her hand down and sucks on the tip of her finger, dragging her tongue along the protrusion. The sliver is deep, but the wood juts from the surface of her skin, allowing her to grip it with her nails to release it. A small bead of crimson escapes.

She inspects the opening of the ceiling one last time before retreating from the footstool and hobbling to her crutches.

The diary is missing.

The possible scenarios pop into her mind. The raccoon family stole it. She had only dreamed she planted it there. Lark's ghost moved it. She shudders at each thought. Another option is worse, though. What if, somehow, Armstrong snuck into the house and removed it? Maybe he found his way inside the day he placed the cookies on her doorstep. Did he sneak in the front door when she was consulting the back stoop?

Once she is in her room, she pulls up their message history. His last text was a couple of days ago, wishing her a Happy New Year. She never responded. She considers typing a message, but a paralyzing fear consumes her. This man is dangerous. It is likely he had at least some hand in Lark's death. If Charlotte is going to confront him, she should ask Darryl to join her. But how can she explain her suspicions without admitting she held onto his sister's diary for weeks?

She will need to confront Armstrong in a public place where there are people she can trust. She sucks a spot of coagulated blood on her finger before crafting the message, inviting Armstrong to join her for lunch at the Angel Pub.

———— • ✦ • ————

Charlotte enters the pub a half hour earlier than Armstrong's expected arrival. On a good day, the walk takes twenty-five minutes. With crutches, it is closer to forty, and her hands are now raw with the beginning of blisters, her flesh a pink sheen. The cold glass of cider soothes her palms as she waits at the bar, her crutches leaning on the stool beside her.

Merle shakes his head. "I still feel so bad. Is it getting better?"

"I walked without crutches from my bed to the dresser this morning."

"Well, look at you."

Cindy waves nonchalantly from across the pub after placing two plates of fish and chips in front of an older couple who sit side by side at their table. She doesn't come by to chat and instead retreats into the kitchen, leaving Charlotte to question whether she is still annoyed from New Year's Eve.

The festive cheer has dissolved from the restaurant. The garland and twinkle lights were stripped as soon as the calendar changed to January. Charlotte's marquee sign reads *Half-priced drinks and apps on Mondays (4 p.m. – 8 p.m.).*

"Are you ordering lunch?" Merle slides a menu in front of Charlotte.

"I will be. I'm meeting someone soon."

"Darryl?"

"Armstrong."

Merle clicks his tongue in disapproval, and Charlotte recognizes the feeling in her stomach as guilt. She realizes how this must appear and how it would look to Darryl if he were to wander into the pub while she was having lunch with Armstrong.

"It's not like that. He took something of mine, and I need it back."

As if on cue, Armstrong strolls into the pub, a smug look on his face. It is clear he believes this is their second date, and for one glorious moment, Charlotte considers tossing her drink in his face and watching the reality wash over him.

"Should we grab a table?" he asks.

They should. He might reveal more if they speak in private. She nods and collects her belongings. Armstrong swoops in with a shoulder and helps her to a seat at a table next to the front window. She angles her chair so that passersby can't identify her. If she's learned anything about Anville, it's that news travels fast and gossip even faster.

After Armstrong orders himself a pint at the bar, he retrieves her crutches, leaning them against the window near his own chair, out of her reach. He settles into his seat and lets out a satisfied sigh. "How's the foot?"

Charlotte wants to slap the smirk off his face. "This isn't a date."

Armstrong's mouth parts. He crosses his arms and leans back in his chair, his lip curling upwards. "Okay, what would you like to call it?"

"I dunno. An interrogation."

He seems to find this amusing and leans in, his forearms resting on the table. "Can I see your badge, miss?"

Charlotte scoffs.

"What exactly am I being interrogated about? You're the one who's been ignoring my texts. I'm starting to think you're playing me."

"Something went missing from my house. The day you dropped that package of cookies off."

He leans forward, resting his forearms on the table. "And you're accusing me of taking it? What was it, your sanity?"

She takes a deep breath to settle her nerves. "You seem to be an expert at lock picking."

He raises an eyebrow.

"Did you break into my house?" she asks.

"I'm not Darryl. Have you checked with him? Or are you not dating anymore, either?"

This was a bad idea. She kicks her foot against the leg of her chair, forgetting for a moment about her injury. An ache shoots up her ankle, and she winces. She isn't sure what she expected to happen when she questioned him. Perhaps she thought she'd be able to read his expressions. Instead, she's contacted a man she has been trying to cut off. And now, she can't decipher the deadpan look on his face.

"Thanks for the waste of time," he says, rising from his chair. He takes a prolonged swig of his beer, his Adam's apple bouncing with each swallow. "Maybe you should file a police report." Then, he struts toward the exit, laughing to himself.

"It was Lark's diary," she calls out, her eyes focused on his empty seat. She waits until he returns to his chair, his head cocked to the side.

"Not something of yours, then."

"Did you take it?"

Armstrong fiddles with his empty pint glass. "Why would I want Lark's diary?"

"You tell me."

"I haven't been inside your house since the night you called the cops, and I was there for two seconds. With you."

225

"What's in the diary that's so important to you?" The adrenaline courses through her, urging her to find answers even if it puts her at risk.

"I should ask you the same thing." He sidesteps the question. She suspects he's been reading through it since he took it from her house, scouring its contents for anything that incriminates him. Maybe he's already destroyed it.

Blood rushes to her cheeks. She is warm in her sweater, and she tugs at the neckline to allow air in. "I saw you that night, you know."

Armstrong draws his eyebrows together.

"Poking around the dumpster. That's what you were looking for, right?"

"I really think you're losing it. Maybe you're spending too much time with the village crazy. Or reading a dead girl's diary."

Charlotte's eyes follow the amber liquid that soars from her glass to Armstrong's face. The cider streams down his nose and chin onto his button-up. She slams the glass onto the table with a thud, and the pub grows quiet. Armstrong wipes his eyes with the back of his hand and rises, abruptly pushing his chair back.

"You, bitch." He closes the gap, leaving an inch between them.

Merle swoops in, grabbing Armstrong by the shoulder. "Let's simmer down."

Armstrong shoots his hands above his head. "I didn't do anything. I'm leaving."

Charlotte places her hands beneath her thighs to hide their shaking. Merle says something to her she doesn't register. When the forgotten Christmas bell at the exit elicits a chime, Charlotte turns in her chair to confirm Armstrong's departure. He spins around and meets her eyes, and he laughs as though they're two friends who have just enjoyed a harmless catch-up.

"You know something funny? You've always reminded me of her."

———————— · ✦ · ————————

Still shaken from her encounter with Armstrong, Charlotte remains at the pub until the lunch rush subsides, picking at fries that Merle declared "on the house." Her seat is now angled towards the window to avoid making eye contact with the other patrons who witnessed the altercation. She was hoping Cindy might come by with a crustless club sandwich and the wholesome smile she hasn't worn in a few days.

"Let me drive you home," Merle says as he clears her plate.

Charlotte shuffles in her seat. The walk home is far from appealing, but she is tired of someone always coming to her aid. This is the first time she has lived away from her parents, and she's practically replaced her dad with Merle.

"Please. I wouldn't feel right after," he begins, gesturing to the exit as if Armstrong is still outside, skulking, "whatever that was."

Charlotte fishes in her wallet for a twenty-dollar bill. She places it on the table before Merle can stop her. "Fine, but you're taking this and don't you dare try to sneak it back to me."

He laughs and stuffs it into his back pocket. Merle helps her to the back door where his car is parked, pausing briefly at the office to fill Cindy in. Charlotte hovers by the door, pretending not to listen to their conversation.

"How long are you gonna be?" Cindy asks, her voice void of animation.

"Fifteen minutes? She can't walk; it's the least I can do."

"Mmm. Pick up paper towels on your way back. The order hasn't come yet." She walks through the door, nearly bumping into Charlotte.

"Sorry, Cindy," Charlotte says, shuffling to the side. "I'm in the way."

Cindy shakes her head and offers a slight smile. "No, you're not." She rubs Charlotte's forearm and then continues toward the bar. Charlotte relaxes into her stance.

"All right, let's do this," Merle says, holding open the door that leads to the staff parking.

The temperature has dropped, transforming wet slush into a layer of slick ice. Guided by Merle, Charlotte takes careful steps to his burgundy sedan. She is thankful for his offer, as walking the entire way home would have likely resulted in another fall.

Merle keeps his car tidy but there is a hint of cigarette smoke that Charlotte hadn't noticed on him before. He turns off the sports radio and increases the heat before pulling out onto the street.

"I gather Armstrong wouldn't give you back the thing?" Merle keeps his eyes on the road.

"He said he never took it."

"But you don't believe him." He shoots Charlotte a glance.

"I think he's full of shit."

Merle anticipates the stop sign a couple of hundred feet ahead, slowing to a controlled stop.

"Thanks for driving carefully. I hate winter driving," Charlotte says, gripping her crutches tightly.

"I've got precious cargo." He laughs. "What did he take, if you don't mind me asking? If it's money, I'm sure we can spot you."

"That's very kind, but it wasn't money. It wasn't even mine," she says, glancing out her side window.

"Huh." Merle makes the right-hand turn onto her street. "Something of the Peters, then?"

She nods but doesn't offer more. She watches Merle, his brows pinched together, and she wonders whether he knew that Lark had kept a diary. She wonders how close they were and if Lark ever confided in him.

"Here we are. Let me help you inside."

Merle doesn't press the matter, and although Charlotte appreciates that, something compels her to reveal more. Merle has a quality about him that puts her at ease—friendly but not boisterous. Curious but never meddling. He is a good listener and asks thoughtful questions. He's likely accustomed to drunken confessions from the locals who frequent his pub. She suspects he knows a lot of the town's secrets.

"It was something of Lark's. With sentimental value," she says as they climb the icy steps to her porch.

"Ah, not something that can be easily replaced, then."

"Exactly."

Inside, Merle offers his arm for Charlotte to hold onto as she shrugs off her coat. He carries her purse to the kitchen stool and comments on the progress made since he last stepped foot in the house to drop off Tux after Charlotte's stay at the inn. Charlotte scans the main level. The contractors have left for the day. She knew it was going to be an early clock out because they needed to wait for the spackle to dry.

"Can I help you with anything before I head out?" Merle asks. He hovers in the entryway, swaying from side to side. "Help you get settled?"

"No, I'm good," Charlotte says. Although she knows she won't feel safe in the lonely house, Merle needs to get back to the pub before he gets in more trouble with Cindy.

When Merle retreats, she advances to lock the door. Through the frosted window, she makes out his distorted frame on the porch. He checks his watch and then turns back toward the door and picks up the bag of salt that leans under the window ledge. He shakes some salt onto the icy steps. Then, he salutes her through the window and proceeds to his car.

Charlotte weaves her way through the living room. It's hardly inviting with its carpenter paper covering the floor and the sheet on the couch. At least Marius and the crew cleaned up their tools.

Home sweet home.

A journal sitting atop the kitchen counter catches Charlotte's eye. She staggers to the kitchen as quickly as her crutches allow and runs her hand over the familiar smooth black covering, pausing at the embossing of Lark's nickname. A piece of paper protrudes like a bookmark, prompting Charlotte to open the marked page.

Thought you might find this of interest.

She flips the note over, but the underside is blank. It is unclear who left it. She tosses the paper aside and scans the date at the top of the page. It is one of Lark's diary entries Charlotte has yet to read.

Chapter Forty-Two

LARK

February 14, 2006

Roses are red, violets are blue. Today was fucked.

When you're an outsider, Valentine's Day can draw attention to that fact in the worst ways. At Anville High, you don't want to be the only person who doesn't get a carnation or candy gram delivered to your desk during homeroom. It's obvious you're a loser when every student sits at their desk chewing hot lips and red licorice—and you, your pen cap. But there's something far worse, which I experienced today. I'm not even sure I know how to process it, so maybe writing about it will help.

Candy grams are platonic. They're meant to be sent to your friends. Students come home with more candy on Valentine's than Halloween because of this. Was I hoping to get a few candy grams this year? Sure, it would have been nice to have a snack for fifth period, but Dani didn't bother sending me one like she did last year, and she is the only one who would have. It's okay, I'm not heartbroken over it.

As for carnations, they are reserved for long-term relationships or secret crushes. I couldn't care less about getting one. In fact, I'd rather not have the attention, which is why it was unnerving to find not one but two placed on my desk this morning. Deep down, I knew who the one was from even though there wasn't a name. He still isn't getting the hint. His message typed on the same red cardstock as everyone else's was unapologetic: *I'll be here waiting until you're ready.* At first, I had assumed the other was from him too and would be accompanied by an equally creepy message. But no, it wasn't from him.

It was from you.

Why did you choose a carnation instead of the candy? I tried to stuff the flower with its sickening, almost artificial smell in my bag. My plan was to throw it in the garbage between classes before anyone snuck a peek. But since Brittany is on the Student Council and the Social Committee, she had seen the note before it was placed on my desk. Hell, she was probably the one who typed up the greetings from the order forms. She told half the school before lunch.

Please tell me this is some kind of prank. Because if it's not, and this is your horrible attempt to cheer me up, you failed miserably. What's worse than getting a Valentine from a stalker? A coded message from your brother.

And now, I'm just waiting for you to get home so I can punch you. Then, ask you what the hell you were thinking when you wrote that message. So, you can tell me it wasn't you. That Brittany did it as a mean joke. But you're never home anymore. You've left me to fend for myself every night Mom is out.

Maybe it's also time that I share my confession with you.

I'm eating Swizzels' Love Hearts, acting like they're the magic eight-ball of advice. *Dream on* the powdered candy tells me. The candy is probably right.

Chapter Forty-Three

CHARLOTTE

Pub fries and cider churn in Charlotte's stomach as she repeats Lark's accusation in her mind. Charlotte recognizes this feeling. The sinking in her gut, like she's lost her footing. It's betrayal, she thinks. Now, the thought of Darryl makes her want to scream, an oscillation from last night when they fell asleep holding each other. She shakes off the thought, not wanting to revisit their connection. How could she be so naïve? How could she think she was capable of having a functional relationship for once? She gave all of herself to him, only to discover she doesn't know him at all. Who *is* Darryl Peters?

She dissects Lark's entry another time, seeking a different interpretation. What was the coded message that he left her? Was this the first time he had said or done something off-putting? Charlotte grasps the front and back cover in either hand and shakes out the pages, willing a red card to fall onto the counter so she can be the judge of the message's meaning.

But nothing. Lark probably shredded it.

She thinks back to the gathering at Leslie's. The women had mentioned Lark and Darryl were strange. Had they suspected something incestuous between the two? Charlotte flips to the next page in the diary. An obscene message in red ink covers most of the page, the words so enraged they almost tore through the paper. *Fuck everyone at Anville High and their mother.* She leafs through a few blank pages where the imprint of the message can still be felt until she encounters a more subdued entry, dated a couple of weeks later in blue. She reads the entry mentioning a bad mark on a biology test. The next entry details how she overheard her mother and Jake having sex. The third describes Dani's cold behaviour, ignoring Lark during gym class. None reveal the result of a confrontation with Darryl. Or Lark's confession. None mentions the carnation and coded message.

A gust of wind shakes the house's foundation and rattles the storm door at the back of the house. Charlotte rubs her arms, her fingers grazing the goosebumps that have formed. She consults the back door. Not only is the main door unlocked, but it is ajar. She closes the door tight and secures the lock.

Did the contractors leave the door open by accident? A few of the guys take smoke breaks out back. Did they find the diary in the attic and write the note for Charlotte? She reads the note aloud in a light tone—*thought you might find this of interest.* She imagines them placing the torn piece of paper in the diary at random, leaving it on the counter for her. It's possible. But something tells her that the person who left it knew exactly what they were doing; they marked this entry specifically to warn her of Darryl. Armstrong would have had time to stop by after lunch. Or perhaps Merle slipped it on the counter when he placed her purse on the stool. She launches the door camera app but there aren't any notifications aside from her and Merle, and the contractors' departure.

Charlotte returns to the back of the house, peering out the laundry room window. There are a few footprints out back, but none that lead to the driveway or the forest that borders the backyard. The oak tree's branches waver, making it look like a creature panting. Charlotte swallows. Lark's proclamation lies somewhere on the trunk of that tree. She had written about it in an earlier entry. Charlotte was so distracted with her own life—with Darryl—these past few days that she had forgotten about it. Etched in the oak's trunk should be Lark's initials and the initials of someone else, someone she was afraid to admit she had feelings for.

Charlotte retrieves her parka, zipping it up to the neck. Once her boots are on, she positions her crutches under her armpits, and with the diary still in hand, she methodically journeys to the back door. The path to the tree is unmarked. A blanket of snow stretches across the half-acre. Standing on the stoop, she guides one crutch into the snow and then removes it, marking the depth. There is at least a foot of snow waiting to swallow her feet.

Charlotte trudges through the snow, taking breaks to ease the tension in her arms and hands. In the distance, she spots a snow squall, concealing the treeline. The oak tree isn't far. She hustles, increasing her pace and extending her crutches farther ahead of her with each movement. By the time she arrives at the tree, her lungs burn, and she can taste iron in her throat.

With its bulky trunk, the tree offers solace from the wind. Charlotte scans the front of the tree for markings but doesn't discover any. Knowing Lark, and the fact that her confession was perceivably forbidden,

Charlotte makes her way to the back of the tree. It isn't until she crouches low, allowing her knees to rest on the snow, that she spots the initials. She bows her head, resting against the rippled bark.

Chapter Forty-Four

CHARLOTTE

When Charlotte spots the initials etched into the bark, the wind grows louder, the snow colder, and the sky three shades darker.

$$L + D$$

But, suddenly, it doesn't matter anymore. Darryl doesn't matter anymore. Charlotte feels cursed. She whips the diary across the backyard, and it lands with a thump, sinking into the snow. Her mind summons her three best friends, and she punches and claws at the tree as if that will bring them back. Her cries are masked by the howling wind, which whistles in her ears, taunting her. She sucks in a deep breath and holds onto it for a moment. She thinks about what would happen if she never let it out, preventing her from accepting more air into her lungs. When it feels like her eyes are bugging out and her head grows heavy, she falls into the snow, expelling her breath. Charlotte lies defeated, feeling more alone than she ever has. She crawls back inside on her hands and knees, deserting her crutches beneath the oak tree, which now solely represents death and decay.

It isn't until she is back inside with a bottle of cabernet sauvignon, her toes thawing within the confines of her slippers, and her hands bandaged that she thinks more about the letter *D* and its significance to Lark. There are two people in Lark's diary whose names begin with D. A brother and a best friend. Darryl and Dani. No matter the outcome, Charlotte is done with Darryl. Things were so much simpler on her own.

She pulls the duvet over her head and turns toward the wall, settling in the fetal position.

Her chest constricts like someone is pushing on it, bidding her sternum to snap. Even after practicing her breathing exercises, her lungs burn as though she has run a marathon.

She slides her hand under her pillow, feeling for her cell phone. Darryl sent two text messages since she returned from the pub.

What did you get up to today?

Wanna hang tonight?

She taps his name on the screen and navigates to the info option. *Block this Caller* stares back at her in red. Her finger hovers above the icon as she considers there are always two sides to every story. She throws her head back. This town has been nothing but trouble since she arrived. She taps the red button and closes her eyes and the world out.

———— ·✦· ————

Charlotte's parents call her immediately the next morning when they receive her text asking if she can stay at the house in Toronto for the week.

"You don't want to do a video call?" Sheryl asks when Charlotte declines the FaceTime and calls them back with audio only.

Charlotte hasn't moved from her bed since she fell asleep last night. The empty wine bottle sits on her nightstand, her attempt to numb the pain. Her eyes, finally dry, pulse from the stress and aggravation of crying and too much drinking. Their redness and puffiness would surely raise concern from her parents.

"I hurt my ankle. I think it's a sprain. I just want to see my doctor." Charlotte's words come through muffled as she lays on her side, the phone resting nearby on speaker.

"Char, baby, are you okay? Do you want us to come home?" Sheryl's voice strains as if she is holding back tears.

Part of her wants to scream *yes*. She misses her dad's jokes and the way he emphasizes the punchline. She longs for her mother's calloused hands as she rubs Charlotte's back. But this is the first time in a long time they've thought of themselves first, and Charlotte can't bring herself to interfere with that.

"No, I just want to stay at your place for a bit while I get it checked. Can I?"

"Of course, you can. Right, Jared?"

"No problem. I'll call the realtor today to see when the next viewing is scheduled for. How long do you need to stay?" he asks as if Charlotte has any intention of returning to the hell hole on Elizabeth Drive.

"Indefinite." She turns onto her back, staring up at the popcorn ceiling. "Can you just leave it open-ended until I see a doctor?"

The silence on the other end of the line allows Charlotte to imagine her parents. She pictures them exchanging worried glances, perhaps writing messages back and forth on a notepad about her well-being and how seriously they should take this.

"Okay, Char, honey," her mother breaks the silence. "We're going to order you a car to take you to our place tomorrow."

Tomorrow. It feels eons away.

"Pack what you need for the week, and we'll talk once you're home. Why don't we say ten tomorrow morning?"

Charlotte nods, briefly forgetting that they can't see her. "Yeah, that works."

"Do you want us to connect with Marius?"

She nods again. "Yes, please."

When Charlotte disconnects the call, she pulls herself to a seated position. Her head throbs from the wine, and her stomach free-falls when she thinks of Darryl. It's a good thing she's getting out of Anville. It's only a matter of time before he stops by. She also doesn't know who planted the diary and who stole it in the first place. If someone has access to the house even after the locks were changed, she's not safe here.

One more day, then she'll put this town and everyone in it, behind her.

Tux pushes the door open and trots toward the bed.

Well, *almost* everyone.

Chapter Forty-Five

CHARLOTTE

Charlotte brushes the empty side of the bed, searching for Darryl in a momentary memory lapse. The doorbell rings, and the nightmare rushes back. She allows her eyes to adjust to the dark room. What time is it? The sun has set, but some light remains. She must have been napping for a while. She feels for her phone, then launches the door camera app. Darryl appears in night vision, his eyes glowing white. She wonders how long he has been there, skulking on her porch. He'll leave eventually. She could be out running errands. She checks the time. She could be picking up dinner.

Charlotte holds her breath when Darryl rings the doorbell again. How many messages from him has her phone blocked? It's been thirty-six hours since she last texted him. She buries her head in the pillow. *Please go away. Don't make this worse than it is.* Silence. The camera app confirms he has left the porch. Slowly, Charlotte rises from the bed and uses its frame to guide her to the window. She peers outside and spots Darryl's truck in the driveway. Ducking, she finds her way back to the bed and listens intently for his truck's engine to purr.

The room grows darker as Charlotte passes the moments, barely uttering a breath, but a pounding disturbs the stillness. Darryl bangs on the back door with force.

"Charlotte? Are you in there?" His voice is sharp with concern, and the sound thrusts her back to the night at Merle's pub when he begged to be let in. Charlotte sensed a darkness in Darryl that night, a desperation. Something animal. What changed to make her question her gut feeling? What made her suppress those thoughts and welcome him into her home and life?

Never again.

Charlotte scans the room for her crutches. Then she remembers she discarded them by the oak tree in her fury. She hasn't left her room since she returned last night. Using the furniture as an aid, she staggers across the room and into the hall. With only the moonlight as a guide, Charlotte feels her way to the washroom for an unobstructed view of the back door.

Darryl peers through the window with cupped hands. With each bang on the door, Charlotte shudders. Her eyes focus on something leaning against the red brick of the house. A steel rod? No, Darryl holds her crutches captive. She watches as he paces the width of the house, his phone pressed to his ear. He might be calling her again, but her phone would block it. She realizes how this must look to him. Like he's stumbled upon a crime scene. Her crutches deserted in the snow. No answer on her phone or at the house. He might think that she's been attacked. Kidnapped. He knows she can't get far on her own without the crutches.

She follows the movement of his mouth, guessing the words he utters. Whoever he called is now on the line, and they engage in animated conversation, Darryl's hands accentuating his speech. Charlotte inches the window open and presses her ear to the screen. Her warm breath escapes her mouth, mingling with the cold air outside.

"Merle, I'm telling you, something's happened to her. I don't know where she is. I found her crutches in the backyard."

She wishes she was at her parents' house. Curled up on the sofa, Tux by her side. If Darryl orders a search party, she'd rather not be here when the entire town arrives.

"What happened with Armstrong? When was this?" Darryl kicks the screen door, and the reverberation startles Charlotte.

"Does he still live above Mac's convenience?" He disappears around the side of the house, Charlotte's crutches tucked under his right arm, and Charlotte can no longer hear the phone conversation. Before she reaches her bedroom window, Darryl's truck roars to life.

Charlotte's chest tightens at the possibility of Darryl confronting Armstrong, but she can't suppress the niggling feeling that it could be Darryl who is dangerous. What if something happened between him and Lark? What if he needed to keep her quiet?

Charlotte won't be able to wait until tomorrow for the black car service her parents ordered. Soon, half the town could be dragged into this mess. It wouldn't surprise her if Merle showed up to check on her after Darryl's plea. Or if Leslie brought her cribbage club over to confirm the rumours from the salon. Charlotte orders a car on her ride-share app and throws a few items into an overnight bag.

It's a fight getting Tux into her carrier, especially with Charlotte's ankle at a disadvantage. Finally, she succeeds, enticing Tux with a toy that resembles a mouse. "I promise you'll like it in Toronto. Lots to look at from the living room window."

Charlotte huffs when the driver cancels, but she orders a new car—fifteen minutes away this time. As she bum-shuffles down the stairs with the carrier and overnight bag on either side of her, Tux moans with each step they descend.

"Sorry, girl. Almost there."

Halfway down, a noise from outside paralyzes Charlotte. A car door slams. She consults her app, but the driver is dropping off a nearby ride, still five minutes away. If anyone is here, she hopes it's Merle. She can provide some sort of explanation for ignoring Darryl and the reason for her hasty exit. Merle can help her to the car, given it might be a challenge to bum shuffle down the driveway.

"I should have known it would be you causing shit." A familiar laugh punctuates the insult. Armstrong. But who is he talking to? Didn't Darryl leave to confront him?

"What did you do to her?" Darryl calls.

Charlotte launches the camera app and spots Darryl on the porch, still holding her crutches. Armstrong and Officer Landry approach and Charlotte increases the volume on her app.

"We got a call from a resident informing us of an unhinged man terrorizing the neighbourhood," Landry says.

"You should ask your partner about terrorizing. He attacked Charlotte yesterday at Merle's. And now she's missing. Won't answer her phone or the door."

Landry closes the gap. "Darryl, why is it always you causing trouble in this town? Ms. Boyd is either not home or uninterested in speaking with you."

"Without her crutches? That makes zero sense."

Landry climbs the steps and then makes himself known. He raps on the door. "Ms. Boyd, it's the Anville Police Department. Officer Landry here."

Charlotte remains where she is on the stairs, trying to appear small. Can he see her through the frosted glass? Is it against the law to ignore a police officer if they call on you? She feels utterly helpless, trapped in the house, with a group of men she doesn't trust just outside.

Landry backs up from the door. "Looks like she's not here. Go home, Darryl. Sleep it off."

"This is bullshit. You idiots investigate the wrong shit all the time."

Landry closes the gap between him and Darryl. "Take a walk, or I'll have to bring you in for disorderly conduct."

"Why didn't you ever question him?" Darryl's body sways from side to side as if he's winding himself up to gain courage. "Armstrong. I know he did something to Lark. And now, Charlotte."

Armstrong laughs. "Prove it."

Darryl lunges at Armstrong, pinning him against the brick.

Landry is quick to intervene, pulling Darryl off. "That's it. You're under arrest for assaulting an on-duty officer."

Armstrong spits in Darryl's face, which compels Darryl to pounce again.

"That's enough, Kyle." Landry twists Darryl's arms behind him, securing them in cuffs. "I'm taking you down to the station. If you're really worried about Charlotte, you can file a missing person's report."

The men retreat from the porch and Charlotte relaxes her shoulders until her phone elicits a chime. *Your driver is arriving.* Charlotte's eyes remain glued to the camera app. The men are halfway down the driveway when a sedan pulls up on the side of the road.

Charlotte opens the chat function to type a message to her driver. Her fingers move quickly. *Be out in five!* But it's too late. A middle-aged woman, bundled in a hat and scarf, opens the door and steps halfway out of the car. Charlotte can't hear the woman, but she suspects she is asking something like, "Uber for Charlotte?"

Darryl looks toward the house. This is it. Her cover is blown. He'll realize she is inside, avoiding him. If she stays where she is, the driver will cancel, and Charlotte will miss her chance to escape. Who knows when the next Uber would arrive, and she refuses to spend another moment in this town. She finishes descending the stairs, rises and stumbles toward the door. Her crutches are leaning outside against the brick where Darryl left them before his wrists were bound. She opens the screen door and makes eye contact with the woman. "Uber? I'm Charlotte. Do you mind giving me a hand?" The woman obliges, pushing past the group of men who stand dumbfounded on the driveway.

Armstrong howls. "Oh my God, this is something special. She'd rather fake her own kidnapping than see you, Peters."

The woman carries the cat carrier and bag out of the house, and Charlotte retrieves her crutches. As she walks, she keeps her focus on the ground in front of her, trailing the woman to the car. When she nears the cruiser, she speeds up her movements.

"Charlotte, are you okay? What's going on?" Darryl asks. She can't bear to meet his eyes. She continues toward the car, and once the woman helps her into the back seat, Charlotte watches as Landry guides a hand-cuffed Darryl into the cruiser.

Charlotte's driver fastens her seatbelt and lowers the volume of the radio. "There's a water bottle in your cup holder. Let me know if there's a station you want to listen to."

Charlotte nods and then eyes the police cruiser in front of them. Darryl turns in his seat, staring at Charlotte through the rear window. His expressionless eyes indicate he has accepted defeat.

Chapter Forty-Six

CHARLOTTE

```
To-Do:
 -Grocery shopping
 -Doctor's appointment
 -Call Merle
 -Ankle exercises
 -Be kind to yourself
```

Charlotte has had a productive morning at her parents' following three restful sleeps in their California king. The fridge is now stocked with the delicacies the Anville Food Mart fell short of—Udon noodles, Matzah balls, olives stuffed with garlic. She placed the grocery order online with a few clicks of her phone when she first arrived, a service not offered in the small winery town she fled.

She relaxes into the seat of the bay window, Tux basking in the sunlight beside her. Her chest feels light, and she can breathe deeply without pain. A takeout coffee cup warms her hands, and she presses its spout to her lips, sipping the mango chai latte, a flavour she hasn't tasted in weeks. She splurged for the large, treating herself after her doctor's visit, where she was fitted for new crutches that don't chafe her armpits or make her feel like she is pole vaulting with every step. In another week, she should be able to walk short distances, especially with the inconspicuous ankle brace her doctor recommended.

When the coffee cup lightens, Charlotte decides it is time for the next to-do item. She owes Merle a call. He and Cindy treated her well when she was in Anville, and an explanation is warranted after Darryl's panicked call to him. If she rings Merle now, the pub should be open but not in the throes of the lunch rush. She powers on her phone for the first time in three days and her stomach lurches at the possibility of missed calls and messages. At least she knows there won't be anything from a certain blocked number. A few text messages flood the screen. She reads one from her mother first:

I think a bit of a technology cleanse makes sense! Call us if you need us but take some time for you. Don't worry about the renos!

Next, Charlotte taps on a message from Dani:

Hey! I just wanted to reach out to see how you are. I heard you left town, and I feel bad we never got to say goodbye properly. I'd love to meet for a drink. We could meet in the middle?

The news of her departure is making its way around Anville. She wonders if Leslie gave the play-by-play of the driveway showdown to her cribbage club. Charlotte navigates to her contact list, scrolling to *M*. The phone rings only once before Merle answers.

"Charlotte? Please tell me you're okay?"

"I'm okay. I'm sorry for the scare the other day."

"Where are you? Are you safe?"

Charlotte explains her whereabouts, omitting the intimate details of her and Darryl's falling out and settling for a vague excuse about her need to visit her doctor. When the answer doesn't seem to convince Merle, she explains she craved a break from Anville.

"Anville or its residents?"

Charlotte sighs. "Maybe one or two in particular."

Merle breathes heavily. "He's not doing so well."

"Darryl?" Charlotte swallows, anticipating his response.

"I know it's not your problem. Whatever happened between you two is your business. I just thought you should know. I'm worried. I think he's drinking again."

"I'm sorry to hear that."

"Sorry for bringing it up. I'm glad you're okay. You know you always have a place to stay if you need it."

Cindy murmurs something in the background that Charlotte can't decipher.

"I should get going; we're hosting our first trivia night. Hey, let me try one on you. What 1973 movie starred a young Tatum O'Neal alongside her father?"

"*Paper Moon*," Charlotte announces the film title before she even thinks. The movie is her mother's favourite.

"Ah, look at you. You should come to the next one."

A tug pulls at Charlotte's chest, a tinge of homesickness despite staying at her parents' house. If her mother were here, they'd put on one of the films Sheryl grew up with and crack open a hard lemonade. All her troubles seem fixable when she watches her mother mouthing the lines from a familiar flick.

Merle thanks her for the call, and then it disconnects before Charlotte can utter goodbye. Based on this conversation, she doesn't believe it was Merle who marked the Valentine's diary entry. He's always been Team Darryl since she first expressed her concerns about him squatting in the garage.

Charlotte swipes through the notifications on her social platforms, and her breath catches in her throat when she discovers a direct message from @DrummerDarryl, which landed in her inbox at two in the morning.

Hopefully, this finds its way to you—I'm not sure if you even go on here. I barely remembered my password. I think you might have blocked my number. I don't know, maybe I'm reading into it, but my calls go straight to voicemail, and it doesn't look like my messages are being delivered.

Fuck, I feel like I'm losing my mind. Did I misread everything? I keep replaying our last night together, trying to figure out where I fucked up. I'm not dumb. I know you are a million times better than me. I'm batting way above my league here. But I thought we had something, and it felt like you did too. So, I guess I'm just wondering what changed. If things are moving too fast or intense, we can take a beat. I get it, we went from zero to 100 in a couple of weeks. I just dig being around you, and I haven't felt this alive in a very long time.

Did Armstrong say something? I hope you'd tell me if he did. Why'd you meet up with him anyway? Merle said he grabbed you. I wish I had been there. Though I probably would have killed him. I get why you left if you're scared of him. But you can trust me, Char. You never have to step foot in Anville again. I'll come to you.

Please call me. I'm a mess.

Charlotte wipes a tear away with the back of her hand. She is being pulled in competing directions, her heart wanting to give in, to seek an explanation from the man she might have been falling in love with.

But no, she needs to protect herself. She allowed herself to get too close to Darryl. She can't make that mistake again. Charlotte closes the app and powers off her phone. Perhaps she needs a few more days offline.

Shaking her shoulders, she considers the next item on the to-do list. She hobbles toward the couch, slinging a green elastic band over her shoulder. As she lies down, she stretches the band around her flexed foot. She points her toe and flexes, repeating the exercise meant to strengthen her ankle ligaments. The routine resembles ballet training for primary students just beginning to learn the technique of pointing their toes. "Good toe, naughty toe," her teacher used to say. She imagines Lark as a young girl, her dark hair pulled into French braids, wearing a pink leotard and tights that sag around the ankles. She imagines Lark as a teenager, performing a solo, backlit, her silhouette centre stage.

Three days without her phone and without the diary have been good for Charlotte. Her mind has felt clearer and her body healthier. There are fewer reminders of the Peters now that she is no longer within the confines of their childhood home, convinced every creak is Lark trying to communicate from the afterlife. Charlotte doesn't want to lose progress, but if she doesn't uncover the truth, then she's failing that little girl with the French braids.

Chapter Forty-Seven

CHARLOTTE

Meet in the middle. That's what Dani had suggested in her text. Charlotte chose a kitschy boardgame café, an hour's commute for both, and now she waits in a pastel-pink booth with a glass of rosé and Jenga.

Dani arrives twenty minutes late, her mess of curls piled on top of her head in a bun. She wears a burgundy blanket scarf that matches her lipstick and her signature white sneakers, an extension of her body. "I'm so sorry. The QEW was a nightmare. Leafs' game tonight." She leans in for a hug, and Charlotte is immersed in the salon's coconut shampoo.

"Jenga?" Charlotte asks, gesturing to the wooden structure.

"Sure, but first, a drink."

Dani unravels her scarf as she consults the chalkboard menu by the bar. She returns with a cocktail in a copper cup. "Cheers," she says and then settles into the seat across from Charlotte. "So, how are you, really?"

"I'm fine. Why, what did you hear?"

Dani waves her hand. "I don't trust talk from the ladies at my salon."

"Oh God." Charlotte cowers. "What are they saying?"

"I heard about the police being called." She raises her brow. "Something about a love triangle?"

Charlotte rolls her eyes and removes a Jenga piece with ease. "Not exactly. And I wasn't the one who called the cops."

Dani lifts her cocktail glass, swirling the ice around. "How many of these do we have to drink before you fill me in?"

"Three?" Charlotte suggests.

Dani forgoes the straw and downs her glass in one gulp. "Drink up, then."

The two erupt in laughter, and Charlotte welcomes this change in her own temperament. The last few days have been riddled with regret, and it takes everything in Charlotte not to scream when she thinks of the Peters.

"Armstrong and I were never a thing, for the record," Charlotte says.

"Thank God for that. He's such a douche." Dani's smirk fades, and she locks eyes with Charlotte. "And Darryl?"

Charlotte shrugs, then distracts herself with another Jenga piece. The structure teeters. "That's a bit complicated."

"Darryl's a bit complicated."

Charlotte nods. Complicated, yes. She thought she could do complicated, but she's learned that Darryl is more than complicated—disturbed, perhaps. She taps at a Jenga piece and, when met with resistance, moves to another.

"Mmm, not so fast." Dani wags her finger playfully. "You have to stick with that one. Those are the rules."

"I didn't know you were such a Jenga expert." Charlotte squints as she pushes the piece through, bracing for the tower to collapse. The block lands on the table with a clink, and by some miracle, the structure remains intact.

"See? That wasn't so bad. How's the ankle, by the way?"

"I'm down to one crutch." Charlotte gestures to the lone support that leans against the window like a third wheel next to a silver Christmas tree yet to be taken down. "But I think in another week, I'll be off it."

"Can I grab your second drink? And yes, I'm keeping tabs."

"Sure. Whatever you're having."

"This was delicious." Dani rises from the booth and saunters over to the bar with their empty glasses.

Charlotte scratches at the pastel paint of the table, exposing white primer beneath. She came here to find answers, but she can admit that she enjoys Dani's company. It's been a while since she allowed herself to let loose and it's comforting to know they are far enough from Anville that the odds of running into Armstrong or Darryl are unlikely.

Dani returns with their cocktails, sliding Charlotte's toward her. "For what it's worth, Darryl is one of the good ones. He's always been like a big brother to me. It's just—he's been through a lot."

Haven't we all? Charlotte thinks. She takes a sip of the citrus drink, preparing for the change in subject. "What about you? Dating anyone in Anville?" She rubs at the film of egg-white froth that covers her upper lip.

"No, I avoid Anville for pleasure," Dani says, tapping a block with her nail.

"Anville's all business for you, eh?"

Dani slides the wooden piece out with precision. "It's just sort of weird when you've grown up with everyone your age. There's too much history."

Dani and Lark's history is exactly what Charlotte is interested in. She plays her turn and then tilts her head to the side. "Any high school exes still roaming around town? Don't tell me you dated Armstrong."

Dani's eyes widen. "God, no. He couldn't be further from my type."

"You're not into blonde jocks then."

Dani frees a block from the middle, and the tower clamours to the table. "Damn." She rises. "I'm not into guys. New game?"

Charlotte nods, impressed with Dani's candour. She watches as Dani makes her way to a shelf to peruse the board games, and Charlotte busies herself by cleaning up the wooden pieces strewn across the table. She understands what Lark saw in Dani—her verve is almost contagious—and considers how, in another life, the three of them could have been friends. Dani returns with a duplicitous smile, holding a retro Snakes and Ladders game, the box dilapidated from overuse.

They finish a round of the classic board game and their second set of drinks, chatting effortlessly about their taste in music, first part-time jobs, and secret party tricks, prompting Dani to juggle items from her knapsack. Dani once again visits the bar on their behalf and returns with two orange concoctions cluttered with every imaginable garnish. "Don't ask. Bartender's choice."

"Drink number three," Charlotte says, pouting.

"Spill it."

Charlotte takes an elongated sip, delaying the inevitable. The orange is sickening, like the syrup drink served at community barbecues. She shakes out her shoulders and stretches her triceps like she's been challenged to an arm wrestle. Dani laughs, which is enough to ease Charlotte's discomfort.

"I heard a rumour. A pretty sick one. And I'm not sure what to believe."

Dani pops a syrup-soaked cherry into her mouth. "Anville loves its gossip."

"And it might just be gossip, but if it's true, then I can't see Darryl again."

Dani sucks in her cheeks. "Want to fact-check it? I don't see Darryl much anymore, but I was close with the Peters. I knew them well."

Charlotte's stomach summersaults. She is unsure of how to broach the subject. Deep down, she hopes Dani can quash the rumour, but Charlotte can't ignore what she read. It was laid out in Lark's curvy handwriting. She studies Dani's face, worrying how she might react to the accusation. The first time Charlotte mentioned Lark, Dani shut her out. Besides, she can't reveal how she learned it. If Dani discovered Charlotte was reading a diary that exposed intimate details of her and Lark's relationship, this friendship would end faster than it started.

Charlotte chews on a cherry stem, thinking back to the cribbage talk at Leslie's. While the women didn't accuse the siblings of being involved, they had said they were off. She chooses her words carefully. "I've heard from a couple of sources that Darryl and Lark were very close."

"Okay." Dani narrows her eyes, and Charlotte immediately wishes she could take it back. When Dani doesn't offer anything, Charlotte feels pressured to continue. "Like too close for a brother and sister." She averts her eyes, focusing on the peeling paint that she inadvertently carved into a heart.

Dani folds her lips into her mouth. "Who did you hear this from?"

Charlotte's cheeks flush like she's been called on by a teacher. "Some of the women at Leslie Tremblay's bake swap. And Armstrong. It's becoming a recurring theme."

Dani nods a few times, then gulps her drink. "This is disgusting," she says, placing it down. At first, Charlotte doesn't know whether she is referring to the cocktail or the gossip, but when Dani downs her glass of water, Charlotte gathers it's the orange syrup nauseating her.

Dani sighs. "I know the rumour. It started in my sophomore year." She wipes the condensation from her glass, and Charlotte leans in, giving Dani the floor.

"I wasn't out in high school. I wasn't even sure I was gay, but I had feelings for a girlfriend, and I was struggling with it."

"Lark?"

Dani shrugs. "I think the feeling might have been mutual. There were signs. But even still, I wasn't ready."

Dani continues to share her story, all the while fiddling with a red game piece from the Snakes and Ladders game they've abandoned. In the second semester of their sophomore year, Dani was concerned with how close she and Lark were becoming, so she pulled away from Lark and started hanging with another group. Dani doesn't mention Brittany and the Tangerines by name, but she admits the group she traded in Lark for weren't nice people.

"I tried to keep my distance, but I loved her. Maybe that sounds silly for sixteen-year-olds, but I really think I did."

Charlotte nods, coaxing Dani to continue, and she finally places the red piece down. "I wrote her a note. It was meant to be romantic—for-bidden love or something like that."

As Dani speaks, she traces the words on the table in front of her as though she is writing the note to Lark firsthand. "I know you're bad for me, but all I want is to be near you." She casts her eye at Charlotte, her long lashes fluttering.

"And she didn't like that?" Charlotte shifts in her seat.

Dani shakes her head. "Especially when she thought it was from her brother."

Charlotte juts out her jaw and, for a moment, she wonders if she misheard Dani. "Wait. You signed it from Darryl?"

"No. The shitty people I was hanging with did."

The realization arrives like a hurtling subway, nearly knocking Charlotte over and stealing her breath away. She brings her hands to her mouth. The Valentine was never from Darryl.

Dani explains she signed the message with 'D,' expecting Lark to identify her. When the Social Committee encountered it, they either assumed it was Darryl or thought it would make for an entertaining Friday, and so, they typed up the note on the card, attributing it to Darryl.

The rumour prompted other pranks to follow in the coming weeks. Darryl's locker was defaced with lipstick and whipped cream, complementing slander about keeping Lark's *v-card* in the family. The Peters' house was egged and paintballed, the latter requiring hydrogen peroxide to remove. One senior with an aptitude for graphic design went so far as to photoshop a "promposal" using the *Cruel Intentions* movie poster, swapping the stepbrother-stepsister duo played by Ryan Philippe and Sarah Michelle Gellar with Darryl and Lark's yearbook shots.

"It was after that sick promposal that I finally worked up the courage to admit it was me who sent the damn flower. But by that point, most of the school had made up their minds about the Peters."

Charlotte's eyes dart from Dani to the graffiti heart and back again.

"I wasn't planning on sharing all that—you probably think I was such a shit in high school."

Charlotte doesn't acknowledge Dani's comment. She mulls over everything she's learned while stabbing at the berries at the bottom of her drink with her straw, unintentionally muddling them.

"I know, it's a lot." Dani melts into the bench.

"A lot for a sixteen-year-old girl to deal with," Charlotte says. She tries to imagine Lark walking the halls amid the school-wide bullying, and for a moment, she disregards Darryl's theory about Lark's death being suspicious. Lark had the weight of the world on her shoulders in the few months leading up to her suicide.

Charlotte knows how quickly someone can slip into a place where the light is impenetrable, a place where you feel insignificant like a tiny grain of sand. Charlotte stirs her drink and realizes the ice clinking against the glass is the only sound at their table. She glances at Dani, her shoulders slumped toward themselves, her expression defeated.

"It was too much," Dani says, her voice barely audible.

Charlotte places her hand on Dani's chipped purple nail polish, the colour reminiscent of Lark's bedroom. Studying Dani's posture, it is clear the woman blames herself for Lark's death. This might be the reason Dani never left Anville. Perhaps cuffing herself to the town and its memories is self-punishment. Why should she be able to escape if Lark never could?

Dani's chin puckers like a peach pit, and she wipes her eyes and nose with her sleeve, a loose thread dangling below. She excuses herself to the washroom and puts up her hand in protest when Charlotte rises. "I just need a minute."

Charlotte collects the game pieces and drops them into the box. Her meddling may have caused Dani harm, but it also cleared up the rumour. She pulls up the direct message she received two days ago from Darryl, scanning its contents with this new knowledge.

She rapidly blinks after she reads Darryl's sign-off. He had said he was a mess. Charlotte recalls Merle's fear that he had started drinking again. She unblocks his number and then crafts a response, staring at the words she has typed. She imagines Darryl drinking brown liquor from a paper bag, as drunks do in the movies, and then pushes the image out of her mind, tapping send.

I came to the city for a break. I owe you an explanation, and I'm sorry this message has come so late. I'll explain everything when I'm back. Maybe tomorrow.

Dani returns, dragging her feet like a sullen teenager, and Charlotte realizes the night must end. Charlotte apologizes for introducing the topic of Lark. Once again, she didn't mean to pry. It had felt nice to confide in a friend. Dani offers a tight smile before wrapping the scarf around her neck. "It's not your fault."

Charlotte reaches for a hug, but Dani's body remains stiff, her arms stuck at her side. Charlotte squeezes tight until Dani finally reciprocates. She rests her chin on Charlotte's shoulder. "There's a lot I would change from that year if I could."

Charlotte's ride arrives first, and she hesitates, lingering for a moment until Dani opens the door, ushering her inside. Charlotte turns in her seat and watches Dani shrink as they pull away into the night.

She opens her message thread with Darryl and types a final thought.

P.S. I miss you.

She leaves the message suspended. Even with the rumour cleared up, Charlotte has reservations about sending it. There is still so much she doesn't know about Darryl. Jumping into this relationship goes against her cautious approach to everything in life. She can argue both sides—on one hand, this might be exactly what she needs—someone who eases her overthinking. But that constant pain in her chest is a reminder that anything can happen in a fraction of a second. Anything can be stolen.

The driver cracks his window open an inch, and the frigid air tosses a strand of Charlotte's hair that has escaped the confines of her bun. She deletes the postscript and closes the message. She leans back against the headrest, closing her eyes tight.

She's not ready to jump in.

Chapter Forty-Eight

CHARLOTTE

Charlotte refreshes the app on her phone's screen, hoping for a red alert to indicate a new message from Darryl. There has been no response since she sent her reply two nights ago. She buries her face in Tux's fur, absorbing the vibrations from the cat's purrs. She would love to remain on the sofa, Tux nestled close, but there are more than renovations requiring Charlotte's attention in Anville.

It is time she comes clean about the diary and quits playing Nancy Drew with the Peters' past. Hearing Dani speak of the horrific bullying Lark and Darryl endured in high school has provided Charlotte with a new perspective. Charlotte unties her robe, letting it fall down her shoulders, revealing her scar. She brushes the imperfection with her thumb. The blemish is the only physical reminder of the pain she felt that night she got behind the wheel.

Charlotte knows the depth of darkness a person can experience. This might be the reason she feels connected to Lark, like they belong to a secret society where the initiation involved having their hearts bludgeoned. She wraps the robe tight, securing the belt. Charlotte understands why Darryl would want to search for an answer, grasping for some meaning, but foul play seems doubtful—especially now that she knows no one planted the diary on her kitchen counter. A call with Marius earlier that morning had cleared that up in an instant. Marius admitted to leaving the diary for Charlotte after the crew had completed a survey of the attic and found it in her hiding spot.

She lies back on the couch, gazing up at the crown moulding that her mother wants to replicate in the living room in the new house. Marius is still waiting for the green light to continue the project. Until then, the house will remain empty with half-finished reno jobs in practically every room.

Hopefully, in time, Charlotte can help Darryl put the past where it belongs. Maybe she can show him he still has a future. She refreshes the screen once again, letting out an audible sigh when nothing changes. Then she navigates to her settings, confirming that she has unblocked his number.

What if there's validity to Merle's concerns about Darryl drinking again? She recalls what Darryl confided in her—that he doesn't like the person he becomes when he drinks.

She'll return to the house. The diary should be under the tree where she left it. Hopefully, the snow hasn't penetrated its binding or erased any of Lark's words.

She packs her overnight bag before cooking herself an eclectic dinner featuring the entire contents of the fridge. She won't allow her groceries to go to waste, and bringing a cooler back to Anville seems like unnecessary baggage.

She is scooping up the last bite—a gooey, fried cheese ball with an olive nestled inside—when she reads an incoming message that almost makes her choke. It's not from Darryl but rather last night's companion, Dani.

Hey, I don't want to freak you out, but I just saw a police cruiser outside your parents' house on my way to work. Are you still in the city? Is everything okay?

Charlotte swallows the olive and huffs. She's gone a few days, and Armstrong is already sniffing around. What will it be this time? More cookies? A love note and carnation like he sent to Lark? She launches the security app's real-time feed and narrows her eyes to get a better look. She is surprised to discover Officer Landry in the fisheye lens, scratching his head and rocking back and forth on his heels. He knocks on the door and shoots a glance left and right before opening it and disappearing inside. Charlotte covers her mouth with her hand and then removes it, the smell of greasy cheese nauseating. The thought of someone entering her home is more than unnerving, and this time, she's caught them in the act.

She rises from the table, abandoning her meal and, out of instinct, approaches her own front door to verify no one is outside loitering. What is Landry up to? The last time she saw him was five days ago when he threw Darryl into the back of his car and watched her leave with an overnight bag. She consults the number for the Anville Police Department, keen to find out why he has come to her house and how he got inside without a key, but a niggling feeling, like an itch she can't scratch, forces her to disconnect the call. She should wait to see if they call her. If he's there on official business, they would let her know.

Charlotte swaps her robe for a pair of sweats and cleans up the mess in the kitchen. Once Tux is secured safely in her crate, Charlotte orders a car. She sits at the bay window, resting her arm on the crate and allowing

Tux to nuzzle her cheeks into Charlotte's knuckles. As she waits to see the driver turn onto the narrow street, a dull buzzing begins in the pit of her stomach. Things were less complicated when her phone was off.

———— ·◆· ————

"A break-in?" Charlotte asks, annoyance in her question. "I don't understand. Who reported it?" The female voice on the other end of the phone is void of emotion and uses the term *ma'am* after every statement. Charlotte strums the armrest of her ride share's sedan, avoiding eye contact with the male driver whom she can sense is watching her. She lowers the volume on her phone and presses it closer to her ear while the woman at the Anville Police Department explains that they were alerted to a possible break-in at her home earlier that evening. One of the neighbours had noticed suspicious activity. *Leslie*, Charlotte gathers. Upon inspection, Officer Landry had found the front door ajar but no apparent forced entry.

"I've been out of town. I'm positive I locked the door before I left." Charlotte's voice is confident, yet she wonders if she might have forgotten to secure the lock in her hasty exit. She had Tux and her bag and, of course, the crutches.

The woman's voice rises an octave as she greets someone at the station, and then she proceeds in monotone, asking when Charlotte plans to return to her home.

"I'm actually on my way right now. Is that—wise?" Charlotte asks. If her home has been broken into, does she really want to return? The woman ignores her question, advising that Officer Landry can meet her onsite to discuss further, and Charlotte is left with a blank line as she considers what awaits her at the house.

For the rest of the drive, Charlotte sifts through the security camera footage from the day. Other than a few passersby on the sidewalk walking their dogs or out for a brisk power walk, no one approaches her home. A car pulls into the driveway in the early evening and then reverses, heading back in the other direction, but that seems to be the most eventful thing that happened all day. Nothing looks suspicious or out of the ordinary unless it happened out of the camera's view.

The driver pulls up behind Landry's cruiser and mumbles something about his sciatica acting up; he can't help her to the door. At least Charlotte has graduated to one crutch, which she is mostly using for stability. She slings her bag on her shoulder and positions the crutch under her right arm. She eases out of the car, and Landry trots over to help her with Tux's crate.

"Not the homecoming you were expecting?" he asks, guiding her to the porch.

"I don't understand what happened."

Once they are seated in the living room, mugs of coffee in hand, Landry walks Charlotte through his report. His tone is friendlier than their last encounter, which might have something to do with Darryl's absence. Landry consults his notepad and runs through the events, taking sips in between. Leslie had called around five thirty in the evening. She spotted a man dressed in dark clothing skulking around Charlotte's backyard. He wore a black toque, but Leslie wasn't close enough to see his face. He seemed young; "limber" was the word she had used.

"Young, like twenty? Thirty?" Charlotte asks.

He skims the paper. "She really couldn't say."

When Landry arrived at the scene, he noticed the front door was open an inch. Upon further inspection, he discovered the backdoor was also unlocked.

"I didn't see anything in my security footage. I have a camera at the front of the house," Charlotte says.

"But not the back?"

She shakes her head. "I haven't installed it yet."

"Is it possible you left your door unlocked when you left? Whoever was here likely knew you were out of town."

Charlotte taps her fingers on her thigh, counting the Anville residents who knew she left. Landry, Armstrong, Darryl, Merle, Dani. Though Dani also mentioned she heard about the love triangle showdown from the salon's clientele, so it could be everyone in Anville at this point.

Landry lets out a grunt as he pushes on his thighs, helping himself to a standing position. "I'll get you to look around and see if anything is missing."

The two survey the house, but nothing noteworthy stands out. The only item of real value in the home is the granite countertop waiting to be installed on the kitchen island but that weighs more than two hundred pounds, so not easily stolen. Most of Charlotte's possessions including her laptop, wallet, and phone, were with her in Toronto.

When they arrive at the front door, Charlotte leans against the banister. "Why would the front door be open if they got in through the back?"

Landry scratches at the stubble on his jaw with his knuckles. "They might have thought about exiting through the front and then noticed the camera. But I can't be sure."

"I swear this place is cursed." She slumps down to a seated position on the stairs. Now what? She should have stayed in the city. Her parents wouldn't want her to sleep here after a break-in, even if it delays the renovations and their move in the spring. A man dressed in dark clothing, wearing a toque. The description sounds similar to the person who she spotted scouring the dumpster.

"I'd offer to drive you back to Toronto—"

"No, no, I'm fine. Thank you."

"I can take you to the Angel. It's on my way to the station. If you're not comfortable staying here, maybe Merle can put you up."

Charlotte squeezes her eyes tight. Her head throbs with a steady pulse like the ticking of a clock. The last thing she wants to do is inconvenience Merle and Cindy, but staying in this house after a break-in is like tempting fate. She opens her eyes, allowing them to focus on Landry, who stands by the door, fumbling in his jacket pocket for his lighter.

"Pack what you need. I'll hang on the porch," he says before pushing open the screen door, inviting the cold to creep inside.

She needs to offload the diary. It isn't her business anymore. The more she reads it, the more she gets tangled in its mess. She opens her message thread with Darryl, their entire history reduced to her last message since she reactivated his contact. She types her note and presses send before she can change her mind.

I'm back in Anville, and I have something that belongs to you. Meet me at the Angel in an hour?

Chapter Forty-Nine

LARK

February 24, 2006

People continue to disappoint me. Maybe I expect too much from them. It just seems the older I get, the more I'm realizing how selfish everyone is. What might seem like an act of kindness, a moment of humanity, ends up showing itself for what it truly is—a lie.

Part of me wants to hide under the covers until someone notices. But I'm starting to think that might take longer than I'd hope. I think it's easier for everyone when I'm not complicating things or "making it harder" for people.

I used to think I was a giver. I used to think that I added to the conversation, that I brought creativity and a new way of looking at things. That I was inspired. I thought I was compassionate and that I could help people when they were bummed.

But now, now I realize I'm a taker. And I just keep taking and taking and sucking and bringing everyone's mood down.

And I'm bad for her.

That's what she wrote on the card. That I'm bad for her. This whole time I thought I was good. That I was a light. That I made her happy.

But it was me who isolated her. It was me who put a target on her back. I made her afraid. If she didn't care about me, then she could just live her life. I was the reason she was so sad that day. I made her see her true self, and she didn't like the way it looked. I'm the reason she cut deep. And I thought I was helping when I grabbed the scissors and did the same—in solidarity, or so I thought. Blood sisters, so to speak. But I made it worse because that's when she pulled away. That was the moment she thought, *Lark is bad for me. Lark's an enabler.* That was the moment she traded me in, upgrading for sunny dispositions. Girls who are too dumb to be curious about life. To question its meaning and where they fit into it.

Dani thinks that I bring her down. Dani thinks I'm bad for her.

And if she truly believes that, then what the hell is the point?

———— ◆ ————

March 2, 2006

Do you know I'm convinced the freckle on the bottom of my foot is actually permanent marker? I have this strange memory of being in the bathtub and marking it. Why I had a marker in the bath, I'm not sure, and why it hasn't washed off after all these years is also questionable, but the memory is vivid, so I have to trust it. I will die on this hill to prove I'm not crazy. To prove that my mind isn't powerful enough to conjure dreams that are more realistic, more lifelike than the memory of what I ate for breakfast this morning.

I must always believe my mind, Darryl. As soon as I don't, as soon as I let others convince me otherwise, all will be lost.

Today, Mom brought home maple syrup from a client of hers at the salon, and she dove into this story about a field trip she joined me on when I was in grade five and how it was one of her favourite field trips she volunteered at. I remember the trip and yes, she did join me, but she's rewritten the whole experience like fiction. At least, I hope she has. I hope it's her memory and not mine that is failing.

The junior students went to a conservation area to tap a tree and learn how syrup is

made. I remember most of the kids getting bored with the demonstration, myself included. A teacher had mistakenly leaked that we'd be getting maple taffy on a stick, and that was all we ten-year-olds could think about. "When do we get the taffy?" we'd whined. I don't know if Mom felt bad that none of the kids were listening to the man spouting off details about the optimal temperature for sap to flow, but her voice got all slow and babyish as she asked him question after question like what he was saying was the most interesting thing she'd heard. She even volunteered to hang the bucket off the spile.

"How do you know if the spile is in deep enough?" This man, Brad I want to say, should have known better. He should have chosen one of the kids—it was a damn school trip. Then, Mom playfully slapped his arm when he made some joke about her being the reason the sap flowed so quickly. I didn't understand the joke like the grade sixes did, but I knew it was sketchy. Or I realized it was after a few of them made comments like, "Lark's mom is really trying to get her an A in science or a lifetime supply of syrup."

But Mom remembers things differently. She kept gushing about the field trip "where we bonded." She said on the bus we had talked about Dad and his pancake routine. *Butter the pancake, cut it into squares, reconstruct it to its circular form and smother it in syrup.* She remembers dumping out the snow that had collected in my boots after trudging through the forest; she said she was happy that I let her when I could have done it myself. She told me I held her hand on the bus home, our pinkies linked. But I don't remember any of that.

Is my mind blocking out the good memories, so all that's left are the shit ones? Or is Mom feeling guilty about the times she let us down, so much so that she can't face the past and has decided to amend it?

Darryl, which one of us is losing grip on reality?

If it's me, I don't know how much longer I can go on.

Chapter Fifty

CHARLOTTE

The *Anville Guardian*'s Arts and Culture section covers the wooden tabletop at the Angel Pub. Charlotte scans a feature on the local theatre company's upcoming musical *Anne of Green Gables*, resting her forearms on the diary beneath the newspaper's creased pages, still cold from days left outside.

At nine in the evening on a Sunday, the pub is quiet. A man sits at the bar, watching the Leafs battle the Senators, and a couple shares a bottle of wine at a table in the front of the restaurant. Charlotte chose a discrete booth in the back after she had unpacked her things in the room Merle offered her for the night. Before that, she had read two final entries from Lark's diary—a ceremonial goodbye.

Darryl enters the pub, his gaze cautiously scanning the tables. A warmth swells in Charlotte's abdomen like the drink she's just sipped isn't cranberry juice but rather a glass of robust cabernet sauvignon. She dreams of reaching out to him and wrapping her arms around him. She wishes she could bury her face in the crux of his shoulder, inhaling the faint smell of weed and aftershave. She imagines planting kisses on his chest and leaving a trail of her lip gloss on his salty skin.

Instead, she waves him over. "Hey, thanks for coming. I ordered you a Sprite," she says, motioning to the glass on the other side of the table. She thought if she ordered them both non-alcoholic beverages in advance, he wouldn't consider something stronger.

He slides into the booth, his eyes cast down at the table. He doesn't touch the drink.

"How are you doing?" Charlotte asks, the question sounding too light for the occasion.

Darryl meets her eyes. His mouth is chiselled into a straight line. He looks tired, his deep-set eyes accentuated by bags the colour of a mature bruise.

"What's going on, Charlotte?" he asks, his tone simultaneously accusatory and defeated.

She chews on her lip. It's a fair question. Just days before their last encounter, they were tangled in her sheets, clinging to each other like they'd never let go. Then, she ghosted him for days until finally, last night, she responded to his emotional appeal with a couple of terse texts. It's no wonder he sits before her, leaning against the back of the booth, arms crossed like this is the last place he wants to be.

She clears her throat. "I owe you an apology. For leaving like that. It wasn't fair to you."

"It's fine. You don't owe me anything."

Charlotte reaches her hand across the table, covering the face of the actress cast as Anne.

Darryl maintains his closed-off stance. "You said you have something of mine. I'm just here to grab that."

Charlotte nods. She practiced what she had planned to say, but now, as she sits across from him, she can't recall the words. "I uh—I found something." She folds the newspaper closed and slides it to the side of the table, revealing the moleskin notebook. "It's Lark's." She pushes it toward him.

Darryl reaches for the diary. "You found it," he says, urgency in his voice. He runs his finger along the insignia. "This is actually it." He opens the book, allowing the pages to flutter. "I haven't seen this since—I looked everywhere for it. Where did you find it?"

"It was hidden in the attic." It isn't entirely a lie, given Marius and his crew did find it after *she* hid it there.

Darryl is enthralled in a page of the diary, barely acknowledging Charlotte. "The truth is in here. It has to be."

Charlotte inches forward in her seat and leans with her elbows on the table. Darryl's eyes dart frantically from page to page as he leafs through the diary. He looks like he hasn't slept in days, and she worries how the contents of these pages will weigh on him. If he's been on the verge of drinking, reading about his departed sister's internal battle will surely nudge him in that direction.

"Darryl?"

He nods but doesn't look up from the book.

"Darryl, I think you need to slow down."

Darryl focuses on something on the page, his lips parting, his eyes widening. Charlotte reaches for his hand, grazing his thumb. "Darryl, please be careful. There are some horrible, horrible things in there."

He flinches at her touch, finally acknowledging her pleas. "You read it? Why would you read it?"

Charlotte blinks. "I—I just read a few entries. I wasn't sure what it was." She shakes her head, shrinking into herself. "It was before any of this. Before I knew you."

"Before you knew me? Wait—how long have you had it?"

Charlotte sinks in her chair as Cindy approaches the table. She places two menus between the couple. "Darryl, I thought that was you. It's been a while." She takes a step back, her eyes flitting between the two customers.

Darryl's mouth softens, and he nods her way. "It's nice to see you."

"It's almost last call for the kitchen. I'll give you a minute with the menus." She takes another step backward and then moves to the couple at the front.

"What happened to these pages? Did you rip them out?" he asks, presenting a fringe of torn sheets at the end of the diary.

"What? I didn't notice that before. Let me see," she says, reaching for the book. If they are entries she's already read, then someone must have removed them recently.

He closes the diary with a thud and then tucks it into his jacket like he's worried she'll snatch it. "So, you've had this for a while and didn't think to tell me."

Charlotte's throat tightens. How can she expect him to understand? She had been afraid he would judge her for reading it. She didn't know how to return it without him knowing she had read what never belonged to her. But this is far worse. He is acting like she conspired to hide it from him.

"Even when I asked you if you'd seen it? That's fucked." He rises from the table.

"Darryl, wait. I was going to give it to you, but then someone stole it. Right from my house." She moves to his side of the booth, blocking him in. "I'm scared. Someone broke in again tonight. Whoever it is, I think they were looking for the diary. I think they know something."

He rubs his eyes with one hand while the other protects the book nestled in his jacket. "I can't do this. I need to go."

Charlotte slides out of the booth, allowing him to exit. "Darryl, I am so sorry. Please, stay. We can figure this out together."

"Maybe we could have, but not now."

Charlotte's eyes follow Darryl as he zigzags through the four-tops, finding his way to the exit at the front of the pub. She waits for him to turn back so she can sneak a final glimpse of him, but he never does. Instead, he thrusts open the door, allowing it to bang against the brick, and he escapes into the bleak January night.

Charlotte slumps into the booth. The diary is in Darryl's hands now. He will devour its pages, scouring for clues and trying to connect the dots. Maybe he'll find closure and a reason for Lark's suicide. Or maybe, just maybe, he'll unearth proof that someone else is responsible.

———— •◆• ————

"Want an upgrade?" Merle stands at the booth, his arm outstretched, offering a glass of red.

Charlotte glances at her full glass of cranberry juice and then nods, reaching for the wine.

"I'm glad you're back, kiddo. It was boring around here without you." Merle sits down opposite Charlotte in the booth.

She laughs into the oversized glass. "Oh? No sprained ankles? Tell me there was at least a bar fight."

"Nah." He shoots a glance at the only patron left and then leans in. "Just me and the Mrs. still duking it out."

It is Charlotte's turn to survey the room, searching for Cindy's whereabouts. When Charlotte doesn't spot her server, she mirrors Merle's lean. "What's going on with you two? You can fix it, right?"

Merle shrugs. "I think so."

Charlotte slides her glass toward him. "Sounds like you need this more than me."

Maxine Nightingale's "Get Right Back to Where We Started From" plays on the TV, celebrating the Leafs' victory and signalling Merle's customer to call it a night. A man pulls on his parka, zipping it up and positioning his hood so that his face barely shows through the small opening. "Night, Merle," he says as he makes his way to the exit.

"Night, Carl. Good game tonight." Merle turns back to Charlotte.

"So? What's going on?" Charlotte can't repair her own relationship, but maybe she can help Merle mend whatever has soured with Cindy.

"Cin found a stash of cigarettes in my car. I quit ten years ago."

"Shit."

"It's not like I'm back to smoking a pack a day or anything. But yeah, this isn't the first time I've slipped."

"Can you get some help?"

Merle shakes his head. "I can quit. I've done it before. It's just from time to time, when the going gets rough, I can use a smoke to take the edge off. That's all this is."

Charlotte isn't familiar with this new dynamic between her and Merle. Usually, he is the one offering her advice for whatever problem she's found herself in. She ponders what might be causing him stress. Weeknights at the pub are never busy, and the rooms are often vacant. Maybe the Angel isn't making them as much money as it used to. She considers probing, and then Merle rises, clearing her cranberry juice and Darryl's untouched Sprite.

"I'm gonna lock up. No rush on the wine. I'll join you for a drink when I'm done cleaning up."

"You can put me to work." Charlotte doesn't want to be left alone with her thoughts. She can't shake the image of Darryl, the way he looked at her, like he didn't know her anymore.

Merle assigns Charlotte the task of tallying receipts from the night. She sits at his desk in the office, listening to classic rock on the radio, as he performs the bar's closing duties that require two good ankles. Halfway through the receipts, she taps the wrong number on the calculator and is forced to start over again. That is what she gets for humming along to Bruce Springsteen. Something catches her eye on the bulletin board, and she recalls the photo featuring a man and woman—the one she didn't have time to inspect the night of her ankle injury. She shoots a glance at the office doorway. Faint whistling reveals Merle's whereabouts. He is still cleaning the bar. She wheels her swivel chair toward the board and reaches for the photo, expecting to see Merle and Cindy.

Merle stares back at her, his familiar wide grin. The hair on the sides of his head indicates this was taken more than a few years ago. But the woman next to him in each photo is not Cindy. Charlotte's mouth goes dry, making it difficult to swallow. She closes her eyes and reopens them, hoping for a different outcome. The person is Lark, wearing her shy smile. They are huddled close together to fit into the frame. Is Lark sitting on his lap? Charlotte can't be sure. The last photo in the series is blurry, with Lark much closer to the foreground, as if she decided to leave mid-shot.

There's nothing necessarily wrong with the photos she's looking at. Nothing inappropriate in their contents. Darryl admitted Lark had spent many evenings at the pub, that it was her second home. Merle thought of Lark as a niece or daughter. But something about these photos has Charlotte's stomach stirring. Something about Lark's blurry form as she seemingly tries to escape the frame, has Charlotte wanting to leave the pub.

She removes the silver thumb tack and holds the matte cardstock in trembling hands. She flips it over and glances at the cursive message written on the back—a message clearly meant for Lark's eyes.

Chapter Fifty-One

CHARLOTTE

Sometimes we get served a shit sandwich, but we can always throw it in the garbage and make a new, tastier one. Remember, Uncle Merle is always here if you need a shoulder or someone to take goofy photos with. Tomorrow is a new day.

Charlotte sits on the bed of her room for the night and reads the message aloud, in her best Merle impression, this time putting emphasis on different words. "Uncle Merle," she says in a sinister voice. Is it strange that he uses 'uncle' in this context? She called friends of her parents Uncle and Auntie. It isn't abnormal to use the term with non-relations. But perhaps it's the way he refers to himself in the third person that makes the hair on the back of her neck stand at attention.

She lets out a lengthy sigh, falling back onto the bed. This is Merle she's talking about. Merle has been like a stand-in dad for her the last few weeks. Not once has she felt uncomfortable with him. He reminds her of her father—his cheery disposition, his playful jokes, his animated expressions when he listens to one of Charlotte's stories.

If any of the pub's workers give Charlotte pause, it's Cindy.

Charlotte sits up with an inexplicable urgency at her epiphany. Prior to Merle's confession about his smoking habit, she had been worried that Cindy was upset with her. Charlotte was convinced that she had something to do with the rift between the couple. She can't help but wonder if the smoking admission was just a cover. She first noticed the tension between the couple on New Year's Eve, right after Merle and Charlotte twirled to some swing song.

It can't be.

She feels sick to her stomach just considering that Merle's intentions are anything but paternal. But if Cindy knows something disturbing from Merle's past, something problematic with his and Lark's relationship, then she might assume history is repeating itself. She might want to keep Charlotte away.

Charlotte no longer feels safe in the antiquated room she found charming during her first stay at the pub. Even though she already said goodnight to Merle and hooked the lock in place, she worries she is exposed. She studies the water bottle and mints on the decorative cherry wood nightstand. The pastel butter mints, normally served at weddings or milestone anniversary parties, are unwrapped and presented in a crystal dish. Charlotte stayed clear of them mainly because she assumed they'd be stale, but she did drink the water. Had the seal broken when she first opened the lid? She can't remember. She stopped drinking her wine as soon as she saw the photo, but she still had about a third of it before that.

She recalls Darryl's suspicions about Lark's death; they found Valium in her toxicology report. What if someone Lark trusted had offered her a drink laced with the depressant? A bartender, perhaps. Charlotte lifts her arms to the ceiling and lets them fall back to the bed. Is her mind playing tricks on her, or do her limbs feel heavier than usual? Is her head foggy, or is she just tired?

She rolls into the fetal position and stares down the subject of a regal portrait that hangs in an intricately designed gold frame. The young maiden's eyes follow Charlotte wherever she moves, and she has the sensation of being watched. Charlotte crawls to the foot of the bed. Using the nearby fireplace mantel, she pulls herself to her knees. She inspects each of the seven Royal Dalton figurines for signs of a planted camera. She picks up the final one, with its cornflower blue bonnet and matching parasol, and sets it down with a thud. "You're losing it." The likelihood of Merle being tech-savvy enough to hook up a teddy cam is low. The man barely knows how to switch the channel on the bar television.

Charlotte approaches Tux, curled up in the armchair, and strokes her back, rousing her. "You're sleeping with me tonight," she says, scooping the cat up in her arms. "And we're keeping the lamp on."

She limps back to the bed, and Tux leaps from her arms, scurrying back to the chair. Charlotte wishes she could call Darryl. She needs to talk to someone. Someone who knows Merle well. But Darryl won't speak to her. She shoots him a text, apologizing again for betraying his trust.

She wonders if he's staying up late to read every last diary entry, if he was able to piece the clues together despite the missing pages. She squeezes her pillow, imagining it is him lying beside her in bed.

The aching in her chest has returned, but this time it feels different like there is a hollowness inside. In recent weeks, Charlotte would have turned to Lark's diary. She would have found solace in the pages written by her kindred spirit. In its absence, she rummages through her bag that lies next to the bed, searching for her own notebook and a pen.

Tomorrow's to-do list:

-Install the camera at the back door

-Earn Darryl's trust back

-Investigate Merle

Chapter Fifty-Two

CHARLOTTE

C harlotte balances one of the takeout cups on top of the other as she carefully opens the door to the salon. Dani rushes to meet her, collecting the top drink. "No crutches?"

"I'm good as long as I walk slow." Charlotte scans the empty room as she follows Dani to the sink. Fortunately, it's another slow day at the salon. She has approximately an hour (according to the online services menu) to find out everything she can about Lark and Merle's relationship.

"Just a blowout today? Any occasion?" Dani asks.

Charlotte doesn't have any plans after her appointment except to return to the house on Elizabeth Drive and pray that no one else decides to do the same. Installing the second surveillance camera is on her to-do list once the snow stops falling, but she refuses to stay any longer at the Angel.

"No plans. I just needed to take my mind off things."

Dani adjusts the tap so that a steady stream of warm water cascades down the crown of Charlotte's head. "I'll bet. Have they found anything out?"

Charlotte opens her eyes and Dani comes into view at an upside-down angle. "Nothing. I stayed at the Angel last night. I was too freaked out to go home."

Dani offers her sympathies while massaging Charlotte's scalp. *She can't imagine how I'm feeling. Anville is normally so safe. Is there anything she can do to help?*

After a few minutes, Dani turns the water off and secures a white microfibre towel around Charlotte's damp hair.

Charlotte sits at Dani's station, sipping on a latte, her arms poking out of a black cape. When Dani joins her, she is equipped with a toolbelt of hair accessories.

"Have you ever stayed there? At the Angel?" Charlotte asks, making eye contact with Dani in the mirror. "They're cute rooms."

Dani smirks. "Only once." She tousles Charlotte's hair with the towel. "Lark and I got hammered one night at the pub. Merle let us sleep it off, and we both told our parents we were staying at each other's house. I don't remember the room, though. We were almost blackout."

Charlotte fiddles with her cape. She wouldn't have expected Merle to serve under-agers until they were "almost blackout," but it's possible she doesn't know the real Merle. "Sounds like a pretty wild night."

"That was the thing about Lark. The highs were high, and the lows were low. She couldn't do anything mediocre. It was part of what I loved about her. But it could also be draining."

Dani sprays Charlotte's hair with a bottle from her toolbelt and selects a wide-tooth comb for detangling. "Tell me if I'm pulling too hard."

Charlotte nods. "So, was that where all the teenagers hung out? At Merle's?"

"Not really. Lark and Darryl did. They were pretty close with Merle and Cindy."

"What about you?"

"I guess by association." Dani works her way through Charlotte's hair, tugging occasionally to free a knot. "It was different with them, though. I think they needed the father figure."

A *father figure*. That was how Darryl had described Merle, too. How Charlotte saw her own relationship with the older man. And perhaps that was all it was with Lark. Dani places the comb back in her utility belt and Charlotte stretches her neck, releasing the tension.

The conversation slows while Dani styles Charlotte's hair with a blow dryer and round brush, clasping sections of her hair in brightly coloured claw clips as she dries it. When Dani finally turns off the appliance, the lull of the white noise waning, Charlotte is wrapped up in her own thoughts.

"What do you think?" Dani asks, presenting a hand-held mirror so Charlotte can see the volume at the back.

"I love it," Charlotte says, staring across the room deep in thought.

"You sure? I can curl it instead."

"Sorry. I'm just thinking about something Darryl said yesterday." Charlotte hasn't heard a word from him despite her numerous texts apologizing. "I'm worried about him," she adds.

Dani places the mirror down and turns her attention to Charlotte. "He's not drinking again, is he?"

"He might be. He's been saying some strange things about Lark. He's convinced it wasn't—that she didn't—"

Dani jumps in before Charlotte can finish the thought. "He thinks someone else was responsible. I've heard this many times over the years. Usually at the pub and usually after he's had way too much to drink."

"So, you don't think it's true?"

Dani scuffs her sneaker against the tile and then saunters over to the neighbouring station where she sinks into the salon chair. "It would make things easier if I did. I could, you know, absolve myself from it all. Pretend like I didn't contribute." She twists her face up and then busies herself, wrapping her hair into a bun. "But no, I don't think someone hurt her like that. I don't think it was a cover-up like Darryl believes. Life isn't some conspiracy theory. Lark was in a lot of pain."

Charlotte knows she should stop there. Dani has punished herself enough, but instead, she leans in, the words escaping her mouth before she has a chance to temper them. "Why didn't you try to get her help? Why did you cut her out?"

Dani jerks her head toward Charlotte. "Because I was sixteen. I needed help, too." She stares down her reflection, narrowing her eyes as if she doesn't recognize the image. "And she cut me out, too. I found a new group, but so did she—started hanging out with Armstrong of all people."

Charlotte's breath catches in her throat. "Why? He was such a creep." After the words leave her mouth, she realizes the use of past tense is odd, but she can't fathom why Lark would see him after the diary confessions. "He *is* such a creep."

Dani shrugs. "She thought so too, at one point. I don't know. Some of my friends saw them drinking at the Angel a couple of times. Another saw him walk her home one night."

Charlotte considers this. An onlooker could describe her and Armstrong in the same way—*they were drinking at the Angel, having dinner at a restaurant, he drove her home one night.* No outsider truly knows the extent of someone else's relationship. Armstrong could have easily pressured Lark into the few occasions Dani described, just like he had with Charlotte.

"Hard to know for sure," Charlotte says.

"I'm pretty sure something happened between them." Dani's lip curls up in a challenge.

Charlotte meets Dani's eyes in the mirror. There is something she isn't saying. "You said Anville likes to talk, right? Maybe that's all it was," Charlotte says.

Dani spins in her chair so that she can face Charlotte. "I saw something."

Then, Dani shares with Charlotte a secret she's tucked away for years. Something that clearly still weighs heavy on her conscience. She tells the story, periodically glancing around the empty salon as if someone might be eavesdropping at the counter.

One night, Dani saw Lark at the convenience store buying the makings of a movie night—chips, candy, a raunchy comedy—all laid out on the counter. Lark didn't notice Dani sneak up behind her in line. Dani spotted something tucked beneath a trashy tabloid magazine.

"It was a pregnancy test." She smacks her lips together. "So yeah, I believe there was something going on between them."

Charlotte rapidly blinks as she tries to make sense of Dani's allegation. "You think Lark and Armstrong slept together." The idea doesn't jive with what Charlotte has read in the diary. If Armstrong was the person vying for her attention, then Lark certainly wasn't into him; she was terrified of him.

Dani swivels her chair, returning to face the mirror. "And if I had been a better friend, maybe I could have helped her."

"Wait, you don't think Lark—that an unplanned pregnancy was the reason she ..."

"I don't think it helped."

Dani continues to speak, but the words are garbled by the time they make it to Charlotte's ears. Charlotte braces herself in the chair, holding onto the armrests. Her body feels warm, the cape secured tightly around her neck, impeding airflow. She allows her head to fall between her knees, the rush of blood making her skull heavy like lead.

"Charlotte? Are you okay?"

Lark wouldn't have slept with Armstrong. Not willingly.

Charlotte's eyes flutter around the salon, eventually narrowing in on Dani's affirmations that Charlotte had scanned on her first visit. She focuses on one message at eye level, scrawled in a curvy script on a gradient blue background.

Honour your life by trusting yourself.

And then, her vision goes black.

———— •◆• ————

Charlotte paws at the back of her nylon cape, attempting to escape its confines. She no longer feels warm, as a cool sweat covers her neck and back. She needs to leave. She needs to find Darryl.

"Charlotte? I think you fainted. Please, let me call someone."

She needs Darryl, but he won't come for her.

"Do you know where Darryl is staying?" Charlotte asks, her voice shaky.

Dani shrugs. "I can call him for you."

"No, please don't. He's staying with a friend. Xander? In the basement apartment, I think."

Dani's eyes widen. "I know where Xander lives. I can take you after my shift."

Charlotte frees herself from the cape and stands up, her legs still weak. "I need to go now. It's important. Write the address down for me?"

"Charlotte, please, sit. I think you should take it easy."

"This can't wait." Charlotte limps toward the door as quickly as her ankle will allow, an urgency buzzing through her.

"You're not going to tell him what I just told you." Dani collects the cape, folding it repeatedly into a square.

"Did you know Lark kept a diary?"

Dani shakes her head.

"I came across it when I moved in. Darryl has it now; he thinks it holds answers. What you told me today is huge. I think it will help him."

Dani bites her lip. "It wasn't my secret to share."

"He deserves closure. I don't have to say it was you who told me. But I'm telling him."

Dani consults the oversized rod iron clock on the back wall of the salon. "Oh, fuck it." She hurries to the front door, switching the open sign to closed. "It's not like I'm going to get any walk-ins." Then she holds out her arm for Charlotte. "Let's go."

Chapter Fifty-Three

CHARLOTTE

The houses shrink but the lots grow as they travel to Xander's neighboring town. The community is made up of bungalows with cinderblock foundations and painted siding. The yellow of Xander's home reminds Charlotte of the pastel mints at the Angel.

Darryl's truck sits in the gravel driveway at the side of the house. Dani slows to a stop, hugging the snowbank, and Charlotte spots a few descending stairs and a door she presumes leads to Darryl's apartment. The basement windows are aglow. Hopefully, that means Darryl is home.

Dani cuts the engine and sips on the coffee she ordered moments earlier from the Tim Horton's drive-through around the corner. "This is the house. Am I coming in?"

Charlotte rubs at the chalk initials on the lid, which identify her drink as hot chocolate. The cups are still holiday-themed despite the new year, and they match the candy cane bows that grace the neighbour's veranda.

She holds Darryl's black coffee in the other hand, its contents burning her flesh.

"That's up to you." Charlotte steadies Darryl's coffee in the crux of her left arm. She pushes open the passenger door with her free hand, scraping the snowbank.

By the time she pulls herself to a standing position, Dani has joined her on the passenger's side, offering her arm. "I guess we're doing this, then."

The path to the side door is covered in snow, and Dani yelps when it seeps through the top of her sneakers. "He ploughs snow for a living. Why the hell can't he clear a path to his own door?"

When they arrive at the stoop, a gust of wind violently whips Charlotte's freshly styled tresses. She attempts to tame her hair, using her forearm, being careful not to spill the hot beverages. Music carries from the apartment, and the drumbeat is amplified as if Darryl is playing along with the song. Charlotte consults Dani, who nods encouragingly. There is no doorbell, so Charlotte knocks lightly with the back of her hand. Dani rolls her eyes and pounds on the door.

"Darryl, let us in. It's freezing out here." When there is no response, she taps at the ground-level window until the volume of the music finally lowers.

Darryl answers the door in a T-shirt and sweatpants, a toque covering his greasy hair. He is unshaven, and the dark circles beneath his eyes are pronounced, yet Charlotte still finds him attractive. Even though they aren't together, she wishes she could make him smile, ease some of his pain. She wishes she were in his arms, her legs wrapped around his waist. She looks away—down at her boots, kicking them together to free the snow that is trapped in the treads.

"What are you doing here?" he asks Dani, then his eyes land on Charlotte behind her. "What's going on?"

Dani pushes past him, letting herself in. "Nice to see you, too. You smell like a liquor store, by the way."

Darryl opens the door wider, allowing Charlotte to enter.

"We brought you a coffee," she says, passing him the cup.

Darryl accepts the drink and bows his head sheepishly.

Merle was right. Based on the state of Darryl and his apartment—the empty bottles and cans scattered over nearly every surface—it is clear he is drinking again. Charlotte scans the living space. She recognizes the milk crates from the garage. A few are turned upside down in a curious arrangement, Darryl's drumsticks placed on top. Charlotte gathers this is his makeshift drum kit and likely how he's been spending his free time in between shifts while guzzling back beers. Charlotte meets Darryl's eyes, and his embarrassment is palpable.

Dani makes herself comfortable at a card table near the kitchenette. "Drink the coffee; you need to sober up."

Darryl hurries to the table, removing plates and beer bottles to free space. "Heard of calling first?"

Charlotte lowers herself into the seat next to Dani. "Would you have answered?"

Darryl ignores the comment and continues to clear the dishes. After a few minutes, he joins them at the table with his coffee. "Is this some sort of intervention?"

Dani laughs. "God, no." She nudges Charlotte, but she doesn't know where to begin. This had seemed like a good idea back at the salon, but now that the three of them are here, hanging out for the first time together, the whole thing seems forced.

"We're here because of Lark," Charlotte says.

Darryl eyes Dani as if expecting further explanation. When Dani only offers a shrug, he returns his gaze to Charlotte.

Charlotte breathes deeply. Delaying this won't make what she has to say any easier. "We think she might have been assaulted."

"We do?" Dani asks Charlotte. "I never said that."

"What is going on?" The tendons in Darryl's neck tense.

Charlotte's voice wavers despite her certainty. "*I* believe she was."

Dani places her hand on Darryl's arm, redirecting his attention. She explains what she witnessed at the convenience store two months prior to Lark's death, assuring him she has no reason to believe Lark was assaulted. Darryl continues to watch Charlotte as if Dani's words mean nothing. As if he and Charlotte are the only two in the room.

Charlotte scootches her chair closer to him. "I'm so sorry. About everything. But I want to help—if you'll let me. Did you know she was pregnant?"

He shakes his head no. His eyes move wildly as he considers what he's learned.

"Have you read any more of her diary?"

Again, he shakes his head. "I couldn't. I had to stop."

"She was afraid of someone. She wrote about it often. She never named the person in the entries I read, but it's clear there was something going on."

"Who?" Dani asks, reminding the couple she is present.

"Armstrong," Darryl interjects, but Charlotte's stomach twists, unsettling her. She had been so sure it was Armstrong. It made sense. The handsome athlete who was used to getting everything he wanted until one person didn't return his feelings. After numerous attempts to win her over, he snapped. But Charlotte can't discount the feeling she had when she discovered the photo in Merle's office or Cindy's recent behaviour.

"I think we need to finish the diary," Charlotte says. She doesn't want to be the one to accuse Merle, but the diary might reveal it.

Darryl buries his face in his hands. "I don't think I can."

Both Darryl and Dani are far too invested to search the diary for evidence. She imagines the two people who loved Lark so deeply being forced to relive the depths of her pain and mine the truth from her firsthand account. Charlotte nods in agreement. "I'll do it, then." She needs the facts to point to Armstrong. It just needs to be him. Because Charlotte doesn't think she can handle an alternate truth.

Darryl retreats to his bedroom and returns a moment later, the book in his tense grasp, his knuckles white. He places it down on the table in front of her, then walks to the mini fridge and cracks open a beer, using the ledge of the counter. Dani gives him a stern look, and he shrugs. "I need something stronger for this."

Charlotte pulls the diary closer. She opens the book, flipping to the pages she has yet to read. The entry is dated March tenth.

This is where she will begin, and she won't stop reading until she discovers the truth.

Chapter Fifty-Four

LARK

March 10, 2006

I've been invited to your prom (you can probably guess by whom). At least his invite was tamer, still a little off, but I think he's finally realizing I won't be Mrs. Armstrong. "I know you'll probably say no, and that's cool, but if you change your mind and feel like dressing up, I'll be wearing a navy suit (if you want to match me)." No thanks, champ. I'll probably just go to the Angel and force Merle to make me mixed drinks and share stories of his youth. Maybe I should just tell Armstrong I like Dani? I'm sure the student body would have a riot with that fact—just think of the prank possibilities.

If it isn't already clear, I'm not going to go, so don't worry about me tagging along with you and your friends. I haven't broken the news to Kyle yet, but I will. He wrote that I should "take my time as I think it over." And then he asked if I wanted a ride to some senior's bush party tonight. Another no from me.

Prom is such a charade anyway—seeing the same people we see every day, only we smell a little fresher not having just done laps in gym class. The whole thing is overrated, but I still think you should go. Dani says they're going to have a chocolate fountain and marshmallows on a stick for dipping. She's attending as a part of the social committee. *Pretty in Pink* was her theme idea, so you can thank her for the nods to eighties fashion. Maybe you should go with a tux in powder blue.

I know Mom wants you to go. She's been talking about it every night this week. She's seeking the stereotypical photo of her son, posing on the stairs with a cute girl on his arm. She wants to help you pick out a corsage and show you how to place it on your date's wrist, even though it will probably clash with her dress. I bet they're getting booked up at the salon for prom dos. That's probably why she's obsessed with it right now but if I have to hear another story about her seafoam-green prom dress and how everyone said she resembled a brunette Farrah Fawcett, I'm not going to make it to my own prom.

Sorry, morbid, I know. I'm just kidding, though, I promise.

Things have actually been looking up, if you can believe it. Kyle is sort of backing off (prom and bush party invite aside). Mom seems happy with Jake. Have you noticed him showing more interest in us? Not that we need him to be a dad but it's nice to know a bit more about him—that he's more than just the uniform. He actually asked Mom to get him a ticket to my recital, so it looks like you won't be the only man in the audience who isn't someone's dad. Most of the school is back to ignoring me. Dani is still in denial, though. Not sure when she'll finally wake up and realize I could actually be good for her.

Sigh.

Overall, things have been okay, and I feel, I dunno. Light? Breezy? I feel pretty good right now, but it could also be the buzz from the vodka cran Merle made me after school. And Jake left a bunch of beer in the fridge that I may have dipped into. And Mom's working the evening shift tonight, and you are at Xander's again, so there's no one here to judge. And after this entry, I think I'll throw on some TV and appreciate the fact that it's March break and I don't have dance tomorrow morning or go to school for a week.

And the doorbell is ringing. And I am betting you forgot your key again.

———— ·✦· ————

March 11, 2006

Where the fuck were you, Darryl? Where the fuck was Mom? You've both let me down more than you could ever imagine, and I've let myself down, too.

It must have been something in the beer. I didn't drink that much. But time became abstract, and my limbs grew heavy like when we used to play that game of concentration, pretending to fill each body part with sand and pebbles. It was terrifying, like a bad high but also, I welcomed the feeling of just letting go of control. Letting my mattress swallow me. I could barely move, but I was still there—on my bed. I was still there but I wasn't. And even now, I'm not sure I can say what happened. Did something happen? Did he tuck me in after he carried me to bed? Why did I let him in? Why did I have a drink with him? I remember him sitting on the corner of my bed, peeling the label off his beer. Perhaps, he was only monitoring so I wouldn't turn onto my back and choke on my vomit?

I remember the smell of his breath. The stink of stale cigarettes and lager, so he must have been close. There was no attempt to mask it with a mint or gum. I don't think he had planned any of it. But what is *it*? I'm not positive that anything even happened.

I only have snippets. Like, I remember an inner pep talk. I told myself to replicate what they taught us in Phys-ed self-defence. When they brought in that guy dressed as the Michelin Man. Did I need to thrust him off me at some point? I can visualize myself bending my legs and pushing into a bridge pose. I can feel the weight of him. The effort it took to breathe. My hip joints pushing past comfort like my legs were being spread open. Was this all just a bad dream? Was something in my drink? Whatever it was has left me with an unrelenting headache today, which I'm actually thankful for because it distracts me from the aches in the rest of my body. I have bruises on my arms as if someone grabbed me. Held me in position. Unless it was just a nightmare. More realistic than the entirety of yesterday. Unless my memory is failing me.

And you're still not home. If you were, I'd hear you drumming alongside the music from your stereo. Mom might be home, but if she is, she's still in bed. Truth is, I haven't left my room. I need you to come home and distract me. Until then, I'll count to thirty and with each number, I'll think of something good. Some morsels of joy to keep my mind off the shame.

1. The dimple on Dani's right cheek

2. Eating soup from our Looney Toons TV trays

3. The smell of Mom's talcum powder

4. Your drumming face. So serious.

5. Tropical skittles, especially the orange ones

6. Bare trees in the winter

7. Landing a triple pirouette

8. Biking with no hands

9. Dani's Mom's moussaka

10. An ice bath for my feet after a two-hour rehearsal on Pointe

11. When you laugh at your own jokes

12. The night you, Mom, and I went to the triple feature at the Drive-in

13. Orange juice and Malibu over ice

14. Thanksgiving or any excuse to eat stuffing

15. Reading on a rainy day

16. Autumn walks when the leaves are changing

17. My lucky number six

18. English class with Ms. Handover

19. My dance girls

20. Binging on chocolate

21. Tagging along with you to band practice

22. Playing Scrabble with Mom even though she makes up words

23. "Fools Rush In" by Elvis

24. The way my hair looks gathered into a slick bun

25. How you anticipate what I am going to say next, finishing my sentence

26. My Chuck Taylors

27. The smell of sunscreen

28. Putting on clothes after they've come out of the dryer.

29. Waking up before my alarm.

30. Dani's expressive eyebrows when she tells a story she's excited about

There's the door. There's you kicking off your shoes. In a second, I should hear you charging up the stairs with no regard for who's still sleeping. You'll swing open my door and ask if I want bacon and eggs from the Angel.

But I don't think I can ever step foot in there again.

Chapter Fifty–Five

CHARLOTTE

Charlotte hesitates for a moment after reading the final sentence. It is underlined for emphasis, making Charlotte's throat constrict as if she's been scolded. She'll have to answer to Darryl and Dani once she admits she's finished. She skims through the blank pages that follow. That can't be all, but sure enough, the rest of the diary is blank, the end of Lark's story.

Dani busies herself at the kitchenette, assembling sandwiches with what little groceries Darryl has in the mini-fridge. Darryl continues to pound on the milk crates, the tempo increasing in intensity.

Charlotte expels a breath and deserts the open book, spine up. Her hand hovers by her mouth, concealing the quiver of her lip. She has many questions swirling in her mind, but she's certain someone raped Lark. Not only did this monster violate her, but they also made her doubt it ever happened.

"I think I'm right." She waits until the drumbeat subsides and for Dani to drop her sandwich. "Someone assaulted Lark. Someone she knew. It's all right here, and then it stops. After the ripped pages, there's nothing."

Dani deserts her station at the counter, asking about the stolen pages. While Charlotte explains what Darryl discovered at the pub the day prior, his leg pulsates with nervous energy like he's tapping a bass drum pedal.

"Who was it?" Darryl asks Charlotte, joining her at the table. "Your best guess?" His eyes are wide as he approaches.

Charlotte chews on the inside of her lip. It could very well be Armstrong. He had been Lark's main concern and had asked her to go to the party that evening. It's possible he stopped by on his way, one last opportunity for her to return his feelings. Charlotte can't imagine Lark inviting him inside and having a drink with him. Lark didn't trust Armstrong. And that night, Lark mentioned the perpetrator smelled of cigarettes. Charlotte has never witnessed Armstrong smoke, yet she does know of one person who recently resumed the habit.

Charlotte consults the last line in the diary once more. Why would Lark be afraid to visit the Angel if it was Armstrong who attacked her? Everything about Lark's account leads Charlotte to believe this was someone she was comfortable inviting into her home. Someone who frequented the Angel—perhaps the owner himself.

Dani reaches for the diary. Protectively, Charlotte places her hand on it. "Are you sure?"

Dani ignores her, grabbing it with eager hands. Darryl moves to read over her shoulder, and Charlotte watches as their expressions mirror each other's, moving from solemn to appalled to utter heartbreak.

Darryl is the first to speak, his voice booming. "It's Armstrong. I fucking knew it."

Dani nods insistently, and then her body convulses, her sobs preventing her from uttering a word.

Charlotte rises, stroking Dani's back. "We don't know for sure." She gestures to the diary. "Lark never mentions his name, but she did in the previous entry. Isn't that odd?"

Dani's voice is shaky when she finally speaks. "I think it's Armstrong, too. I remember that party. I went with Brittany. Armstrong never showed up."

That is the only proof Darryl needs. He whips a drumstick across the room, knocking over a beer bottle and sending it shattering across the floor.

Charlotte shudders at the sound. "I get that you're furious right now—"

"He murdered my sister," he snaps.

Charlotte inches closer, placing her hand on his arm. "Darryl, we don't know any of that. All we know for sure is that something happened to Lark that night in March."

Darryl softens at Charlotte's touch, and his eyes finally find their way to hers. "He drugged her. Can't you see that? She had drugs in her system the night she died, too. If she was pregnant, that would be proof of what he did to her. Maybe he wanted to get rid of that proof."

"But what about her last line. The Angel. Did Armstrong even go there in high school?"

"He went there. Maybe not as much as us, but he'd go," Darryl says.

It is Dani's turn to approach Darryl, and she, too, rubs his arm. "Lark left you a note. Didn't you tell me that? That she left a note under your pillow. Addressed to you? Armstrong may have raped her, but he didn't kill her, Darryl."

Darryl's brows bunch together, and he darts from the room. He returns, holding his wallet. "It never made sense to me." He fishes through the leather pleats until he pulls out a folded piece of paper. He unravels it and flattens its creases on his pant leg before scanning the note he has likely read many times over the years. He slams it on the table in front of Charlotte. "What's unique about Lark's diary?"

Charlotte eyes Dani, imploring for help with Darryl's riddle.

He jabs a finger at his name in one of the entries. "She addresses me. As if she's writing to me."

Charlotte and Dani seem to arrive at the realization at the same time. Charlotte's hand flies to her mouth and Dani gasps like she's had the wind knocked out of her. Darryl slides the note into the diary, and the edge forms one of the torn pages. A perfect fit.

"It wasn't her suicide note. It was her diary entry. Or at least part of it. We're still missing two pages."

The note suffocates in Dani's grasp as she reads Lark's confession aloud. Lark's tone is solemn, fervent. Yet, it isn't much different from the tone in her other entries. She speaks of feeling trapped and out of choices, but there is an undercurrent of hope. Dani elongates the final sentence, rising as though it were written as a question. "'I wish I could explain everything to you, but that will have to wait'?" She releases her grip, and the paper soars to the table. "Wait for what?"

Darryl gathers his keys, wallet, and coat. "I'm going to see Armstrong."

"You are not." Charlotte holds out her hand for Darryl's keys. "Please, not like this." She moves closer, her eyes pleading.

Darryl's nod is so subtle that most would miss it, but Charlotte catches it. He turns his hand over, placing the keys into her grasp, and his hand lingers for a moment. It is the most they have touched in a week, and it sends pulses through Charlotte's core.

Dani retrieves her bag and coat, heading to the door. "We'll take my car. But we're not going to Armstrong's. We're going to the police."

"The police won't do anything now," Darryl says, zipping up his coat. "They haven't for years. Not without any proof. Armstrong will have the other pages."

"He's probably burned them by now," Dani says.

"I bet he's kept them," Darryl says, moving to the door. "Like a fucking trophy."

Charlotte drops Darryl's keys onto the table. She can no longer feel her fingers save the ice-cold tingles that envelop them. She inhales a shaky breath and steadies herself against her chair.

Dani's eyebrows shoot up. "I've got an idea." She breaks into her elaborate plan, which Charlotte tries her best to follow, ignoring her body's warning signals. They will text Armstrong from Charlotte's phone, asking him to meet her at the Angel. There is no doubt among the group that he will come. Clearly, the officer is still interested in Charlotte.

Charlotte breathes deeply, engaging her diaphragm. She can't allow Darryl to confront an armed police officer and quite possibly the wrong suspect, but her body is failing her at the worst moment.

Dani continues to share her plan, her excitement swelling. With Armstrong distracted at the pub, Dani and Darryl will break into his apartment and search for the pages. Once they have the proof, the police will have to listen to them.

"He still lives above Mac's convenience?" Dani asks.

Darryl nods.

Charlotte's body seems to sway. She sinks into her chair as the room spins around her. She can't distract Armstrong. She can barely stand. "I don't think I can."

Darryl nods in agreement. "It's not safe. I don't want Charlotte going near him."

"What about Officer Landry? Can he help?" Dani asks.

Darryl laughs wildly. "Like he'll go against his partner." He swigs the last of his beer and drops it on the counter with a thud. "Landry's no use to us. He's still holding a grudge after Mom broke it off with him."

Dani is at Charlotte's side before she can register the words she just heard. *Mom broke it off with him.* Darlene Peters broke up with Officer Landry? When did they date? Dani strokes Charlotte's forehead. "Char, are you okay? You're looking pale again."

"Sandwich." It's all Charlotte can muster; she knows if her mother were here, she would force-feed her Dani's sandwich until the colour came back in her cheeks. If she eats something, she might be able to shake this, think straight. She bites into the white bread. Ham. Processed cheese. Pickle. Mustard. In between slow chews, she finally extracts the thought. "I didn't know they dated," she says. But it's too late, Darryl and Dani have moved on.

"I think that could work. Except ..." Darryl eyes Charlotte with concern. "You stay here," he says. "Text Armstrong to meet you at the pub for ..." He consults his phone. "Seven thirty. Ten minutes after you're supposed to meet, ask him to order you some food and that you'll be there in twenty. And then you never show. That'll give us at least forty minutes to search his place, but chances are he'll stick around longer and drink away the embarrassment."

The women nod at Darryl's amendment. This way, Charlotte is safe.

I think I chose the wrong guy. I'm sorry about what went down between us. Darryl fed me lies about you. Can we meet at the Angel? 7:30? I'm hoping for another chance. The trio's carefully crafted invite is a blend of apology and come-on, appealing to both Armstrong's compassion and ego.

I guess. See you in twenty.

Once Armstrong responds, Darryl and Dani leave the basement, en route to Anville to scope out Armstrong's apartment. Charlotte sets an alarm on her phone for 7:40 p.m.—when she has been instructed to send the first text about running late.

She moves to Darryl's bedroom, a small den off the main area with the same cot-like bed he was using in her garage and sheets pinned to the small windows acting as curtains. She pulls the Afghan quilt up to her chin and rolls onto her side. This is where she will wait for Dani and Darryl, willing their plan to work. If they find the diary entries, which, if she's being honest with herself, seems like a long shot, it will mean that Merle is innocent. She closes her eyes; her heart rate has finally slowed, but the whole episode has drained her.

———— • ♦ • ————

Charlotte wakes to the chimes of her alarm and a missed text from Armstrong.

Still coming? I have a booth at the back.

She jolts upright and responds, letting him know she's on her way. She explains she forgot her phone at home and had to go back. She tells him she'll be there in fifteen minutes and to order the mozzarella sticks. Then, she informs Dani and Darryl that she's bought them some time and asks if they made it inside. Dani responds.

Just got in. Idiot actually left his door unlocked.

This is good. Now, when Armstrong does return, he won't suspect someone has been inside. Charlotte starts the countdown on her phone, but before it runs out, she receives another text from Armstrong.

Are you close? I'm a space cadet, too. Forgot my wallet at home. Gonna run back and grab it.

Fuck. This was not a part of the plan. She quickly types out a message.

Don't worry, I can spot this one. I'm close. Ten minutes tops.

Time is running out. Even if Armstrong waits another ten minutes, he'll need to go back to his apartment eventually to get his wallet. She sends Dani another text, asking how it's going and letting them know it's time to wrap up their search.

As she awaits a response, she counts slowly to ten, breathing deeply all the while. The tingling sensation has left her fingers, and she no longer feels light-headed. She swings her legs to the side of the cot, planting her feet on the parquet tile. The first message to arrive is from Dani.

Can you stall? He has filing cabinets, and we need to pick the locks.

The only way to stall would be to meet Armstrong at the pub. Charlotte picks at a hangnail on her thumb. She isn't only anxious about seeing Armstrong. Merle will be there, too. She launches her ride-share app and is disheartened to find that on this side of town there are currently no available cars. It would take her about ten minutes to drive to the Angel if she left right now using Darryl's truck. She bounces her knee up and down in a sporadic rhythm, her nerves returning at full force. That would require getting behind the wheel, and she hasn't driven in years.

The evening sky is clear and still when Charlotte ventures outside. The naked branches of a maple tree sway slightly in the wind. Charlotte heaves open the door and climbs into the elevated seat of Darryl's truck. She places her phone in the cup holder and her purse in the seat beside her. How unnerving it is to swap her passenger role for driver. A message comes through from Armstrong as Charlotte turns the key in the ignition.

Okay. Don't leave me hanging too long. I'm on my third drink already.

The sound of the car starting sends her stomach into flutters and her shoulders immediately tense. Once she adjusts her seat so that she is close to the steering wheel and has a clear view through the windshield, she counts backwards from ten like she is preparing for lift-off. Her grip tenses around the gear shift as she swings it into reverse. She holds her breath as she eases her foot off the break, allowing the monster of a vehicle to creep backwards until she meets the road.

There's no turning back now. Darryl and Dani need her.

Lark needs her.

Chapter Fifty–Six

CHARLOTTE

Charlotte's knuckles are white, her so grip intense on the steering wheel it's like she'll never let go. She hugs the curb, slowing to a stop by Dani's salon. Here, Armstrong won't notice the truck and she can pretend like she arrived at the pub on foot. She relaxes her shoulders and mentally checks off the task on her to-do list. She drove the truck. A throaty laugh escapes her. She actually drove it!

But the job isn't over. Now, she must distract Armstrong so he doesn't return to his place and find Dani and Darryl searching his apartment.

The pub is buzzing, the bar full of blue-collar workers who have finished assembling, repairing, or patrolling for the week, taking advantage of Merle's happy hour special. Charlotte gets away with a polite nod to Merle before retreating to the back of the pub, where Armstrong picks at fries. He raises his eyebrows when he spots her across the room, a look of genuine surprise on his face like he expected to be stood up.

"You came," he says, his mouth stretching into a wide smile.

"I did." She slides into the booth across from him where there is a glass of red waiting for her. "What are we drinking?"

"I got you that Californian you like." He shrugs. "Merle may have helped."

She raises the glass to her lips, then pauses. How long has the wine been sitting here, she wonders. Armstrong or Merle would have plenty of time to slip something in. She sets it down.

"Shit. I got it wrong, didn't I? Was it merlot you liked?"

Charlotte tosses her head. "No, it's just I already started with beer at home. Do you want another?" She rises from the table.

"If you're buying."

Charlotte joins the men at the bar, wedging herself through a small opening near the register. A policeman moves to the side to let her through.

"Ms. Boyd," he says, tilting his beer to her.

Charlotte jerks her head toward the voice and discovers Officer Landry standing there. She makes polite conversation until Merle approaches, his cheeks flushed. "Hey, you, ready for another glass? Cindy will come to the table, you know. Gotta rest that ankle."

"It's a lot better. I just need two beers."

"Two, eh?" Merle says, raising his eyebrow. He leans over the bar, eyeing Charlotte's guest, who waves back in response, a smirk on his face.

"You got it." He cracks the bottles of lager on the opener secured to the wall and then slides them over to Charlotte. "Be careful, there. He may get the wrong idea."

Charlotte twists her mouth. As she turns away, Landry mumbles to Merle. "Leave them alone; they're just having fun. You remember being young and in love, don't you?"

Charlotte passes Armstrong the bottle and takes her seat. Her phone buzzes in her coat pocket where she left it, and she transfers it to her lap, opening the message from Dani.

So far, it's a bunch of baseball cards, but there's more to go through. Are you still texting with him?

Charlotte glances up at the eager cop. He flashes another smile, and she fumbles with the phone. "Sorry, it's my parents. Asking about the renos. One sec." She types her response and presses send.

Don't freak out, but I'm at the pub with him. Buying you more time.

She places the phone face down on the seat beside her. "So, how have you been?"

Armstrong peers at her through narrowed eyes. "I thought you were still mad at me."

"Mad?" She sips the bottle.

"The last time we were here, you accused me of breaking into your house. Then, you left Anville for like a week."

"Right. I was dealing with some personal stuff."

"Have you seen Darryl since you've been back?"

Charlotte pauses to sip her beer. "No. And I don't plan on it."

He nods, his smile returning. "Are you back for good?"

She considers the question. Her parents aren't planning to return for another two months, so she is expected to stay at least until then. But she hasn't given thought to what's next after the renovations are done and her parents no longer need her help. A week ago, when her world was turned upside down, she would have left Anville as soon as she had the opportunity. But now, she isn't sure where she and Darryl stand.

"For a while," she says, which seems to satisfy him.

Cindy carries over a plate of mozzarella sticks and places them on the table. "Charlotte's favourite," she says in a sing-songy voice. Charlotte hasn't seen her warm smile in more than a week. "Glad to have you back," Cindy says, and Charlotte returns the smile, thinking the same thing. "Thanks for talking to Merle, by the way."

Charlotte scrunches up her nose in confusion.

"He hasn't had a cigarette all week," Cindy clarifies. "I'm sorry if I've been short lately. It was weighing on me that he'd picked up that horrid habit again. Anyway, he mentioned you talked some sense into him." She winks, then retreats to another table.

Is it true, then? Merle and Cindy were fighting about his smoking? It had nothing to do with Charlotte? She glances toward the bar and Merle raises a glass to her, a carefree smile on his face that reminds her of her dad.

Charlotte's phone vibrates on the seat beside her.

Nothing but a bunch of rookie cards. I think it's a dead end, but Darryl wants to keep looking. I haven't told him you're with Armstrong. I think he'd lose it.

When Charlotte looks up from her phone, Landry is standing next to Armstrong. "Any more scares since yesterday?" he asks Charlotte, and it takes her a moment to realize he is referencing the break-in.

She shakes her head. "I've got a camera for the back of the house now." She doesn't bother sharing that she hasn't installed it.

"That's smart. Good for you." He swigs his beer—a lager, but she can't tell the brand as he's completely peeled the label off. "Cheers, you two have fun." He saunters back to the bar, and Charlotte watches as he finds his spot on the stool next to a pile of label peelings.

She turns back to Armstrong. "When did Officer Landry date Mrs. Peters?"

Armstrong cocks his head to the side. "Uh, it was my senior year. It was only for a few months. They didn't last after Lark."

Charlotte feels a wave of dizziness, a sharp pain surfacing at her temple.

"Did you know that Jake is the reason I got into policing? He was actually my reference when I applied to the college."

"Jake Landry," Charlotte says aloud, his full name sounding both foreign and familiar. No one has ever referred to him as Jake before. Just like no one refers to Armstrong as Kyle. She consults her phone again and her fingers can't move fast enough for her thoughts.

It's not Armstrong. Meet me at your salon asap.

"Are you okay?" Armstrong sets his beer down, his eyes searching Charlotte's for clarity. "Is it the mozzarella sticks?"

She shakes her head no. She wants to run as far away as possible from this pub. But Darryl and Dani need to leave Armstrong's apartment before it's safe for her to bail. She glances at Jake Landry, and everything is clear, like a windshield defogging. Jake had been at the Peters many times in the lead-up to Lark's passing. He was showing interest in their family—interest in Lark. He was earning her trust. He had given her a beer more than once. Wouldn't it have been easy to slip something into her drink that night? Lark had recalled the cigarettes on her attacker's breath, the way he peeled the label of his beer.

"It's true." Armstrong nods to himself. "I wouldn't be a cop if it wasn't for him. He took me under his wing."

Charlotte nods, but she's barely listening to him. Instead, she is thinking about the times Landry had access to her house. How he stumbled upon the break-in. But how does Charlotte know there was a break-in to stumble upon? She never heard Leslie's accusation directly.

"How'd he take you under his wing?" she asks as she watches Landry at the bar.

"Honestly? I was a bit of a mess after Lark. He was going through some stuff too—hell, he had to bury his girlfriend's daughter."

Charlotte sucks in a sharp breath. "Right. That's heavy." She shoots a glance at Landry, who tucks a cigarette between his chapped lips.

"Didn't you say he was the first to the scene that night?" The insignificant detail that Armstrong shared on their first outing feels vital now. If Landry was first to the scene, he was close by, perhaps expecting the call to come in. He would want to be the first to arrive so he could give his report. Rule it a suicide.

Across the bar, Landry rises from his seat, pulling his coat on.

"Can you imagine?" Armstrong shoves a mozzarella stick in his mouth. "Anyway, he mentored me. Let me shadow him. After that first patrol, I was hooked."

Landry stops at their booth, and Charlotte averts her eyes for fear he'll be able to read her thoughts.

"Heading out?" Armstrong asks.

Landry's cigarette dangles from his mouth, muddying his words. "Yeah, I'm calling it early. But you kids have a good night."

Charlotte can sense Landry's eyes on her, but she keeps them lowered, focused on her phone. She doesn't believe she could hide the discomfort from her expression if she were forced to look him in the eye.

"What the fuck?" Armstrong asks, drawing Charlotte's attention across the table. His eyes are fixed on his phone. "My neighbour just texted that he saw a girl leaving my apartment."

Charlotte tenses. "Last night's date?" she jokes. Then she takes to her phone.

Someone saw you leaving. Please tell me you're both out.

"I should go check this out. I left my wallet on the kitchen table," Armstrong says.

Landry cocks his head to the side. "Interesting. Another break-in. Wonder if she's our girl, Charlotte?"

Charlotte stiffens at the sound of her name on his tongue. She shrugs. "Could be."

Landry's gaze remains on Charlotte as he zips his coat up. Then, he directs his attention to Armstrong. "I'll come with you to scope it out."

"You'll wait for me here?" Armstrong asks Charlotte, a pleading look in his eyes.

She assures him she'll stay at the Angel and order them another round, but then she tracks the two men as they exit onto the street. As soon as they are gone, she grabs her phone and dials Dani. When there is no response, she tries Darryl. But it's no use. His phone goes straight to voicemail. Staying at the pub isn't an option.

Chapter Fifty-Seven

CHARLOTTE

Back in Darryl's truck, Charlotte starts up the engine and turns the heat on full. Armstrong lives above Mac's convenience—that's what Darryl had said. She pulls open the navigation app on her phone and searches for the store, which is a ten-minute drive. She shakes out her shoulders. Two drives in one day, something she would never imagine doing if the situation wasn't dire. As she waits for the car to warm and the windshield to defrost, she calls Dani, who answers after the third ring.

"Charlotte, are you with Darryl?" Dani's greeting is unnerving.

"You're supposed to be with Darryl. I'm the one on Armstrong duty."

Dani expels a long breath. "I know, but I couldn't get him to leave the apartment."

"You left without him? Is he still there?"

Dani's silence reveals everything. She has no idea if he's left, and with Darryl's phone going straight to voicemail, they have no way of contacting him.

"Armstrong and Landry are heading there right now. But I don't think it's Armstrong we need to worry about."

"What do you mean?" Dani asks.

"It's Landry."

Charlotte puts the phone on speaker and adjusts her seatbelt. "I'm going there now. Stay by your phone."

Dani protests, forcing Charlotte to end the call early. She doesn't have time to convince Dani that this is their only option, and calling the police seems ludicrous when the person responsible is one of them.

———— ·✦· ————

Charlotte pulls into the two-story strip mall. It takes her a minute to spot Armstrong's truck among a cluster of SUVs. Charlotte scans the parking lot for Landry's cruiser, but it is nowhere to be found. As she parks in front of a laundromat whose open sign glows neon green, she considers whether the two officers drove together.

The apartment entrances stagger between storefronts, and Charlotte approaches the one next to the convenience store. She opens the door into a small vestibule with four mailboxes to the left and a narrow staircase ahead that presumably leads to the second-floor apartments. She climbs slowly, steadying her breath, unsure what she will stumble upon.

At the top of the stairs, Charlotte is met with four apartment doors. She creeps down the hallway, stopping at the first door on the right. There is only the light hum of a television show, so she moves on, quickening her pace. It is her arrival at the third door that gives her pause and sends a chill down the nape of her neck. The door is ajar, as if someone didn't have time to close it. She pushes the door open slightly, poking her head in with caution. The open-concept kitchen and living room are exposed, revealing nothing abnormal, but Charlotte can hear a faint struggle at the back of the apartment. She immediately recognizes Darryl's voice, which is strained and unstable.

She slinks through the tidy, minimalist apartment, eyeing a walleye mounted above a black futon couch. She slows when she is close enough to hear the confrontation in the back room. Keeping her distance, she presses her cheek to the wall of what she assumes to be an office, a black filing cabinet in view.

"I swear, I never touched her." Armstrong's voice is garbled. "I think I—loved her." A thump echoes against the cabinet, numbing Charlotte. Shakily, she moves closer to the doorway. When she pushes the door wide, Darryl comes into view, pacing the length of the room while clutching his battered fist.

It isn't until Charlotte enters that she notices Armstrong slumped against the wall, originally masked by the filing cabinet. Thick crimson drips down his face and his eyes are swollen shut.

"What did you do?" she asks Darryl as she kneels at the officer's side.

"I had to," Darryl says, his eyes wide and unfocused, his jaw protruding as he clenches it. "Is he dead?" he asks, moving to the window, his eyes searching left to right.

Charlotte jostles Armstrong's knee. He doesn't move, except for his head, which falls against the cabinet. Panicked, Charlotte seizes his wrist, searching for a pulse. "He's unconscious. What the hell happened?"

Darryl grabs a tartan scarf draped over Armstrong's desk chair and wraps it tightly around his hand. "We need to leave before someone notices."

"Someone already did." Charlotte rises. "They saw Dani. That's why Armstrong came back."

Darryl rushes toward the door. "Are you coming?"

Charlotte shakes her head. "We can't leave him like this. He could die."

"Let him," he says, continuing to the exit.

"He didn't do it, Darryl. We were wrong."

Darryl freezes mid-walk, his brows pinched together. A creak in the floorboard in the main room causes Charlotte to pause. The two stand there unmoving, exchanging glances. Charlotte notices Landry before Darryl, the cop's reflection in the hallway mirror, giving his position away. He adopts a stance, his gun held at attention, and meets Charlotte's eyes. Slowly, Landry brings a finger to his lips as if they are accomplices and Darryl is the problem.

Charlotte locks eyes with Darryl, her lips pursed and neck muscles tense. Darryl must sense her warning because he backs away from the doorway slowly, his arms raising above him in surrender. Charlotte follows his lead, and they wait for Lark's attacker to enter the room.

"Why is it always you?" Landry asks Darryl in a sing-song voice. "Breaking and entering, yet again?"

Neither Darryl nor Charlotte speaks. Landry's playful banter implies he has yet to see his partner's beaten body, which is thankfully behind him out of view. Charlotte hopes it remains that way.

"Are you going to tell me why you broke in?" Landry presses.

Darryl only shrugs.

Landry directs his attention to Charlotte. "And why are you here? Were you the girl the neighbour saw? Is that why you were late meeting Armstrong for your date?"

Charlotte swallows. If only she could stop time in this moment. Explain to Darryl that it was Officer Landry who had both a motive and the opportunity to hurt Lark. They need to get out of this apartment. Landry is armed.

She returns her focus to the officer. "Mind lowering your gun?" Charlotte asks, her voice meek. "It was just a misunderstanding."

"Let's have a chat while we wait for Armstrong." Landry points his gun toward the doorway, and Darryl and Charlotte comply, shuffling past him. When they arrive in the hallway, Charlotte spins around, catching the cop's attention before he has a chance to survey the room. "Officer Landry, we can explain everything."

"You do that then, Ms. Boyd," he says, motioning toward the living room. "Take a seat on the couch."

In the natural light, Charlotte notices Darryl's cheekbone is red and his lip swollen. Armstrong must have gotten in a few punches before Darryl knocked him to the floor. She wills Landry not to notice. They must get out of the apartment before Landry realizes Charlotte is on to him.

Landry frisks Darryl, and when he's satisfied, he gestures for him to join Charlotte on the futon. "Who wants to go first?"

Darryl shoots Charlotte a glance, and she nods. It's not that she has a plan, but she doesn't trust Darryl to think clearly.

"Why are you in Armstrong's apartment?" Landry asks.

Charlotte adjusts on the sagging couch. "Darryl and I got our wires crossed. He thought we were meeting at Armstrong's, and Armstrong and I thought we were meeting at the pub. Like I said, it was a misunderstanding."

Darryl eyes Charlotte as he chews on his swollen lip.

"You're going to have to give me more than that," Landry says, and he cocks his head to the side. "Since when do the three of you hang out?"

Charlotte swallows. "We needed to give Armstrong something."

"What, exactly?" Landry asks.

Charlotte's temple throbs. "It's nothing, really. We'll just catch up with Armstrong later." She rises to leave.

"Sit down, Ms. Boyd. We're not done yet. What did you need to give him?"

She fiddles with her earring. "Information?" the statement comes out as a question, and she can't ease the shakiness in her voice.

"Information about what?"

Charlotte reaches for Darryl's hand. "We should go."

"My sister's alleged suicide," Darryl chimes in, disdain dripping from his words.

Charlotte shoots Darryl a look and then returns her gaze to Landry who appears as though he's seen a ghost. The colour drains from his face and his eyes bug out, their murky brown on display. He redirects his attention to Darryl who still chews on his lip, glaring at the officer.

"Are you still on this? It's been years. And now you've pulled her into it?" Landry drags over a chair from the kitchen table, sighing as he does so. Then, he collapses in front of Charlotte with a huff. "Listen, I don't know what he told you, but Ms. Peter's case was closed more than fifteen years ago. It was a suicide, plain as day. Listen, I take responsibility, too. I should have checked on them more. Darlene was having her own troubles."

"What's that supposed to mean?" Darryl asks.

Landry keeps his focus on Charlotte. "When we arrived on the scene, Darlene was passed out in her bed—Valium in her system—the drugs easily accessible for Lark. We reckon the girl took a pill or two herself before deciding to hang herself in the backyard. What else can I say?"

"She was pregnant." Darryl spits out the words. "Did you know?"

Charlotte shakes her head at Darryl, her attempt to stop him from revealing too much.

Landry smirks. "That's the information you have? A hunch that your sister was pregnant?"

"It's more than a hunch," Darryl growls.

Landry rubs his eyes with his palms. "It wouldn't be the first time a teen offed herself because she got knocked up."

Charlotte notices a flash in her peripheral, and before she can stop him, Darryl charges at Landry, sending his chair toppling over. Landry scrambles to his feet, pushing Darryl off him. With the back of his pistol, he whips Darryl in the nose.

"You just don't learn." With the second blow, Darryl crouches to the floor, his face in his hands, and Charlotte watches in horror as his blood pours onto the cream carpet.

"Please, stop!" Charlotte barely recognizes the words as her own.

Landry repositions his chair and lowers into the seat. Dabbing at the corner of his mouth with his thumb, he chuckles to himself. "Once again, you've assaulted a police officer." He waves his gun in the air. "Now, anything goes."

Charlotte stiffens in her seat. She can feel her pulse in her jaw. "Maybe we should all go to the station. I don't feel comfortable."

Landry leans in. "You're not taking this to the station. If you do, it will just get assigned to me."

She sits up tall. "We have proof. Not here, but we can take you. Lark's diary."

Landry raises an eyebrow.

"That's what you've been looking for, isn't it? First, in the dumpster—is that why you referred me to your cousin's business? So, you could take your time picking through it? Then, you needed another look in my house, so you staged a break-in?"

Darryl's head bobs to the side, and he makes eye contact with Charlotte. This is all news to him. They haven't found the proof they need, but Charlotte is certain Landry doesn't have the pages either or he would have stopped his search. She doesn't need to possess the proof; she just needs Landry to believe she does.

Landry shuffles his chair closer to the couch and Charlotte can almost taste the cigarettes on his breath. "All right, you've had your fun playing detective. It's cute, really."

Charlotte slides off the couch, crawling over to where Darryl sits, holding his face.

Landry's thick form moves quickly, tracing Charlotte's steps. "I wouldn't leave if I were you."

Darryl attempts to stand, arriving on all fours, but Landry kicks Darryl's side so that he falls to the floor. "You, too." He flashes the gun again. "No one is leaving this apartment."

Charlotte scurries back to the couch, settling for the seat near Darryl. His nose is likely broken with the amount of blood that still pours in a steady stream. She wants to hold him. Tell him that everything will be okay; together, they can make Landry pay for what he's done. But the reality is this man has gone unnoticed for years because of his position, and she doesn't know who they can turn to for help. She needs to alert Dani. They need someone on their side.

"I know you raped Lark," Charlotte says, her face tilted up towards the man who violated Lark.

Landry expels a slow breath that fills the space between them. "You read this in the diary? Where is it?"

Charlotte holds his gaze. "Hidden somewhere safe. It's all in there. She was attacked by her mother's drunk boyfriend."

"That's a lie. It didn't go down like that."

"We have the diary. Lark explained everything."

"She was into me too," Landry says, perhaps trying to convince himself.

"You drugged her, raped her."

Landry crouches down, so close that his nose is almost pressed against hers. "You know what I think?" A crooked smile snakes across his face. "That it doesn't matter what I did. Did I rape her?" He shrugs. "It's my word against you two idiots." He rises, backing up slowly, pointing the gun first at Charlotte, then Darryl. "No, I think I responded to a break-in—the third this month. And when I confronted you, you both attacked me." He takes his own gun and slams it into his face. "Self-defense." He slams it again, and blood seeps from his nose.

Charlotte lets out a deep scream for help when she realizes this might end soon—her future decided for her by a weak man. The cold steel shocks her, followed by the sharp sting of the impact. Her view changes from Landry's ruddy face to the white of the ceiling, then a goose-down feather caught in the carpet fibres. Darryl's guttural cry follows, and Charlotte understands she's been hit by Landry's gun, a piercing bite travelling up her right cheekbone.

"Get away from her." The voice is steady and authoritative. "I mean it."

Charlotte rolls onto her back, craning her neck to find the source.

Armstrong stands at the doorway to the office, his own firearm raised. He creeps slowly across the hardwood. His eyes are still swollen, forcing him to squint. His thin lips are pursed.

"Is that true?" he asks Landry, with a pleading look like a young boy confronting his father. "Tell me."

"Lower your gun, Kyle."

"What did you do to Lark?" Armstrong presses, his gun unmoving.

Landry shakes his head. "They're lying." He motions to Charlotte. "This one's been playing you."

Charlotte shakes her head. Armstrong lowers his gun a few inches.

They're losing him.

She whimpers, bowing her head to her knees.

Darryl pushes his chest off the floor, raising his chin to Landry as high as it allows. "My mother didn't take drugs. It doesn't make sense. It must have been you. You killed Lark."

Armstrong shoots a look at Landry, who raises his hands above his head. "I didn't kill her, I swear. I wasn't there that night."

"What did you do to her?" Armstrong's strong composure falters, his frame weakening. "She wanted it, too," Landry mumbles.

Armstrong's head dips. Charlotte imagines the pedestal he's placed his role model on

crumbling to dust.

Darryl pulls himself to his knees. "You're a rapist and a murderer."

"You're fucking done." Landry raises his gun to Darryl.

A piercing sound takes Charlotte's breath away, and she shields her eyes. A gunshot. But who? When she opens her eyes again, they meet the blood across the room, soaking into the carpet. Landry's body lies unmoving, and Armstrong faces him, his gun still pointed at the man whose life he just ended.

Beside her, Darryl shakes his head, rubbing his arms and breathing heavily. His breath continues to quicken, and Charlotte recognizes the terror in his eyes. She has been exactly where he is. Darryl is hyperventilating, showing signs of a panic attack.

She crawls over to him, rubbing his back. "Head between your knees."

Armstrong crouches beside Landry, checking his vitals. "He's gone."

Charlotte continues to rub Darryl's back. "It's okay, it's okay. It's over now."

Armstrong staggers forward, rushing to the floor where Charlotte and Darryl cling to each other. He slides his gun back into its holster.

"Are you okay?" He looks from Charlotte to Darryl and back again.

Darryl collapses against Charlotte. She holds him close and kisses his head. "It's over now."

Chapter Fifty-Eight

CHARLOTTE

Three months later

Darryl reaches his hand backward, summoning Charlotte to join him at Lark's grave. The recent warm weather has surrendered most of the snow, but the ground is soft and damp, and the earth squelches beneath her boots as she weaves through the headstones to join him. Darryl kisses two fingers and then presses them to the rose-coloured granite where his sister lies below.

Charlotte studies his features. The pain is still evident in his eyes—it will probably never leave—but his forehead is free of wrinkles, his brows relaxed. He stands taller, true to his height. He seems happier, and Charlotte relishes in that change because she might just be a part of it. After a moment, he backs away, pulling Charlotte with him, but she isn't ready to leave yet. While she never met Lark in the flesh, she feels like she knows her like a best friend. Lark's words lit a flame in Charlotte. They helped her discover herself. They also led her to Darryl. She runs her hand along the smooth stone, which is cold against her fingers, and she utters an almost silent thank you for only Lark's ears.

As they walk the path back to Darryl's truck, he leans toward Charlotte, resting his chin on the top of her head. "Angel's for lunch? I don't have class until four, and Merle wants us to test his new chilli."

She grins at him. "Class," she repeats. It is the first week of his nursing school prep course before he attends full-time in the fall. She consults the time on her phone. "How about lunch with your mom?"

He nods, pulling her in for a kiss and she rises on her toes to meet him. With her arms wrapped around his neck and the warm breeze unearthing scents that have long been sheltered by the snow, Charlotte feels hopeful.

When they arrive at the truck, Darryl dangles his keys. "Your turn?"

She sighs and leans against the truck bed. "Do I have to?"

"No," he says, opening the passenger door for her. "You never have to."

She hesitates, staring at the open door. He's given her an out, as he always does. She snatches the keys from his hands and glides to the other side of the truck. "Fine, but you're driving home."

Charlotte is a child in the driver's seat until she adjusts the position so that she has a clear view of the world. She glances next to her, feeling comforted that Darryl is an arm's length away, ready to take the wheel if she needs it.

As they drive on the highway, she doesn't have the impulse to run through her tasks for the day like each is a level in a video game she needs to beat. Instead, she thinks about them differently, with composed content. When Darryl goes to class, she will return to her parent's house on Elizabeth Drive and see the contractors out. She will feed Tux the wet food she likes, the one that makes her skitter around the living room

333

while Charlotte prepares it. She will video call her parents to unveil the kitchen's makeover and tell them about her third therapy session. She will visit Dani at her new salon in the city. Later, she'll head to the gym to coach the ten-to-twelve-year-olds before returning to Elizabeth Drive, where Darryl will be waiting for her.

They will fall asleep as they always do, a tangle of limbs, their breathing in sync.

Chapter Fifty-Nine

LARK

May 4, 2006

I think Mom knows. She heard me spewing my insides this morning for the fifth time this week. When I opened the door, she searched my eyes. "I know what this is. I remember these mornings." She retreated to her room and locked the door, and I could hear faint arguing. I think she called Jake on the phone. I think she broke up with him because I could hear her yelling for him to never come over again. To stay far away from her. Far away from me, her baby.

Do you think he confessed to her? Of course, his version would be different.

"Always so beautiful, Lark," she said last night at dinner, stroking my hand, but then she grabbed my wrist, her grip clenched tight. "I looked like you once. I was beautiful, too."

She knows, Darryl. And when she stares into my eyes, I can tell she thinks everything is my fault. What did he say to her? I'm worried she's torn every good memory she has of me, crumpled them up, and glued over them with this altered event.

I'm no longer her Birdie.

I'm something she wants to forget.

Well, I can forget, too. I ripped the pages from my diary this morning, hoping it would ease some of the pressure in my chest.

This is the first entry of my new diary—the old one is hidden away, somewhere only I can find it.

I can have a new start, too. I truly believe that. I know that you and I can get through this together. As soon as you're home, Darryl. I'll tell you everything. You'll know how to make it right.

Since I came home this afternoon, Mom's been napping, a bottle of Valium spilled open on her dresser. I had to look up what the pills even do. I'd never seen them before. They help her sleep. Did you know she needed help sleeping? I wonder if she knows that I haven't slept straight through the night since Jake. Ten years ago, if I had a nightmare, I would have run into her room, burrowed under her comforter, and pressed my tummy to her back so I could feel her spine on my navel. I miss her.

I actually took one of her pills; can you believe it? And I can feel myself getting heavier as I write. I just want to have a nap until you're home from your show, and then we'll make a midnight snack and I'll tell you everything. I'm sorry it took me this long.

I think I hear Mom stirring.

Or was that the front door?

THE END

Acknowledgments

I dedicated this book to my husband and partner in crime, Sean Sommerville. In a lot of ways, this novel is a love story and so, it felt fitting to offer What She Left Behind to the boy who wooed me with his guitar-playing beneath the stairs of our high school in my senior year, and now, nearly twenty years later, the father of our three amazing children. So, thank you, to Sean and to Hannah, Ellie, and Calvin who allow me the time and space to craft my stories, and my marketing manager Hannah who tells her teachers, friends, and the random person walking their dog that their mother is an author, and they should buy my books.

To my parents, Wendy and Bill Pickrell who read the novel over one weekend, calling and texting me their thoughts throughout and indulging me in an impromptu book club discussion when they'd reached the end. You are my biggest fans and I love you so much for that, and for instilling in me a love for reading (Dad) and the dark and twisted (Mom). To my sis, Jamie-Lee Warner for allowing me to pick your brain on art therapy so that I could bring the scene with Darlene's picture to life.

To my teenage self who was the inspiration for Lark. This is a thank you for capturing your feelings and thoughts in your journal in high school, for staying true to yourself, for being "weird" and for believing at your core that that weirdness would help you find true friendships (because it absolutely did). For wishing on pinecones instead of the stars because why can't manifesting our aspirations through ordinary objects like pinecones work just the same if not better?

To each member of my writing critique group "Let's Cross the Finish Line" for your critical eye, dedication to each of our successes, and sense of humour when this industry reveals how bonkers it can be. Your insights and laughter mean so much to me and I'm so happy we connected nearly four years ago: Audrey D. Brashich; Jessie Wright; Jody Gerbig; Katy Mayfair; Mary Taggart, Natalie Derrickson; and Robin Morris.

To my beta/first readers for falling in love with my characters and helping me fine-tune this story: my uncle and fellow author Randy Coates; critique partner and creative writing classmate Nataly Shaheen, Rising Action pub-sibling Hannah Sharpe, bookstagrammer and reviewer, Sabrina Ladak-Jiwani (@BooksOverBeaus), pub-sibling and editor extraordinaire Marthese Fenech, and my mother-in-law and avid reader Beverley Barton Sommerville. Your comments clarified what I was missing and made me confident in what was working well.

To the entire team at Rising Action Publishing Collective for championing me and this story: the remarkable women co-founders Alexandria Brown and Tina Beier, and Abby Sharp and Coleen Brown – I am so thrilled I get to work with you; the extended team at Simon & Schuster; Nat Mack for my gorgeous cover (go ahead, just look at it again); Katrina Escudero at Sugar23; my pub-siblings and fellow Rising Action authors – special shout-out to Marie Still and Maggie Giles for reading an ARC and giving me the nicest blurbs; the editors, marketers, publicists, foreign, and subsidiary rights agents and sales agents whom all contributed to bringing this story into the world.

I want to send a HUGE thank you to the writing and reading community, especially in the greater Toronto area. This community is incredibly special and I'm so honoured to be a part of it. Shoutout to the Toronto Area Women Authors group run by Lydia Laceby for welcoming me with open arms. Thank you to Samantha Bailey for the initial invite and for being the most supportive author I know – your blurb for both my books and co-hosting my debut launch meant the absolute world to me, and I devour all your books. I'd also like to thank authors Jessica Hamilton for your thoughtful blurb for book one and two, Ashley Tate and Jacquie Walters for engaging with me on social and again, for your lovely blurbs, and Amy Jones for being the first author to read my work and give me the confidence to share with readers. Thank you to the Off Topic Publishing community (Finnian Burnett, Ivanka Fear, Jennifer Mariani, Lindsay Harrington, Lori Green, Marion Lougheed, and Renee Cronley to name a few) and The Shit No One Tells You About Writing podcast community and its hosts Bianca Marais, Cecilia Lyra and Carly Watters. And thank you to the book lovers, bookstagrammers and booksellers for reading and recommending my books and to my favourite indie store Blue Heron Books and its owner Shelley Macbeth for supporting local authors and inviting me into your fabulous community.

And lastly, thank YOU dear reader for taking a chance on this book. I hope you enjoyed reading it as much as I enjoyed writing it (which was a lot).

About the Author

Brianne Sommerville is a Canadian author who writes thrillers. She studied English literature and theatre before entering the world of public relations and marketing. She lives in Toronto with her partner and three littles under five and knows every episode of Peppa Pig by heart. *What She Left Behind* is her second novel. Her debut, *If I Lose Her*, released in 2024.